HIDE AND GEEK

The Treasure Test

Random House   New York

HIDE AND GEEK

THE TREASURE TEST

T. P. Jagger

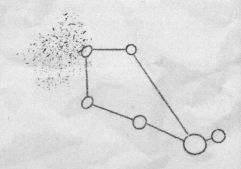

Text copyright © 2023 by Working Partners Ltd.
Jacket art copyright © 2023 by Chris Danger

All rights reserved. Published in the United States by
Random House Children's Books,
a division of Penguin Random House LLC, New York.

Random House and the colophon are registered trademarks
of Penguin Random House LLC.

Created by Working Partners Limited, 9 Kingsway, 4th Floor,
London WC2B 6XF, England

Visit us on the Web! rhcbooks.com

Educators and librarians, for a variety of teaching tools,
visit us at RHTeachersLibrarians.com

Library of Congress Cataloging-in-Publication Data
Names: Jagger, T. P., author.
Title: The treasure test / T. P. Jagger.
Description: First edition. | New York: Random House, [2023] | Series: Hide and
geek; 2 | Audience: Ages 8–12. | Summary: After eleven-year-old Gina Sparks and
her fellow GEEKs, Edgar, Elena, and Kevin, save their town of Elmwood,
New Hampshire, someone from the next town says the GEEKs are frauds,
but the GEEKs are determined to prove their puzzle-solving skills.
Identifiers: LCCN 2022031038 (print) | LCCN 2022031039 (ebook) |
ISBN 978-0-593-37797-0 (trade) | ISBN 978-0-593-37798-7 (lib. bdg.) |
ISBN 978-0-593-37800-7 (ebook)
Subjects: CYAC: Rumor–Fiction. | Best friends–Fiction. | Puzzles–Fiction. |
Friendship–Fiction. | LCGFT: Novels.
Classification: LCC PZ7.1.J38445 Tr 2023 (print) | LCC PZ7.1.J38445 (ebook) |
DDC [Fic]–dc23/eng/20220923

Printed in the United States of America
10 9 8 7 6 5 4 3 2 1
First Edition

For Ramona and Lincoln—
because Mom got the dedication in the first book

𝔗𝔥𝔢 𝔈𝔩𝔪𝔴𝔬𝔬𝔡 𝔗𝔯𝔦𝔟𝔲𝔫𝔢

Friday, April 1

CEREMONY TO SIGNAL BAMBOOZLELAND'S RETURN

By GINA SPARKS

Did you ever zip through the dips and drops of the Log Mill Run wooden roller coaster? Did you knock into other dinosaur riders at Bump-a-Saurus Wrecks? Or did you simply enjoy gazing across Fair Valley from the top of the Ferris wheel? No matter what your favorite Bamboozleland rides used to be, come out on Monday, April 4, and celebrate, because those rides are about to return!

The discovery of the Van Houten fortune in Elmwood last September brought much-needed tourism to the town. And the business community took notice! Soon Deepsight Development Enterprises purchased the Bamboozleland property, planning to restore and reopen the park. This additional source of income stemming from the publicity surrounding the fortune will provide a more significant, long-term boost to the local economy.

The entire town is invited to the ground-breaking ceremony at Bamboozleland amusement park. The ceremony is scheduled to begin at one o'clock in the park's amphitheater. See you there, Elmwood!

Six months ago, after my friends and I nearly got ourselves killed in a secret treasure vault hidden in an abandoned amusement park, I thought things would go back to normal. I'd return to being plain old Gina Sparks, freckle-faced and fact-loving journalist–the girl with a notebook in her hand and a pencil in her hair bun. My three best friends–Elena Hernández, Edgar Feingarten, and Kevin Robinson–would settle back into their normal routines. I figured the treasure-hunting excitement was over.

Man, was I wrong.

Really, the only thing that returned to normal was middle school lunch. The French fries were still soggy, the milk was still fresh from the cows at Feingarten

Family Farms, and—of course—Sophina Burkhart still couldn't leave us alone.

"GEEKs!" Sophina called, though not in the mean way she used to do before she and Kevin became sixth-grade class co-presidents.

I looked up from jotting notes in the leather-bound journal I always carry with me. I'd pretty much gotten used to the *GEEKs* label, but, well, it was kind of unfortunate that Sophina had figured out that putting the first letter of my name together with Elena's, Edgar's, and Kevin's spelled out *GEEK*.

Sophina sauntered over to our table, followed by her typical pack of minions—Kyesha Killman, Bella Ronelli-Compelli, and Mandy Sykes. Sophina's usually straight, shoulder-length blond hair had been curled on the ends and bounced with every step, and her lips glittered with pink gloss. She eyeballed us. "I must admit, you all clean up pretty well. Not as well as me, of course, but still . . ." Sophina patted down one of Edgar's loopy red curls and smoothed the collar of Kevin's polo shirt. I reflexively ran my hands down the front of my brand-new sweater, which my mom had given me as a special surprise that morning. "At least you look better than usual." Her eyes flicked over Elena, who wore a red hoodie with a cartoonish Albert Einstein on the front. "Well, *most* of you."

Elena scowled and tugged on her braid, which was

4

a sure sign she was about to launch a French fry at Sophina's head.

"Stay focused," she whispered to herself. "Bamboozleland. After lunch."

She loosened the grip on her braid. But her other hand twitched near the pile of fries on her lunch tray.

"Anyway," Sophina said, "I just wanted to stop by and tell you that when we get to Bamboozleland for the ground-breaking ceremony, you'd better not trip on the stage or anything. I don't need you GEEKs ruining my big moment. I heard Annalise Richardson from Channel 6 News will be there, so I figure I'll get a live interview." She flipped the ends of her perfectly styled hair and gave her best beauty-queen smile. "It will be my time to shine! Toodles!"

Sophina gave a tiny finger-wave and pranced off, her minions trailing behind her.

FACT #1: The special ground-breaking ceremony was to celebrate the soon-to-be redone and reopened Bamboozleland amusement park.

FACT #2: Bamboozleland was only getting reopened because *we* (the GEEKs) had saved Elmwood by finding the Van Houten fortune. So . . .

FACT #3: The GEEKs were being honored during the ceremony. But . . .

FACT #4: Sophina was *also* being honored, even though she hadn't actually helped find the treasure. All she'd done was call the police to come investigate, hoping to get us in trouble. The Elmwood chief of police—who happened to be Elena's dad—found us in the secret treasure vault, sitting on a bad guy.

As soon as Sophina was out of sight, Elena groaned and said, "Oh, sweet Einstein! That girl drives me bananas!"

Edgar shrugged. "At least she's nicer than she used to be. Thanks to her endorsement on the morning announcements, drama club's up to *four* members."

Kevin nodded. "Yeah, and she's not a bad sixth-grade co-president. My approval rating is higher than ever." He patted the tight curls of his high-top fade. "I know a lot of that is because we hunted down the Van Houten fortune, but it's also thanks to Sophina's support for my schoolwide calculator initiative. Ninety-five-point-two-four percent of sixth graders now believe we're doing a good job, and Gunner Bradley only disapproves because I wouldn't give him my strawberry Jell-O cup yesterday."

"Fine," Elena said. "You guys win. Sophina's not as annoying as she used to be." She crossed her arms. "But she's still annoying."

I kept quiet, but I knew none of us really had anything to complain about. It wasn't just Kevin who was doing great. Edgar was pretty much a shoo-in to get the lead role in *Oliver!*, the first play scheduled for the newly renovated Elmwood Theater. Elena had started a YouTube channel where she shared wild science experiments, and she'd topped fifty thousand subscribers after launching a video series called *Cool and Sometimes Dangerous Science Stuff You'll Never Learn in School*. And me? Well, thanks to my blog posts chronicling the GEEKs' search for the Van Houten fortune, I'd won the New England Youth Journalist of the Year award. That had given me a spot in the exclusive New England Journalism Mentorship Program, which included an all-expenses-paid two-day trip to New York City in July, where I would get to shadow a journalist from the *New York Times*. Incredible, right? I was still pinching myself.

But even with all that, I wouldn't have minded things going back to at least a *little bit* of normal. Sure, all the attention had benefits—it was way more fun going to school now that everyone liked us. But I was used to seeing my *name* in print, not my picture. As a journalist hunting for scoops, I found it tough to blend in and observe when everyone recognized me.

But a return to normal would have to wait, because right then the bell rang, signaling the end of lunch.

The cafeteria filled with the noise of sneakers

stampeding across the tile floor, trash being tossed into garbage bins, and excited voices calling out things like "Field trip time!" and "Bamboozleland, here we come!"

As we left the cafeteria, classmates gave us fist bumps and friendly "Hey, GEEKs!" as they headed for the school buses that would take us to Bamboozleland.

Gunner Bradley zoomed up and threw an arm across Kevin's shoulders. "Dude, this field trip gets me out of math class. Any day without fractions is a day I approve!"

Kevin looked so happy, he didn't seem to mind Gunner's poor view of math. As Gunner zipped away and bounded onto one of the buses, Kevin beamed. "One hundred percent sixth-grade approval rating!"

Edgar thrust his arms into the air in celebration. "As Shakespeare never wrote but should have—'tis a fine day for thou to be a GEEK!"

And, at that moment, it seemed like Edgar was right. But we would soon learn how quickly things could change.

2

Bamboozleland is laid out in a large circle, the paths like spokes in a wheel leading toward the carousel in the park's center, which is where we'd discovered the hidden treasure vault six months earlier. However, for the special ground-breaking ceremony, the park's center would have been too crowded, so the ceremony was being held in the amphitheater at the eastern edge of the park.

The amphitheater was a semicircle of crumbling cement steplike seating that descended in tiers toward a stage at the bottom. Schoolkids and townsfolk and news crews were settling in, waiting for the ceremony to begin. A microphone stand had been placed in the center of the stage, and a pair of large speakers faced the audience. A curtain hung from a steel frame along the back of the stage, and the other GEEKs and I gathered behind it.

Kevin smoothed the front of his shirt. "Do I look presidential enough?"

"Seriously, Kev?" Elena said. "You're the Elmwood Middle School sixth-grade class co-president, not president of the United States."

"I know," Kevin replied. "That's why I didn't wear a tie. Though, maybe I should've worn a suit coat. It's kind of cold."

"It's April in New Hampshire," Elena said. "What did you expect?"

Elena had a point. The sun was shining, but it was still barely above fifty degrees–a pretty typical early spring afternoon in the Fair Valley. I was glad for the fuzzy, extra-thick sweater my mom had given me.

While Kevin and Elena continued to debate clothing choices and the weather and Edgar hummed songs from *Oliver!*, I opened my notebook and plucked the pencil from my hair bun, ready to jot notes if I noticed anything newsworthy.

As I scanned my surroundings, I spotted my mom at the other end of the backstage area. She's the owner, editor, and do-it-all journalist of our town's weekly newspaper, the *Elmwood Tribune*. She and Kevin's mom were talking to two men. The first was a tall, thin, middle-aged man with glasses–our friend Max Van Houten.

The *real* Max Van Houten—not the con artist who'd impersonated him and almost swindled our town out of its finest treasures. Max had inherited the Van Houten Toy & Game Company after his aunt Alice had died.

The second man was a beak-nosed guy with perfectly groomed gray hair, dressed in a tailored black suit, complete with a baby-blue tie and matching pocket square. Thanks to an article my mom had written in the previous week's *Tribune,* I recognized him as Lambert J. Schoozer—the businessman preparing to restore Bamboozleland. Kevin's mom, who's on the Elmwood select board and was emceeing the day's ceremony, seemed to be listening intently. As Mr. Schoozer spoke, I saw her eyes widen and her smile suddenly waver.

I headed that way, my reporter radar pinging.

I'd only made it a couple of steps before I got attacked.

"Rah-oo!" A stubby-legged cannonball shot toward my kneecaps, long ears flapping.

"Sauce!" I knelt and let myself get tackled by my dog.

Sauce—part basset hound, part Scottish terrier—slurped his tongue across my face. I laughed as his long Scottish-terrier mustache tickled my cheek. I was glad my mom had brought him. I figured Sauce deserved to be honored at the ceremony too. After all, it was Sauce's keen hearing and sense of smell that had kick-started our search for the Van Houten fortune in the first place.

I gave Sauce a quick scratch between the ears and stood up. "Come on, boy. Let's go see if Mom's getting a scoop!"

Sauce gave a happy bark and followed me.

I eased in behind my mom, eavesdropping on her interview. She held her phone out, recording Mr. Schoozer as he spoke.

"So," Mr. Schoozer was saying, "when we get done with it, Bamboozleland will no longer be just another tiny, outdated amusement park." He pointed across to the western section of the park, where an old wooden roller coaster called Log Mill Run climbed into the sky. "We'll tear down that splintering mess and replace it with the looping, lunging Space Spiral!" He gestured toward the center of the park. "Instead of a slow, boring carousel, our central attraction will be the Death Drop, where harnessed riders will plummet toward the ground, free-falling for over a hundred feet. And we won't just have better rides. We'll also expand, creating space for *more* rides. Bamboozleland will grow from a dud to a destination!"

Wait a second. . . . Grow? No wonder Kevin's mom had looked surprised!

It was my mom's interview, but I couldn't keep quiet. "Hold on." I stepped forward. "You just said Bamboozleland will expand. I thought the plan was just to restore the original park."

As a journalist, I knew I should have phrased that as a question, but I was too shocked to think straight.

Mr. Schoozer winked and flashed a white-toothed smile. "If a baby Bamboozleland is good, a big Bamboozleland is better! With all these woods around"—he swept out his arms—"the growth potential is phenomenal!"

I blinked, stunned. "But the woods are—"

"Excuse me." Mr. Schoozer held up a finger and pulled out his phone, which buzzed in his hand. He glanced at the screen. "I need to take this call." He turned his back and drifted away.

I looked at my mom, then at Max. "They can't expand!" I said. "The money from selling Bamboozleland was supposed to be used to buy more of the woods to extend the nature preserve, not the amusement park!"

"I know, Gina Bean." My mom put her hand on my shoulder. "Let's not worry about that right now, though." She smiled. "Today is a day to honor you and your friends."

"That's right," Max said. "If it weren't for you and Elena and Edgar and Kevin, we wouldn't even have an expanding Bamboozleland to worry about. For now, let's celebrate!"

I forced a smile. "Okay." I reached down and scooped Sauce into my arms, reminding myself of how bad things had been for Elmwood just a few short months before. "Mom, is it all right if I take Sauce to say hi to Elena and the others?"

"Of course, Bean. But be quick. The ceremony's about to start."

I hurried back to my friends, Sauce wriggling in my arms.

As Elena, Edgar, and Kevin scratched Sauce's head and got licked across their faces in return, I told them what Mr. Schoozer had said.

Edgar frowned. "I want Bamboozleland to be restored to the way it *was*–the way I remember it when we were little."

Elena gazed dreamily toward the center of the park. "Not gonna lie–the whole Death Drop thing sounds uh-maz-ing. But still . . ." She sighed. "Not at the expense of the nature preserve."

"I don't know." Kevin scratched the back of his neck. "A bigger Bamboozleland would be good for Elmwood. More rides means more visitors, which means more support of local businesses."

Elena raised an eyebrow.

"I'm just saying there must be a way to make Bamboozleland bigger without cutting too much into the surrounding woods," said Kevin confidently. "In politics, you learn the art of compromise. Compromise makes it so everyone can be happy."

"Or *no one*," Elena mumbled.

Elena and Kevin can argue forever about almost anything—they actually *like* to argue. So I was glad when their Bamboozleland-versus-nature-versus-politics debate got interrupted by Kevin's mom calling out, "Okay, kids! Now's your big moment!" She stood at the edge of the curtain on the amphitheater stage, waving us over.

My heart pounded with an unexpected burst of nerves. I wasn't like Edgar, who loved the stage and the spotlight. Or like Elena, who confidently posted her science YouTube videos to tens of thousands of subscribers. Or like Kevin, who could stand in front of an entire gym of middle schoolers and get them fired up about building a school vegetable garden that would provide fresh produce to families in need.

I glanced around and spotted Sophina a little bit off to the side of our group. She was smiling and winking and snapping selfies that were probably uploading straight to Instagram.

I definitely wasn't like her, either. I was a journalist! I preferred being in the background!

I swallowed the nervous lump in my throat and gave Sauce an extra-tight squeeze.

As I followed the others out from behind the curtain, my mom called out, "Go get 'em, Bean!"

"Hooray for our treasure hunters!" Max added.

I looked back at them and gave a tiny wave. That's when I noticed Mr. Schoozer. He was pacing back and forth, still on his phone, one hand waving wildly at nothing and no one.

He did *not* look happy.

3

"Come on, Gee! Don't be shy!" Elena tugged me and Sauce out onto the stage before I could make any more observations.

As we lined up onstage, Kevin's mom began a speech about our treasure hunt and the discovery of the Van Houten fortune. She said it would be displayed at the soon-to-open Van Houten Museum. I barely listened. Partly because I was too nervous. And partly because I couldn't stop myself from observing everything around us. In fact, it took all my self-control to keep from pulling the pencil from my hair and jotting notes.

The amphitheater had filled completely. Every tier of seats was packed with clapping, cheering people. Along with all the kids and teachers from school, I spotted plenty of other familiar, smiling faces from

Elmwood–Mrs. Dupree from the Maple Leaf Diner; sweet Ms. Kaminski, the retired town librarian; Cy Porter, the security guard from Van Houten Toys; and Bob Hensworth, a local astronomy expert who looked a lot like a flannel-wearing Santa Claus.

Off to my left, my mom had joined a pool of mostly local reporters, as well as a TV crew from Channel 6 News. A hollow-cheeked man with stringy hair poking from beneath a Red Sox beanie used his bony elbows to clear out other reporters in order to snap photos with a camera that had a zoom lens nearly as long as my arm. Two other cameras hung around his neck. Standing at the front of the pack of reporters was a boy about my age, taking notes on his phone. He wore a navy-blue hoodie with GROVE PARK MIDDLE printed across the chest. I recognized him–and his dark wavy hair, which swooped across his forehead like it was ready to take flight. He was from the neighboring town of Grove Park, and if I remembered correctly, his name was Finley.

Back in January, Finley had won second place at the same ceremony where I'd received the New England Youth Journalist of the Year award. He'd done some great investigative journalism, writing an exposé about the Fair Valley School District buying expired food at discounted rates, with a school official pocketing the leftover money.

I was so caught up in my memory of Finley's article that I guess I must have been staring. He glanced up from his notetaking, and his dark eyes met mine. My cheeks grew warm, and I looked away, my gaze flicking over to a pretty, smiling woman who stood next to him. She was tall and wore a red pantsuit. Blond highlights streaked her long brown hair. Like Finley, she looked familiar, though I couldn't think of where I'd seen her before.

"Gina Sparks!" My name boomed through the speakers.

The crowd started clapping and cheering again.

Elena stuck her fingers into her mouth, gave a shrill whistle, and started chanting: "Go, Gee! Go, Gee!"

I snapped my attention to the center of the stage. Kevin's mom was smiling at me and holding out a royal-blue ribbon that had a shiny golden medallion hanging from the end. The medal was round but looked like it was made from a bunch of tiny rods. I grinned when I realized it was meant to look like a Bamboozler, the 3D puzzle toy that had made Van Houten Toys famous and was the namesake of Bamboozleland.

Sauce wriggled in my arms as I walked to the center of the stage. I dipped my head, and Kevin's mom hung the medal around my neck. Then she held up a small paper bag. "And for the treasure hunt's canine contributor, Evelyn Dupree has donated one of her famous Maple Bacon Barbecue Burgers courtesy of the Maple Leaf Diner!"

Sauce barked a joyful "Rah-oo!" and lunged for the bag. The crowd laughed. Even my non-canine nose could pick up the burger's sweet, tangy scent.

I carried Sauce off to the side and let him scarf his burger as the others received their medals. Sophina held hers up and blew kisses toward the Channel 6 camera crew, waving like a beauty queen. Elena rolled her eyes.

Once the clapping and cheering died down, Kevin's mom said, "Of course, we're gathered today not only to celebrate these wonderful children but also to celebrate the fact that this place where we've gathered—Bamboozleland—is going to be restored and reopened." She paused a moment as fresh cheers erupted, especially from the kids in the crowd. "For today's ground-breaking ceremony, each of these children we've honored"—she swept her hand toward where the other GEEKs, Sophina, and I now stood in a line along the front of the stage—"will dig up a single shovelful of dirt. This act will symbolize the fresh start for this beloved park." She turned and looked toward the backstage area. "Henry, could you bring out the ceremonial shovels?"

Henry Hinkler, the owner of Hinkler's Hardware,

came out from behind the curtain. The crowd gasped and started cheering again. Mr. Hinkler carried five shovels that had gleaming golden handles and scoops, which flashed in the afternoon sun.

Kevin's mom held up her hand until the crowd quieted. "And last but not least, Bamboozleland could never be rejuvenated without the efforts and vision of its new owners, Deepsight Development Enterprises. Let's give a warm Elmwood welcome to Deepsight Development's CEO, Mr. Lambert J. Schoo—"

Just then, Max Van Houten bounded onto the stage. He hurried over to Kevin's mom and whispered something in her ear. She frowned and stepped back from the microphone. They held a quick, quiet conversation.

The crowd began to murmur and buzz.

I turned to Elena. "What's going on?"

She shrugged.

Max hustled off the stage, and Kevin's mom stepped back to the microphone. Her lips held a forced, too-tight smile. The crowd immediately quieted. People leaned forward, their eyes on the stage.

"I'm sorry," Kevin's mom said. "There's been a . . ." Her eyes cut toward the backstage area and she coughed, clearing her throat. "There's been a bit of a technical issue. I'm afraid today's ground-breaking ceremony has been postponed. Thank you for coming, everyone. Have a nice day."

The crowd immediately began to buzz again. The amphitheater filled with cries of "What technical issue?" and "What's going on?" And I'm pretty sure it was Gunner who shouted out, "Can I have one of the shovels?"

I caught a glimpse of reporters jotting in notebooks and Finley–the boy from Grove Park Middle–typing notes into his phone. Annalise Richardson–the newswoman from Channel 6 News–was saying something into her TV camera, somber and serious, right before her cameraman panned around the confused crowd.

Kevin's mom whisked us backstage, where Max and my mom waited, and Mr. Hinkler wandered around clutching five golden shovels to his chest, his forehead wrinkled in confusion.

"Where's Mr. Schoozer?" I asked, looking around, seeing absolutely no sign of the Deepsight Development CEO.

Max shifted his weight from foot to foot. "I don't know. He just got off his phone and told me that maybe reopening Bamboozleland wasn't such a great idea after all. Then he left."

Elena threw up her hands. "The Schooz-meister can't just change his mind and then–*bam!*–take off!"

"It's completely irresponsible!" Kevin added.

"Sorry," Max said. "I've told you all I know."

"But I was going to be on Channel 6 News!" Sophina whined.

Edgar pointed. "You might still get your chance."

Annalise Richardson strode into the backstage area, trailed by her cameraman. "What can you tell us about this sudden cancellation?" she called out.

"Come on," my mom said, herding us away from the Channel 6 News crew. "I like reporting the news, but I don't need to be on it. Let's get out of here!"

4

Kevin's mom stayed behind to distract the news crew, and Sophina stayed too, still hoping for a live TV interview. Max and my mom swept me, Sauce, and my friends out of the park, so we could regroup in private at the old North Star Bank building, which was going to be the site of the new Van Houten Museum.

The not-yet-open museum had tall white pillars out front and a large dome that rose from an otherwise flat roof. On the inside, the dome was painted with a spectacular mural of the night sky. Once opened, the museum would display all the priceless artifacts that had been part of the hidden Van Houten fortune–things like a sword that had once belonged to Alexander Hamilton and an unpublished manuscript written by Robert Louis Stevenson, the author of the classic book *Treasure*

Island. The museum would also highlight the history of Elmwood and the town's most famous toy, the Bamboozler.

As Max swung open the museum's thick oak doors, we were still trying to figure out why Lambert J. Schoozer would have changed his mind about Bamboozleland in the middle of the official ground-breaking ceremony.

"What if the entire ceremony was a sham?" Elena asked.

"But why would Deepsight Development want a sham ceremony?" my mom asked.

"Maybe it was a publicity stunt," Edgar said.

"If so, Mr. Schoozer's an even better actor than you, Edgar." I adjusted Sauce in my arms. "I saw his face during the phone call. He looked really angry."

Kevin rubbed his chin. "Deepsight Development is a business, so maybe it was just a last-minute money-saving decision. With a little more information, I could probably come up with a mathematical formula to evaluate the cost of the ceremony compared to other financial considerations."

Realizing I should record everyone's theories in my notebook, I set Sauce down. I should've kept a better hold on his leash.

As soon as Sauce's paws touched the dark granite floor, he sniffed the air, and—"Rah-oo!"—he lunged forward. His leash tugged from my hand.

"Sauce!" I cried. "Come back!"

Like always, he totally ignored me.

I took off after him, dodging around glass display cases filled with priceless artifacts.

Sauce is surprisingly fast for a chubby, stubby-legged basset-terrier combo. Fortunately, my sneakers had better traction than his paws on the polished floor. His toenails tick-ticked as he skittered across the foyer, ears and leash flapping, me hot on his trail.

"Sauce! Bad dog!"

Sauce shot through an open doorway on the far side of the foyer. I dashed through after him. I was just in time to see him try to slam on the brakes. He twisted and turned. His paws scrabbled and skidded on the slick floor. Then he smacked butt-first into a table that had a square, very antique-looking wooden clock sitting on it.

The impact of Sauce's butt sent the clock sliding toward the table's edge.

No, no, no!

The clock stopped, half hanging off the side.

I breathed a sigh of relief.

But the clock had some sort of carving sticking out of the top, which made it top-heavy. The clock tipped over the edge.

I lunged.

I'm not much into sports, but if I ever decide to play baseball, I might make a pretty good outfielder. I caught the clock with my fingertips right before it smashed against the floor.

Sauce rewarded me with a lick across my left eyebrow, then trotted away across the room.

I stood, trembling, and gently set the clock back onto the table.

"That nearly gave me a heart attack!"

My eyes snapped toward the familiar voice. Mrs. Sánchez, the rosy-cheeked and round-faced Elmwood librarian, stood behind another table on the far side of the room, her palms pressed against her chest.

"I'm so sorry!" I said. "Sauce got away from me, and I couldn't stop him in time."

"Well, I'm just glad no one *and* no things got damaged." Mrs. Sánchez gave a relieved smile as she sank back into her seat. The table in front of her was covered with artifacts. Beside them sat Sauce's motivation for tearing off across the museum—an open bag of peanut-butter-filled pretzel bites.

Sauce stared at the bag, jumping up and down, tail wagging.

"Oh, you little cutie, how could I say no to those begging brown eyes?" Mrs. Sánchez tossed Sauce a pretzel, which he snatched midair.

I walked over to the table, recognizing a portrait of King Louis XVI of France, which we'd found in the treasure vault. "What are you working on?"

"I'm helping Max. We're trying to learn as many details as we can about each item. Then we'll follow up with the appropriate experts before finalizing the museum displays." Mrs. Sánchez pushed up her glasses, which had thick, bright-orange frames that matched the wide diagonal stripes of her sweater. "I'm used to cataloging books. Now I'm cataloging swords and two-hundred-year-old paintings. It's amazing!"

"Well, I'm sorry we interrupted." I scooped Sauce from the floor, held him tightly, and double-wrapped his leash around my hand. "You know Sauce and his nose."

Mrs. Sánchez laughed and fed Sauce another pretzel bite. "I certainly didn't mind the break. Though, I *am* thankful you caught that old clock. It's one of the items whose background remains a mystery, but I'm sure it's priceless."

"I bet you'll figure it out." I smiled as I headed for the door. "Especially if I can keep Sauce from destroying it first."

Mrs. Sánchez laughed. "Enjoy the rest of your day, Gina."

As Sauce and I rejoined everyone in the foyer, my phone pinged in my pocket. My friends' phones all chimed at the same time. I pulled mine out. It was a group text from Sophina:

She included a link to Twitter.

I frowned. It seemed we were trending.

And not for a good reason.

"Look at this tweet." Kevin held up his phone. "'GEEKs in Elmwood planted their treasure, then faked their search. #LyingGeeks #FakeFortuneFind.'"

"What?" my mom asked. "They're saying you faked the treasure hunt? Who are they using for a source?"

"Probably a one-legged iguana with internet access." Elena waved her phone above her head, nearly smacking it into Max's face by accident. "We all know the treasure hunt was real. I mean, the proof is all around us! None of this makes sense."

"This one's even worse," Edgar said. "It has photos!"

We huddled around Edgar's phone. Someone had posted two pictures side by side. One was a photo from the Van Houten treasure vault with a highlighted circle around a bejeweled necklace. The second was a half-blurry Halloween photo my mom had posted to Facebook back when I'd dressed up as Marie Antoinette in fourth grade. I gasped. In the photo, a circle highlighted the glittering necklace I'd worn as part of my costume.

"This isn't a photo fact!" I cried. "I was wearing plastic costume jewelry! And the necklace I wore doesn't even look like the one from the Van Houten fortune. The photo's just too out of focus to show it!"

"And look at this one." Edgar scrolled down to a photo of James Hatcher—the man who'd pretended to be Max Van Houten and nearly conned his way into stealing the fortune. In the photo, James was leaning forward, speaking with Edgar's mom as the two of them stood beneath a Feingarten Family Farms sign.

Elena smacked her forehead. "Fake Max went to the farmers market. He was only buying cheese!"

"Exactly," Edgar said. "But look what it says on Twitter."

30

"People can't actually believe this junk, can they?" the *real* Max Van Houten asked. "Could this be why Mr. Schoozer canceled the ground-breaking ceremony and took off?"

I groaned. "He wouldn't back out of rebuilding Bamboozleland because of some lies, would he?"

"You know how powerful misinformation can be," said Kevin darkly. "I always knew I'd have to face a campaign like this one day. I guess I just thought I'd be a state elected official first."

"I'm sure we can get it straightened out," my mom said.

I swallowed the lump in my throat. I hoped Max and my mom were right. But when I checked my phone again, the scroll of #LyingGeeks tweets just kept growing.

I needed facts. *Real* facts. Especially when everyone else seemed to be busy creating fake ones.

I was going to have to take matters into my own hands.

When I got home, I dug through boxes of old dress-up clothes, searching for the plastic gold necklace. All I had to do was find it to prove that the Halloween photo didn't show the necklace from the Van Houten fortune.

Unfortunately, my search came up empty. The necklace could have fallen off my neck while I was out trick-or-treating, or it could have gone into a giveaway box, or even become one of Sauce's unauthorized chew toys.

I didn't know what had happened to the necklace. I just knew it was long gone.

Frustrated, I stayed up past midnight, scrolling through every tweet and post I could find about the GEEKs and our treasure hunt and Elmwood, trying to figure out where all the lies were coming from. The trail of tweets eventually led to a single blog post that had been made less than an hour before the groundbreaking ceremony. As I read it, my fingers tightened around my phone. *This isn't journalism,* I thought. *It's a smear campaign!* I threw my phone down onto my bed. Tears stung my eyes.

I didn't know who had written the blog or why. But one fact was perfectly clear—the Fair Valley Tattler was *not* a fan of the GEEKs.

The Fair Valley Tattler

ANONYMOUS • Monday, April 4 • 12:07 p.m.

FVT FINDS FAIR VALLEY FRAUD!

Looking for the latest lowdown? Want to know what's REALLY going on in Fair Valley? Then the FVT is the blog for you!

For anyone planning to attend today's Bamboozleland ground-breaking ceremony, you are likely anticipating a celebration of a handful of local Elmwood sixth graders—the so-called GEEKs—who ALLEGEDLY uncovered the long-missing Van Houten fortune. You may even be wondering:

What will be done to honor these local heroes?

However, the FVT has discovered that a DIFFERENT question should be asked:

Did the GEEKs actually do anything worth honoring?

New evidence points toward a single, shocking answer:

NO.

Thanks to an anonymous yet credible source, the FVT has learned that the entire "search" for the Van Houten fortune was a TREASURE-HUNTING HOAX planned by the GEEKs themselves! Is it mere coincidence that the mother of one of the GEEKs is Bernita Robinson, a politically connected member of the Elmwood select board? Or that another is Christina Sparks, the owner of the *Elmwood Tribune,* which has published an endless stream of gushing "insider" reporting about the GEEKs' adventures? And have you wondered about the Elmwood chief of police who conveniently stumbled upon the GEEKs as they reportedly restrained a "criminal" with no prior criminal record? Well, that would be Chief Luis Hernández—yet ANOTHER parent of one of the GEEKs!

According to our source, the FORTUNE-FINDING FRAUD was cooked up by the GEEKs and numerous influential Elmwoodians as a publicity stunt to enrich both the perpetrators and the entire town. Furthermore, in yet another disturbing twist, the FVT has a source within Elmwood who confirmed that the GEEKs' exploits included multiple occurrences of breaking and entering, as well as possible vandalism. Such criminal activity should be condemned, not commended.

Now we are all left to wonder: Is the treasure itself actually real, a gift to the town from the Van Houten estate? Or is it as FAKE as the GEEKs' search to uncover it?

Wherever the facts lead, two things we know for sure: Shame on the GEEKs. Shame on Elmwood.

The FVT will continue to investigate and report as additional details are uncovered. Stay tuned.

The Fair Valley Tattler—Finding. Verifying. Truth.

5

When I arrived at school on Tuesday morning, I was met with total chaos.

A white Channel 6 News van sat along the curb. Parked behind it was a blue van from Channel 13, along with a third that had a graphic for WACJ Talk Radio on its side. TV cameras rolled. Our social studies teacher, Mr. Singh, herded a group of reporters off the sidewalk, including the hollow-cheeked, stringy-haired reporter in the Red Sox beanie I'd noticed at the ground-breaking ceremony. Once again, three different cameras hung around the reporter's neck, including the camera with the massive zoom lens. Students milled around, looking at each other's phones. The air filled with the hum of their voices. I dodged through the churn of bodies on my tiptoes until I spotted Edgar's curly mop of red hair sticking above the crowd near the flagpole.

As I forged a path through the mob, I noticed that the things I'd gotten used to over the previous six months were gone. There were no more smiles or nods or cheerful calls of "Hey, GEEK!" Instead fingers pointed, eyes narrowed, and more than one voice whispered, "Did you hear about . . . ?"

Had *everyone* seen the lies about the Van Houten fortune? Did everyone *believe* them?

When I finally made it to Edgar, Kevin and Elena were there too. Unfortunately, we weren't the only ones who'd used Edgar's height and hair to spot him in the crowd. Just as I joined my friends, the stringy-haired reporter cried, "There they are!"

Fingers pointed. Cameras click, click, clicked. The entire herd of reporters surged forward, pushing past Mr. Singh. Shouted questions buzzed through the air like a swarm of killer bees: "Was the treasure hunt a hoax?" "Where did the treasure actually come from?" "Are the artifacts even real?"

"No comment," replied Kevin, and I was impressed with how well he was holding his nerve.

Edgar kept his head down and did his best to look like he wasn't enjoying himself, but I saw a little twinkle in his eye. "I've always told Ollie there would be paparazzi in my future," he murmured to me. "I just didn't know they'd come so soon."

I almost laughed despite myself. Leave it to Edgar to talk to Ollie—his beloved prizewinning heifer—about being pursued by paparazzi.

The reporters pressed in around us, questions firing. "Kevin, were you only elected sixth-grade co-president due to voter fraud?"

Kevin's calm finally broke. "What? No! I ran a completely legitimate—"

"And did you or did you not make illegal photocopies of campaign flyers in the teachers' lounge?"

Kevin tugged at his collar. "I had Principal Gawkmeyer's per—"

The stringy-haired reporter cut him off. "What is your response to the allegations of breaking and entering at the theater, and even at Bamboozleland?" He held up one of his cameras and clicked a photo. "Are the GEEKs criminals, or only liars?"

"How is anyone supposed to answer a question like that?" I shot back. "Interview questions aren't supposed to be multiple choice with only bad answer options!"

Phones were held high, recording the madness. A Channel 6 News microphone stabbed toward us through the crowd. We were getting overrun.

"With me, young scholars! With me!" Mr. Singh

sliced through the throng in a flash of polka-dotted bow tie and curlicue mustache. "Into the school!"

Mr. Singh is not an intimidating presence—he wears bow ties and blue jeans with socks and sandals every day—but somehow our social studies teacher swept us along through the press of reporters and into Elmwood Middle. He ushered us to the quiet of his empty classroom. "I'm sorry you had to experience that," Mr. Singh said. "You know journalism is the first draft of history. Sometimes they don't get it right."

Kevin sniffled. "I saw an online petition calling for my resignation from student council."

Elena paced back and forth. "Well, somebody tweeted that I faked the treasure hunt to promote my YouTube channel, and that made me lose ten thousand subscribers in a single night!"

Edgar frowned. "The director of *Oliver!* didn't call last night, even though he said he would let me know about casting. I thought maybe he was just busy, but . . ."

As I listened, I felt like I had been lucky compared to my fellow GEEKs. Then I began to wonder about my spot in the New England Journalism Mentorship Program. Could that get taken away because of all the lies being spread about us and our discovery of the Van Houten fortune?

Mr. Singh tried his best to comfort us, but it was no use. Then the morning bell rang, and things only got worse.

Principal Gawkmeyer managed to keep the reporters and news crews out of the school, but as the halls
filled with students, there was a return of the pointing
fingers and whispered accusations. "There are the lying
GEEKs!" "Did you see the photos?" "They're making the
whole town look bad!" "We're going to lose Bamboozleland, and it's all the GEEKs' fault!"

By lunchtime, we slumped into our seats at our regu-
lar table, which was empty except for the four of us. Not
a single other student wanted to be associated with the
GEEKs. None of us spoke. I usually like the cafeteria's
mac and cheese, but that day I pushed it around on my
tray with a plastic spork, not eating. I didn't even have
the energy to jot notes in my journal.

Suddenly some girl in a pink baseball cap and massive white-framed sunglasses clattered her tray down
onto the table, slid into the seat next to me, and hissed,
"You GEEKs had better fix this!"

I squinted at her. *"Sophina?"*

"Shhh. Not so loud." Sophina slid her sunglasses to
the end of her nose, her green eyes studying us over the
top of the frames. "Thanks to you GEEKs, I have to stay
incognito. Since I'm connected to the treasure hunt *and*
I'm sixth-grade co-president with Kevin, people keep
asking if I was in on your plot. Even Kyesha, Bella, and
Mandy are acting like I have the plague. And can you

believe that Gunner Bradley went so far as to suggest I owe the entire sixth grade daily cake pops for life?"

Sophina's parents owned the Burkhart Bakery, which made excellent cake pops.

"This isn't about you, Sophina!" Elena snapped. "People are spreading lies about *us*."

"Well, *are* they all lies?" Sophina asked.

Elena's lips flattened. Edgar's eyes bugged out. Kevin's mouth dropped open.

Heat flushed through my entire body. "Of course they're all lies!" My voice shook. "You saw the treasure vault yourself!"

"Politics can be a dirty game, but you know me better than that," Kevin scolded.

"Good." Sophina crossed her arms. "Then fix it. I'm not going to have my entire life ruined because of you GEEKs." She glared at us and gave a dramatic sigh. "Thank God spring break is next week. At least it will be easier to avoid the school gossip. But by the time we're back in school, I expect you GEEKs to have this fixed . . . or else!"

Before any of us could respond, our phones buzzed. It was a group text from Max.

Edgar read the text, threw out his arms, and used his best British accent to declare, "As the Bard once wrote, 'at the length, truth will out'!"

I was pretty sure that Edgar (and Shakespeare) meant that sooner or later we'd get the truth. And it looked like maybe he was right. Because for the first time that day, a pair of facts was finally in our favor.

FACT #1: Max wanted to meet us at the Maple Leaf Diner after school.

FACT #2: Max had convinced Lambert J. Schoozer to be there to hear our side of the story.

A tiny bell jangled as we stepped into the Maple Leaf that afternoon. For the first time ever, the hamburger-scented air didn't make my stomach grumble. Even though I hadn't eaten anything at lunch, I was too nervous to think about food.

For a moment, I thought the diner was empty. Then I spotted Max and Mr. Schoozer sitting hunched over a table in the far corner, away from the large front windows.

Mrs. Dupree bustled from the kitchen, wiping her hands on her floral-print apron, her white hair a cloud floating around her head. A smile flashed onto her smooth brown face. "Sweeties, you made it!"

My heart lifted in my chest. Finally someone who seemed happy to see us!

"Hey, Mrs. D!" Elena said. The rest of us echoed with greetings of our own.

Mrs. Dupree guided us toward Max and Mr. Schoozer. "You kids go ahead and get down to your business. I'll get you some burgers and fries." She winked. "On the house."

We thanked her and settled into seats. Max smiled at us. "Kids, meet Lambert J. Schoozer from Deepsight Development Enterprises." Then he swept his hand toward us. "Lambert, please meet Elmwood's favorite famous sixth graders—Gina Sparks, Elena Hernández, Edgar Feingarten, and Kevin Robinson."

Mr. Schoozer didn't smile, but he offered a tiny nod. "Thank you for coming."

My stomach tightened. Would we be able to convince Mr. Schoozer of the facts?

Kevin started us off. "Mr. Schoozer, thank you for meeting us here today. We want to do whatever we can to assure you of our innocence and integrity. These rumors going around are nothing more than a disinformation campaign, possibly organized by a political rival who is jealous of my sky-high approval ratings. But you have my word that everything we told the world about the Van Houten fortune is true."

Mr. Schoozer studied Kevin, clearly impressed.

"And all the work being done to catalog the artifacts will prove they're real," I added. "Whereas things like this"—I pulled up the old, blurry Halloween photo on my mom's Facebook page—"are being lied about. The only thing this picture proves is that I had something gold around my neck. But it was just a cheap plastic necklace. I wasn't wearing part of the Van Houten treasure."

Mr. Schoozer raised his eyebrows. "Well. Do you have the necklace you *were* wearing?"

I sighed and shook my head. "I tried, but I can't find it."

Mr. Schoozer frowned, and my heart sank. Would our reputation be ruined because of a silly Halloween costume?

Edgar pulled up the picture of his mom selling cheese to James Hatcher—the fake Max Van Houten—and explained that photo too.

After listening in silence for a few minutes, Mr. Schoozer finally held up his hands. "Look, you make legitimate arguments. And it's not that I don't believe you. It's that nobody *else* seems to believe you. The public tide has turned against Elmwood, and instead of the town becoming an attraction, it's quickly become a liability."

I held up my phone. "But the photos . . . the facts."

"I'm a businessman." Mr. Schoozer linked his fingers together, elbows on the table, back straight. "I have to determine which investments will turn a profit, and which will not. Bamboozleland has unexpectedly flipped to the wrong side of that ledger. When I meet with Deepsight's board of directors later this month, I'm afraid I'll be recommending that we pull from the project." Mr. Schoozer stood to leave. "I'm very sorry."

"Excuse me," a gentle voice said. I turned. There stood the tall, pretty woman who'd looked so familiar at the previous day's ground-breaking ceremony. She held a box of Mrs. Dupree's maple leaf cookies. "I couldn't help but overhear."

How long had the woman been there? I'd been so engrossed in presenting facts to Mr. Schoozer, I hadn't noticed her enter the diner.

The woman set her box of cookies on the table and reached out to shake Mr. Schoozer's hand. "I'm Lily Grove. The mayor of the neighboring town here in Fair Valley–Grove Park."

That was why she looked so familiar! My mom had covered Lily Grove's reelection campaign the year before. Mom had written a feature article on it because someone from the Grove family had been in charge in Grove Park since, well, since forever. Because it was the *Grove* family who'd founded Grove Park way back in the middle of the 1700s.

"I'm pleased to meet you, Ms. Grove," Mr. Schoozer said. "But really, I must be–"

"Please, call me Lily." Lily rested her hand on Mr.

Schoozer's arm. "And do stay a moment. From what I overheard, I think I may be able to help."

She can help? I exchanged glances with the other GEEKs. Their eyes were wide and hopeful, just as I imagined mine must be. Lily Grove had been the one responsible for getting the beautiful new library built in Grove Park, which was where Edgar and I had uncovered one of the clues during our hunt for the Van Houten fortune. If she could push for a project like that, what might she be able to do for Elmwood and Bamboozleland?

Lily patted the box of cookies she'd set on the table and chuckled. "It's a good thing Mrs. Dupree's cookies pull me into Elmwood each week. If I hadn't come to the Maple Leaf today, just imagine the opportunity we'd have missed!" Somehow she managed to guide Mr. Schoozer back into his seat as she said this.

"And what opportunity would that be?" Mr. Schoozer asked.

Lily opened her box of cookies, took one, and then handed the container around the table as she started to speak. "I'm sure you won't be surprised that I've seen the terrible things being posted online. And even though I don't know these children directly"–she smiled at me and the other GEEKs–"I've met most of their parents, and I know the town of Elmwood. There's absolutely no way the rumors are true."

Right then, I wanted to leap from my seat and wrap

47

Lily Grove in a giant hug. Someone in authority believed in us and believed in Elmwood!

Unfortunately, it seemed Mr. Schoozer held a different opinion. He cleared his throat. "I'm sorry. On April sixteenth–only two Saturdays from now–I have a meeting with the Deepsight board, during which we have to decide the fate of Bamboozleland. It doesn't matter what I believe or you believe or anyone else at this table believes. The news became so bad so fast, there's just no way to quickly convince the people out *there*"–he waved vaguely toward the diner's front door–"that the story behind the Van Houten treasure hunt is true."

"That's the problem!" Elena blurted, waving a cookie around. "People want to think they're right more than they want to know the actual truth!"

Lily slowly chewed a bite of cookie, swallowed, then dabbed a few crumbs from her lips with a napkin. "Here's the thing." Lily rested her elbows on the table, taking a moment to look each of us in the eye. "What if we could replicate your treasure-hunting success while the world is watching? What if instead of telling them they're wrong about you, we give everyone a show of your skills that makes the truth undeniable, while using it to promote Bamboozleland at the same time?"

Mr. Schoozer suddenly looked less anxious to leave. "How would you do that in less than two weeks?"

"It's quite simple, actually," Lily said. "Here's what I propose . . ."

And then she outlined her plan.

When Lily finished, everyone started firing questions.

"What's in it for you?" Elena asked. "Because the last 'nice' adult who offered to help ended up being a treasure-stealing con man who wanted to kill us."

Lily laughed. "Oh, Elena, there's definitely something in it for me! You see, what's good for Elmwood is good for Grove Park. Our towns are so close! If Bamboozleland reopens, it's not only Elmwood's restaurants and shops that will get more business—Grove Park's will too."

"But according to your plan, you'd only have a week to get everything ready," Kevin pointed out. "How would that be possible?"

"It's all in my last name," Lily said. "I'm a *Grove*. Grove Park is in my blood. I know its history like the back of my hand, so a week should be plenty of time to prepare. By a week from today—next Tuesday—we can kick things off, which should work well since it will be during spring break."

"But won't people think it's just another hoax?" Edgar asked.

"I'll find someone to document everything," Lily said.

Max rubbed his chin. "You'd need someone who's objective and trustworthy."

Lily didn't hesitate. "I know the perfect person for the job—Finley Brown." She turned to me. "He's a wonderful journalist. He could go everywhere with your group and post daily updates to the public. Gina, you know who Finley is, right? Don't you agree he'd be perfect?"

I nodded, unable to speak. Finley had proven his bona fides as a journalist. Maybe that was why the thought of being around him 24/7 made me a little nervous.

Mr. Schoozer leaned forward. "That could be positive publicity. It could win back the public trust *and* build renewed interest in Bamboozleland. So . . ." He rubbed his chin. "Ms. Grove will have until next Monday to prepare, and then the challenge will run from Tuesday to Friday." He nodded at me, Elena, Edgar, and Kevin. "If you succeed, then on April sixteenth I can recommend that the Deepsight board move forward with Bamboozleland. However, if you fail . . ." Mr. Schoozer's voice trailed off. His unspoken words hung like a storm cloud over our heads, his meaning clear. He arched an eyebrow. "Are we in agreement?"

We exchanged glances. What choice did we have except to try?

Kevin raised his hand. "I make a motion to vote on—"

Elena thumped her fists on the table. "The GEEKs are in! Book it!"

And for once, Kevin didn't argue.

Mr. Schoozer gave a sharp nod and stood. Max gave a thumbs-up. Lily Grove smiled at each of us and said, "I'm going to have to buy a couple more boxes of maple leaf cookies just to celebrate." And Mrs. Dupree showed up with four Maple Bacon Barbecue Burgers and two baskets piled with steaming French fries.

My stomach rumbled, my appetite returning for the first time that day. I grabbed a burger and took a bite. Warm barbecue sauce dribbled down my chin. I closed my eyes and gave a slow, contented sigh.

I couldn't imagine a better meal to celebrate a brand-new treasure hunt.

The Grove Park Herald

Friday, April 8

TREASURE-HUNTING TEST FOR ELMWOOD GEEKS

By FINLEY BROWN

Following recent allegations of fortune-finding fraud, four local sixth graders known as the Elmwood GEEKs are about to be put to the test. To prove that their discovery of the Van Houten fortune was no hoax, the GEEKs must navigate a new treasure hunt, this time coming to Grove Park and leaving behind the potential aid of Elmwood locals.

Lily Grove, mayor of Grove Park and part of the Grove family legacy in Fair Valley, is preparing the challenge. "My test will focus on the history of Grove Park," Grove said. "The children will have no home-field advantage. More important, I have written a sworn affidavit that neither the children nor anyone close to them has any knowledge of the tasks ahead. If they succeed, they will have done so based on their own wits and skill. They will prove to all of us—and to the world—that their discovery of the Van Houten fortune was fact, not fraud."

The stakes in this challenge are high. Lambert J. Schoozer, CEO of Deepsight Development Enterprises, summed it up: "The fate of Bamboozleland is in the balance. If the kids succeed, Deepsight will move forward with its plans to redevelop the park. If they fail, Deepsight will shift its attention and resources to more promising projects."

The challenge will kick off at 2:00 p.m. on Tuesday, April 12, with the presentation of the first clue. This opening ceremony will be held on the Elmgrove Bridge, which connects the towns of Elmwood and Grove Park. The challenge will conclude at noon on Friday, April 15, at the Bamboozleland amphitheater, with preliminary festivities beginning at 11:00 a.m.

Will the GEEKs succeed? Can four sixth graders bring the return of Bamboozleland, ensuring economic security for their town? This reporter will be along for the ride to find out. I will bring daily, objective updates on the GEEKs' progress until they have cracked the clues or collapsed under their false claims. One week from now, we will all know whether the Elmwood GEEKs really are the real deal.

7

A week after the deal at the diner, Elmgrove Bridge was crowded. Both ends of the bridge had been blocked off with orange traffic cones, and townsfolk from Elmwood and Grove Park filled the space between, along with a collection of news crews and journalists. The White Bend River flowed lazily beneath. A small platform with a microphone on it had been set up in the middle of the bridge. Along with Lily Grove and Mr. Schoozer, Elena, Edgar, Kevin, and I stood on the platform beneath a banner that read:

THE GROVE PARK CHALLENGE
FIVE CLUES. FOUR DAYS. ONE CHANCE.

My phone buzzed in my pocket. Lily was adjusting the microphone, getting ready to begin the event, so I quickly slipped my phone out and peeked at the screen. It was another group text from Sophina:

DON'T MESS THIS UP, GEEKS!!!!

My jaw tightened. Sophina acted like everything going on was our fault, even though it was just a bunch of lies.

"Don't pay attention to her," Elena said to us. "We got this!"

Edgar stood tall, looking cheerful as usual, but Kevin—who was blinking a lot and kept biting his lip—was clearly struggling to keep a brave face. I thought I knew why. In the past few days, the petition to remove him as class president had gained hundreds of signatures—more than were in the entire student body of Elmwood Middle. People from Texas to Alaska were calling for his resignation.

"It's okay, Kev," I whispered. "We're going to fix this. Together."

He nodded and flashed a little smile my way. "Yeah. Together."

As I slid my phone back into my pocket, Lily cleared her throat and spoke into the microphone. "Thank you, everyone, for coming out today as we—"

"If the GEEKs fail this challenge, will they

publicly confess to their fortune-finding fraud?" someone shouted. It was the stringy-haired reporter with the Red Sox beanie.

Lily held up her hand. "Quiet, please. This is not the time for questions. In light of the accusations made against the GEE–" Lily coughed. "In light of the accusations made against these fine young people, they deserve a chance to prove themselves. This challenge has been created to provide that chance."

No one called out any more questions, but the reporter who'd interrupted the first time pushed his way forward and started snapping pictures.

Lily frowned at him a moment but then continued. "Due to the allegations of breaking and entering that these young people have faced from their original treasure hunt, my clues will *not* lead them to anywhere forbidden–the places they must go, they will be allowed to go. They may ask people questions in order to learn information that might be relevant to solving the clues, but they may *not* share any part of the clues with others in order to gain assistance. To ensure that our young treasure hunters solve the clues for themselves, Grove Park's favorite youth reporter, Finley Brown, will be with them every step of the way, documenting their progress and posting updates. He has been told nothing about the hunt and will not help in any way." Lily turned to her left. "Finley, would you please join us onstage as

Mr. Lambert J. Schoozer prepares to explain the details of the challenge?"

The crowd clapped as Finley–once again wearing his navy-blue Grove Park Middle School hoodie–stepped forward and up onto the stage. My heart did a little flip-flop at the sight of him.

As Mr. Schoozer stepped toward the microphone, he turned back and mumbled to Lily, "You never told me the reporter was just another kid."

"It wouldn't be reasonable to send a strange adult to follow four children all around, now, would it?" Lily whispered.

Mr. Schoozer glanced toward Finley and frowned but didn't complain further. Then he flipped his frown into a toothy grin, straightened his tie, and faced the crowd. "People of Fair Valley, it is an honor to be here today. And, of course, it's an honor to have these children"–he gestured toward the GEEKs–"willing to prove their puzzle-solving prowess. Like all of you, I'm looking forward to following the reports of their progress throughout the week. Here's how the challenge will be conducted."

The crowd stayed quiet as Mr. Schoozer laid out the basic facts.

FACT #1: The GEEKs had seventy hours to solve five clues–from 2:00 that Tuesday until noon on Friday.

FACT #2: The final clue would lead to the very first Bamboozle Bolt—a palm-sized golden lightning bolt. (The crowd oohed and aahed when Mr. Schoozer held the Bolt above his head and it flashed in the sun.)

FACT #3: If we showed up at the amphitheater by noon on Friday with the Bolt, that would mark our successful completion of the challenge, and Mr. Schoozer would tell the Deepsight board to move ahead with the restoration and renovation of Bamboozleland.

FACT #4: The Bolt would also be a lifelong pass to Bamboozleland for all four of us. (And—for an appropriate fee—the Bolt would then be made available to anyone else who wanted "a lifetime of *bolting* to the front of the line!")

When Mr. Schoozer finished explaining the challenge, he turned to Lily. "Ms. Grove, would you like to present the first clue?"

Lily handed me a large white envelope with a wax seal and called out, "Let the treasure hunt begin!"

The crowd cheered and started chanting: "O-pen it! O-pen it!"

I slid my finger under the envelope's flap, but Kevin grabbed my forearm. "Not yet," he whispered. "Not here."

"But–"

"Kev's right," Elena said. "Too many people. We need to go somewhere we can focus."

"And fast," Edgar said. "Every minute counts!"

I looked out at the chanting crowd, then down at the envelope in my hands.

"O-pen it! O-pen it!"

"Okay, GEEKs, we grab our bikes and go," Elena said. "In three . . . two . . . *one!*"

Elena practically dove off the back of the stage. Edgar, Kevin, and I followed after her. So did Finley. All of us GEEKs had stashed our bikes behind the stage, and Finley's was leaning against the bridge's railing nearby. We jammed on our helmets and pedaled toward the Grove Park end of the bridge, weaving our way through the crowd. I clutched the sealed clue against my handlebars.

Kevin glanced over his shoulder. "Some people are trying to follow us!"

I risked a peek and saw the stringy-haired reporter and some others running after us, trying to keep up.

"I know where you can get some privacy," Finley called as we reached the end of the bridge. "This way!" He veered right, shooting down a ramp that led to a walking path along the river. The rest of us followed.

Clear of the crowd, we raced underneath the bridge and tore off along the path.

"Woo-hoo!" Elena shouted, jabbing a fist into the air as she pedaled. Her braid flapped behind her in the wind.

When I looked back, people crowded the bridge, watching and pointing. The stringy-haired reporter stood at the bottom of the ramp we'd pedaled down. He stared after us, the shadow of the bridge slashing across his face, his cameras dangling from their straps around his neck.

"Seventy hours," Kevin said. "Five clues. That gives us an average of fourteen hours per clue. Take away eight hours a night for sleeping for three nights, that's nine hours and twelve minutes. I'll set a timer."

I couldn't help but smile. It was kind of funny that Kevin pushed so hard for the schoolwide calculator initiative when he never needed one himself. But he was right to keep us on track. I refocused on the path, following Finley and my friends. As we wound along beside the river, I mentally reviewed everything I knew about Grove Park, most of which I'd jotted in my journal while researching the town over the weekend.

Grove Park had been founded by Thomas Grove in 1758, about twenty years before Elmwood. Its current population was 8,471 people—about four times as big as Elmwood. The town's largest employer was Fair Valley Technology Solutions, a company started by a former executive from Van Houten Toys who'd decided to move from toys to tech. The town was sandwiched in a horseshoe-shaped curve of the White Bend River. Across the river on the eastern edge of town was Cloud Tapper Hill, which was so big that it might as well have been a mountain. Back in fifth grade, I'd even made the long hike to the top during a field trip. We'd followed the red trail markers all the way up to Wizard Rock–a massive, odd-shaped boulder that looks like a stooped old man.

After a few more minutes of riding, Finley branched off from the path, leading us up a short trail to a bench tucked between some trees. We all coasted to stops and dropped our bikes to the ground. None of us spoke for a minute as we panted, catching our breath.

Then Elena decided we'd rested long enough. "Come on, Gee!" She knocked her knuckles against my helmet. "Are you gonna open the clue or what?"

"Yeah, let's see what we've got," Edgar said.

Everyone leaned in.

I took a deep breath. "Okay, here goes nothing." I popped the wax seal on the envelope and pulled out our first clue.

Where the river meets a poet, you will find a clue,

But only in the lonesome nest from which the sparrow flew.

A good lady retired there into eternal rest,

And that's the place where you will face your first and early test.

A chariot of silver rises skyward to a spire,

And you will only have arrived when you can go no higher.

A bird will give its light to guide you when the clock chimes five,

Shining on a secret buried in a lost archive.

Kevin pointed to the clue's second-to-last line. "Wherever the next clue is hidden, we'd better hurry. It's already nearly three o'clock, and we need to be in the right spot 'when the clock chimes five.' Otherwise, we'll have to wait an extra twenty-four hours to get a second shot."

"At least we're already by the river." I pointed to the first line of the clue. "But do poets just wander around down here?"

Finley laughed. "Not that I know of." He clapped his hands over his mouth. "Oops. Sorry," he mumbled. He pulled out his phone to take notes. "I'm only supposed to be a silent observer."

"Don't sweat it," Elena said. "I don't think your accidental slip got us any closer to the answer. Besides, I'm more interested in the silver chariot taking me skyward. 'Cause *that* sounds epic."

Edgar pointed to the clue's third line. "It mentions *eternal rest.* Could we be looking for a graveyard?"

I groaned. "Don't you remember what happened the *last* time we searched for something in a graveyard?"

Everyone frowned as our minds flashed back to when we'd been trapped in a mausoleum during our search for the Van Houten fortune.

"Relax, Gee," Elena said. "This time we're not being chased by an evil con man."

Kevin pulled up a map of Grove Park on his phone. He trailed his finger along the river. "We're somewhere around here." He zoomed in on the map. "And there's a church farther upriver as we loop around the northern edge of town. Grove Park United Methodist. Maybe there's a graveyard there."

Elena snatched her bike from the ground and jumped on. "Well, don't stand there like a bunch of pickled mailboxes. Let's go!"

Pickled mailboxes made absolutely no sense, but we all hopped onto our bikes and pedaled after Elena anyway. As we chugged along, following the curve of the river, we passed a nook carved out along the bank with a small riverside harbor. A handful of houseboats and motorboats were tied up to a pair of docks, and a half dozen canoes were stored upside down in a rack that had a sign reading CANOE RENTALS.

"*Wait!*" Edgar shouted from the back of our line. I heard the skid of his tires as he slammed on his brakes.

"What is it?" Kevin asked. "We need to get to that graveyard."

"What we *need* is a river and a poet," Edgar said.

64

"And look!" He pointed to an old wooden houseboat. The cabin had once been painted blue with red trim, but the paint was dingy and peeling, and the boat's metal roof seemed to be more rust than steel. At the bow, a worn yellow recliner sat abandoned underneath a fraying, faded, red-and-white-striped awning.

"Congratulations, Edge," Elena deadpanned. "It's a boat."

"It's not just a boat," Edgar said. "Look closer."

"What are you—" Elena stopped.

She, Kevin, and I must have all spotted the words painted along the boat's hull at the same time.

"The Bard!" we all shouted.

"Edgar, you're brilliant!" I added.

Finley scrunched up his eyebrows. "I don't get it."

"The Bard is Shakespeare's nickname," Edgar explained, which was something the GEEKs already knew, thanks to Edgar's constant Shakespearean quotes and almost-quotes. "And Shakespeare is only the most famous poet of all time. So . . ." He flung his arms wide. "The river meets a poet!"

Everything about the clue seemed to click into place at once.

"Boats are often called *she,*" Edgar said, "so even though Shakespeare was a guy, maybe *The Bard* is the *good lady* from the clue."

"And look how beat-up it is," I said. "I don't think it's

65

been used in a long time. Maybe it was retired here *into eternal rest* in the harbor."

Elena bounced up and down. "And some boats have a nest, just like in the clue!"

Kevin shook his head. "You're talking about a crow's nest, which is only on ships with masts, and *The Bard* doesn't have masts. Plus, the clue talks about a nest for a sparrow, not a crow."

Elena shrugged. "Close enough. Let's go!" She coasted from the trail down to the dock, dropped her bike in the grass, and started clopping along the dock toward *The Bard.*

"Hold on, Elena!" I said, trailing after her. "Don't you think–"

"Quite a bit, Gee. But right now it's *action* time!" Elena hopped from the dock and onto the boat, followed by Edgar.

I glanced around, didn't see anyone else in the area, and joined them. Still, even though Lily had said the clues would only lead us to places we were allowed to go, I wasn't in love with the idea of hopping onto some boat when we didn't know who it belonged to.

Kevin grumbled, "Here we go again," then joined us too.

Finley stayed behind on the dock, taking notes on his phone.

The boat creaked and rocked gently underfoot as we

searched the deck for anything that might have to do with a sparrow or a silver chariot or a nest. Nothing.

"We need to check the inside," Elena said.

Edgar was standing near the door to the boat's cabin, which had a curtain pulled across its cracked window. He reached for the rusty doorknob.

Wham!

The cabin door crashed open. Edgar staggered back. He stumbled over a rusty bucket and–*whump!*–fell buttfirst onto the deck.

A wild-eyed man with a bristly white beard and a gray stocking cap popped from the doorway. "Trespassers! Interlopers!" He waved something long and silvery above his head.

"Holy swordfish!" Elena cried.

That's when I realized the man was swinging a massive frozen fish like a sword.

Edgar crab-walked backward. "We're sorry! We didn't kn–"

"Off with ya!" the man yelled. He thumped his frozen fish against the side of the cabin, then thrust it in Edgar's direction. "You've got five seconds to be off my house or you'll end up in the river!"

Kevin stepped forward. "We apologize, sir. We didn't mean to disturb you. You see–"

"*Five . . .*"

"We're on a treasure hunt and–"

"*Four . . .*"

"The clue said–"

"*Three . . .*"

Elena tugged on Kevin's sleeve. "Kev, I don't think he cares."

"*Two . . .*"

"But as sixth-grade co-president–"

"*One!*" The man stepped toward Kevin, fish raised.

"GEEKs out!" Elena yelled. She towed Kevin behind her and leapt to the dock.

All of us sprinted away, our feet thumping across the wooden boards.

"And don't come back!" the man yelled.

We didn't need telling twice. I vaulted onto my bike. The others did the same.

And that's when I noticed all the people watching us.

In the time we had been on the boat, a crowd had gathered up on the docks, phones out, taking pictures and recording. The stringy-haired reporter stood at the front of the group. He lowered his camera. "This time, you've been caught in the *act* of attempted breaking and entering!" he called. "There's obviously a pattern here. Does your status as local celebrities somehow give you the right to trespass on private property?"

We should have known that guy would trail us along the river! I thought.

"I thought the clue was leading us here," Edgar protested.

The rest of the crowd jeered and shouted questions too, but Lily Grove arrived and tried to herd them out of our way. "Come now, folks," I heard her say, "give them a fair shake. I'm sure it was an honest mistake."

"We need to get out of here," Kevin said.

"We're not far from the café where my mom works," Finley said. "We can take cover there. Follow me!"

For the second time that afternoon, we followed Finley away from all the unwanted attention. We left the path along the river, pedaled down a few side streets to lose anyone trying to follow us, and then rolled to a stop outside the Pink Barn Café, which–yes–totally looked like a giant pink barn.

"Hurry," Finley said. "Let's get inside before we're spotted."

"What about our bikes?" I asked. Mine has a basket on the front, which is great for holding my reporter's notebook and a spare leash for Sauce (or occasionally even for giving Sauce a ride around Elmwood). But the basket also makes my bike pretty recognizable.

Finley held open the door. "I guess they come with us."

It was a good thing the Pink Barn was bigger than the Maple Leaf, so there was room inside for five kids and five bikes. It was also a good thing it was almost four o'clock on a Tuesday afternoon, so the café was nearly empty. A single customer sat on a stool at the counter, eating a sandwich and munching from a bag of potato chips. The waitress behind the counter wore blue jeans and a pink-and-white-plaid shirt with a PINK BARN logo on the pocket. Her dark wavy hair, which was pulled back into a high ponytail, was an unmistakable match for Finley's, despite her few streaks of gray.

"Finley, what on earth?" the woman said.

The man at the counter looked at us, turned back to the woman, and chuckled. "Didn't know you offered ride-through service now, Cassandra."

"Sorry, Mom," Finley said. "Emergency. Can we go to the back?"

Finley's mom rubbed her temples. "Will I get a full explanation at some point?"

"Tonight," Finley said. "I promise."

Finley's mom sighed. "Keep your bikes out of the kitchen."

"No problem, Fin's mom!" Elena said.

"And thanks!" I added.

Finley's mom smiled and gave a tired shake of her head.

We wheeled our bikes down a short hallway and leaned them against the wall. Finley led us into a cramped room with a small round table and two folding chairs. A row of hooks along one wall held a few pink aprons, plus one of the pink-and-white-plaid shirts like Finley's mom had been wearing.

As soon as the door closed behind us, Kevin said, "This is bad. It's already nearly four o'clock, and we're no closer to the next clue."

"Not true, Kev," Elena said. "Thomas Edison made all kinds of attempts when inventing the light bulb, and he famously said, 'I have not failed. I've just found ten thousand ways that won't work.' We tried the houseboat of an angry guy with a frozen-fish sword, and now we know that place won't work. See? Progress!"

"We do need to hurry, though," I said. "We only have about an hour to get to the right place before five o'clock."

Edgar plopped into one of the folding seats and un-strapped his bike helmet. Sweat plastered his curly red hair to his forehead. "When we stopped at the boat, we were on our way to the church to check for a graveyard. Why don't we look there?"

"All in favor of the church?" Kevin asked, raising his hand.

Elena, Edgar, and I raised our hands too.

Kevin pulled up the Grove Park map on his phone again, and we plotted our route, making sure we'd keep off main roads as much as possible. Finley convinced his mom to let us wheel our bikes through the kitchen, so we could sneak out the back of the Pink Barn, in case anyone was watching for us out front.

This time, Elena led the way, taking us down alleys and side streets, keeping close to the river but never so close that anyone could spot us from the river-walk path. As Elena was zipping across one intersection, she slammed on her brakes, putting a foot down as she skidded sideways.

Finley, Edgar, and I swerved around her. Kevin smashed his brakes, stopping mere inches from a collision. "What in the world are you doing?" Kevin demanded.

Elena pointed to the street signs at the corner of the intersection. "We're on Edison Road," she said, "but look at the other one."

"Hudson Road." Kevin shrugged. "So?"

"My abuela used to live in New York, and her apartment was close to the river–the *Hudson* River. So what if Hudson Road is the *river*"–Elena tossed up some air quotes with her fingers–"we're supposed to be following?"

"But what about the poet?" Kevin asked.

"I know Edison is an inventor, not a poet," I said. "But maybe other streets are named after different people. One might be a poet."

Grove Park United Methodist Church was near the river, but that wasn't a lot to go on. And what if Elena was right about Hudson Road?

"It could be worth a try," Kevin mused.

"Route switch!" Elena cried. "Follow me, GEEKs!" She took off.

We passed old houses with trim lawns. Long porches stretched across their faces, and windows poked up from roofs that were two or three stories up. Bright early-spring flowers bloomed along fences and sidewalks.

At the next intersection, we crossed Twain Street.

"Mark Twain was a writer," I said, "but he didn't write poetry."

Then came Carver Lane.

"George Washington Carver," Elena said. "Another famous scientist and inventor."

Then Holiday Way.

Kevin shook his head. "That street's not named after a person."

"It could be," Edgar said. "Billie Holiday was a famous jazz singer."

And then . . .

I pumped my fist. "*Woot-woot!* Frost Street!"

Elena quirked an eyebrow. "So . . . brrr?"

I rolled my eyes. "I mean *Frost* like *Robert Frost.* You know—'Two roads diverged in a wood, and I– / I took the one less traveled by, / And that has made all the difference'?"

"So we found our poet?" Kevin asked.

"Yep."

There were no cars driving by, so we dismounted our bikes in the middle of the intersection and looked around. Finley started taking video to capture the scene.

Edgar spun in a slow circle, sweeping his arms wide. "How are we supposed to know which house is the right one?"

The houses on all the corners were large and grand, with fancy trim, but the house on the northeast corner caught my attention.

A redbrick walkway led up to a large wraparound porch, and the house itself was built of the same red brick, which was accented with cream trim. A pair of chimneys rose from the sharply angled roof, and an octagonal turret towered at one corner of the house, rising above the second story, reminding me of the square turret at the Van Houten mansion in Elmwood. But it wasn't the red bricks or architecture that made the house stand out from its neighbors. It was the sign attached to the wrought-iron fence surrounding the house's manicured yard:

THE HISTORIC WHITE BEND INN
IS UNDERGOING RENOVATION

Could the White Bend Inn be where we need to look? My gaze wandered up to the turret. What I saw removed all doubt.

"Look." I pointed to the turret's top floor. "Check out that window."

Each side of the turret had a large, stained-glass window, and the one facing west included a bird with bright blue feathers on its back.

"The clue! *A bird will give its light!*" Edgar said. "That house is the sparrow's nest!"

Elena frowned. "That bird is a swallow, not a sparrow. Sparrows don't have blue plumage."

"Lily Grove isn't a science expert like you," Kevin said. "She probably doesn't know the difference. And the clue mentions *a spire*, which matches with the turret. This house is the only empty one on the corner too. In other words, *lonesome*."

Elena shrugged. "I guess the wrong bird is better than no bird." Then she clapped her hands together, her eyes brightening. "So we're going in?"

Kevin held up his hands. "Slow your roll, Elena. There have already been too many reports of us breaking and entering."

"Relax, Kev," Elena said. "Lily said we're allowed to be at the places where the clues lead. If this is the right place, it'll be open for us." She wheeled down the brick path and leaned her bike against the porch. Then she bounded up to the inn's massive double doors and turned the knob.

The doors swung open on well-oiled hinges. Elena grinned back at us as she walked in. We followed.

The high-ceilinged foyer was paneled in dark maple. A massive chandelier hung high above our heads. Tarps covered chair- and table-sized lumps along the walls, and the smell of sawdust hung in the air.

"Now we just need to get to the bird window," Edgar said.

"Easy cheese sauce!" Elena said. "We'll take the stairs!"

"How do you plan to do that?" I pointed.

"Oh, sweet Einstein!"

At the far end of the foyer, there was a large rectangle of unstained floorboards where there quite clearly *should* have been stairs. The landing for the next story was at least twelve feet above the floor.

Finley—who'd been trying to stay out of our way—couldn't seem to resist saying, "I guess when they say this place is undergoing renovations, they mean it."

"Well, we have to find *some* way up," Kevin said. "The clue says the light will guide us when the clock chimes five. We only have twenty minutes!"

10

Elena, Edgar, Kevin, and I scurried around the White Bend Inn like squirrels looking for a lost nut. We searched for another set of stairs or an outside fire escape. Nothing!

"What about the *chariot of silver* thing from the clue?" Edgar asked.

Elena snapped her fingers. "An elevator!"

We charged around the first floor again. Elena and I opened every door, peeked in every closet. Kevin and Edgar circled the entire outside of the house. Finley observed. Eventually we all regrouped in the inn's huge kitchen and slumped against a countertop island in the center of the room.

Kevin trailed a finger aimlessly through the sawdust on the countertop. "The first clue, and we've already failed."

I swallowed the lump lodged in my throat. I looked at my phone. Thirteen minutes until five o'clock.

Elena clenched her jaw. "We haven't failed yet. Even if we don't get up in the turret today, we can figure it out tomorrow. Sure, we'll be behind, but–"

"Wait!" Kevin sprang across the kitchen, practically hurdling over the island. "Sparrow!" He pointed at a section of wall at the end of a stretch of kitchen counter.

We raced over to look. Tiny marks had been notched into the wall, each one neatly labeled:

Sparrow, age 4 . . .

Sparrow, age 5 . . .

Sparrow, age 6 . . .

And so on.

"My mom used to measure my height just like this against my bedroom wall. Sparrow was a child!" Kevin said. "That's why the word *Sparrow* was capitalized in the clue."

I traced a finger over the name. *Sparrow.* One of the notched height markings had been made right on top of a knot in the paneling, and I pressed it, feeling the slight groove cut into the wood-paneled wall.

Click.

I yanked my hand back. *What in the . . . ?*

About three feet above the floor, a section of the wood-paneled wall slid upward, revealing an open-faced steel box.

"What's *that*?" Kevin asked.

Edgar yelled, "A silver chariot!" at the same time that I said, "A dumbwaiter!"

"A dumb-*huh*?" Elena asked, her eyebrows scrunching in confusion.

"A dumbwaiter," I said. "I read about them in the Spiderwick Chronicles! It's kind of like a miniature elevator to carry food from one level of a house to another."

Kevin grimaced. "And this is how we're supposed to get up to the turret? There's no way it was made to hold the weight of a person."

I used the light on my phone to peer through the tiny gap above the steel box. "It's got a pretty thick steel cable."

"But this house is being renovated because it's ancient," Kevin protested. "What if the cable snaps?"

Finley cleared his throat, and we all jumped. I'd nearly forgotten he was there.

"I know I'm only observing," Finley said, "but I just wanted to say that Lily wouldn't make you do anything unsafe."

"Finley's right," Edgar said. "And I know I was wrong about the poet-river thing with that houseboat, but *this*? With the name *Sparrow* and the silver dumbwaiter, this has *got* to be right. So that also means it's got to be safe."

Elena pumped a fist in the air. "We're riding the silver chariot!" She slung a leg up and into the dumbwaiter.

"Should we at least send the smallest person first?" Kevin asked.

Elena paused. Everyone's eyes turned to me. Elena was the daredevil, not me. But . . .

I squared my shoulders. "Kevin's right. We should go smallest to biggest."

Edgar dragged a wooden chair over from the corner of the kitchen. I climbed onto the chair and crawled inside the dumbwaiter. It was dark and musty inside, and it bounced slightly as I settled into place. I sat, hugging my knees to my chest, the cold steel of the dumbwaiter pressing against my back. It was surprisingly large inside, though Edgar was going to be a snug fit.

"Ready?" Elena asked.

I willed myself to relax and gave a thumbs-up.

Then the door slid shut and everything went black.

For a moment, only the sound of my rapid breathing filled the dumbwaiter. Then there was a bump, a lurch, a grinding of gears from somewhere overhead. My heart pounded. With a creaking, metallic groan, the silver chariot began to rise.

I pulled my knees so tightly to my chest, I could barely breathe. What had I been thinking? I wasn't *that* much smaller than Elena!

The dumbwaiter continued its grinding, groaning journey inside the walls of the White Bend Inn. I squeezed my eyes shut, even though it was already too dark to see.

Then, with a *clunk,* it was over. The dumbwaiter joggled to a stop, swaying slightly. I opened my eyes. A faint line of light sliced a vertical streak along the wall beside me. I reached out and pushed. The dumbwaiter door swung open, and I let out a sigh of relief.

Without a chair to climb down on, I tumbled from the dumbwaiter and *thunk*ed onto the floor. I stood, brushing dust from my knees.

On the wall beside the dumbwaiter door was a rectangular panel with two tarnished brass buttons, one above the other. I pressed the bottom button. The dumbwaiter jerked into motion, creaking its way downward, a silver chariot descending for its next rider.

I listened to the growling motor and watched the thick steel cable slide past as the dumbwaiter disappeared down the dark shaft. Then, as I waited for my friends, I opened my journal to scratch a few quick notes, using a trick my mom had taught me for recording facts—my *observations*—and what I'm thinking about them—my *cogitations*. Because there was plenty to see and think about in the old, dusty turret of the White Bend Inn.

Tuesday, April 12

Observations & COGITATIONS

(Grove Park Challenge, Day 1, White Bend Inn)

- Eight stained-glass windows wrap around the turret; make a rainbow of light
- Dusty plank floor has scuffed trail of footprints
  ↳ LILY'S TRACKS FROM HIDING A CLUE?
- Boxes piled high along walls; more clutter includes two large chests, antique brass floor lamp, ornate grandfather clock, furniture
  ↳ WILL WE HAVE TO SEARCH THROUGH ALL THAT JUNK?
- Waist-high wooden rail circles most of the way around large hole in center of room; more missing stairs; ladder lying on floor below
  ↳ LILY MUST HAVE USED THE LADDER TO GET TO THE TURRET BUT THEN MADE SURE WE'D HAVE TO USE THE DUMBWAITER INSTEAD. TRICKY!

11

I had to hand it to Lily—she'd forced us to take the tough route with the . . . *Wait! The dumbwaiter!*

I slapped my journal shut and looked toward the opening in the wall. The cable was sliding in the opposite direction. Elena was the next smallest and must have been nearly up.

An armchair with worn, velvety green cushions and wood trim sat to the left of the dumbwaiter. I shoved it over, its wooden legs scraping fresh trails along the dusty floorboards. I parked the chair under the opening to the dumbwaiter right as the next chariot rider popped into view.

I tossed up goofy, exaggerated jazz hands to greet Elena. "Hey, Ele—" My hands froze in midair. *"Finley?"*

Finley gave a shy smile and unfolded himself,

stepping onto the velvety chair and down to the floor. "Elena and I are about the same size, so the others decided I should go next. You know—to document."

I dropped my hands to my sides, ears burning. *Great time for jazz hands, weirdo!*

But if Finley thought I was acting strange, he didn't show it. He just shoved his hands into his pockets and didn't say anything else.

I reached out and pushed the button on the wall, sending the dumbwaiter back down. I glanced sideways at Finley. He was staring at the creaking cables. We stood there in awkward silence for a long, *long* moment.

"Um," I said finally. "I read your article."

Finley jolted. "How did you—"

"It was really good journalism—the way you got the cafeteria workers to trust you enough to open up and tell what was going on."

Finley's shoulders relaxed. "Oh, well . . . I've always wanted to be a journalist, maybe even in radio or TV. Like a modern Edward R. Murrow."

Finley knew who Edward R. Murrow was? I'd always figured I was the only sixth grader in the world who geeked out about famous journalists!

"Who's your favorite journalist?" Finley asked.

I watched the rainbow of light play across the floor from the turret's stained-glass windows, willing my heartbeat to steady. "You'll laugh," I finally said, "but it's my mom. She's–"

"Three cheers for the silver chariot!" Elena sprang from the dumbwaiter and bounced off the chair like it was a trampoline. Dust from the chair's cushion billowed into the air. "Chariot rides rock!"

I'd been so caught up in talking with Finley that I hadn't even noticed the dumbwaiter's arrival.

Elena looked from me to Finley, and back to me. She arched an eyebrow.

My face grew warm. "We should look around!" I blurted. I could tell my pale, freckled face was blazing red. "Look but don't touch," I said, hoping it didn't matter that I'd already moved a chair. "We don't want to mess something up that would keep us from finding the next clue."

"Roger that, Captain." Elena gave a finger-waggling salute.

We didn't have to wander around for long before Edgar arrived in the dumbwaiter, crammed into the steel box tighter than a ten-word headline on a newspaper.

"Jeez, Edge," Elena said, helping drag Edgar from the dumbwaiter. "Did Kev have a growth spurt while we were up here, and now he's bigger than you?"

Edgar shook his head. "I needed his help getting in." The right side of Edgar's face had a giant red spot where it had been smashed against the side of the box. "There was shoving and tucking involved."

We all laughed, and I sent the dumbwaiter back for Kevin.

When Kevin crawled out a minute later, his eyes were wide, his forehead beaded with sweat.

"You okay, Kev?" Elena asked. "You look a little–"

"I'm fine!" Kevin insisted. He straightened his shirt and cleared his throat.

Just then, a loud *DONG!* echoed through the turret, vibrating my entire body.

"It's five o'clock!" Kevin declared. "The bird will give its light!"

"Lily must have wound the grandfather clock when she came up to hide the clue," I said as the clock continued to chime.

We stampeded over to the window with the blue-feathered bird in the middle. The sun had dropped just far enough in the sky to send its rays directly into that window.

"Follow the light refracting through the swallow's blue plumage," Elena ordered.

The glass around the bird shone in greens and yellows and reds, with the feathers on the bird's back the only splash of blue. All of the colors seemed to dance in the turret's dusty air, but my eyes followed the blue-tinged sunbeam that traveled across the room.

A wooden chest sat among the old furniture. It was banded with thick iron straps and looked like a pirate's chest straight out of *Treasure Island*. The blue light fell onto the chest's open clasp.

Edgar got to it first and opened the lid. Bundles of envelopes and papers sat inside, yellowed with age.

I reached in and started handing stuff to the others. "Look for anything that could be the next clue."

When I picked up a packet of envelopes knotted together with brown twine and accidentally started to hand it to Finley, he took a step back. "Notetaking only." He smiled and held up his phone. "Remember?"

"Sorry." I returned his smile and set the envelopes back in the chest. "Guess you look too much like another GEEK."

Finley pinched his bottom lip, glancing around at the others.

"Don't worry, Fin," Elena said. "Gee just gave you a compliment!"

Finley's face reddened, but a slow smile pushed up his cheeks.

For the next few minutes the turret was filled with the rustle of papers and murmured comments like "Nothing in this pile" and "This is just a bunch of fifty-year-old receipts."

Unable to pass up anything connected to newspapers, I got distracted by a brief obituary clipped from the *Grove Park Herald* in 1955.

Hattie Simmons, beloved innkeeper of the White Bend Inn, passed away from undetermined causes on Monday, September 26. She was 75 years old. Mrs. Simmons was preceded in death by her husband, Gerald Simmons. She is survived by her estranged daughter, Maxine Van Houten, of nearby Elmwood.

I read the last line again, unable to believe my eyes. *Her estranged daughter, Maxine Van Houten?* Hattie Simmons was Maxine's *mom?* Why would the brilliant Maxine Van Houten have been estranged from her own mother?

I showed the obituary to the other GEEKs. "Hattie must be the *good lady* from the clue. The one who retired into eternal rest. But why would Maxine have been estranged from her mother if she was such a good person?"

"We can't worry about that right now," Edgar said. "We still need to find the next clue."

"Well, check this out." Elena held up the stack of envelopes I'd nearly handed to Finley. She waved around the top envelope. "It's addressed to Maxine Van Houten from Hattie Simmons!"

"Reading other people's mail is a crime," Kevin said. "I—*we*—can't risk that. Not with all the other accusations."

"The envelope's already opened," said Elena. "So the next clue could be inside. Besides, the only surviving relative of Maxine Van Houten is *Max*. He's not gonna press criminal charges against us for peeking at his dead grandma's mail."

Elena didn't wait to see if Kevin had a counter-argument. She pulled a yellowed sheet of flowery stationery from the envelope.

"I can do a dramatic reading!" Edgar plucked the letter from Elena's hand. He stood, placed one hand over his heart, and used his best little-old-granny voice: " 'My dearest little Sparrow . . .' "

We all laughed. Then Edgar kept reading, and our laughter died away.

By the time Edgar got to the final lines, his voice had softened, its drama and fake accent long gone. He had sunk back to the floor, sitting with the rest of us. " 'My little Sparrow, I know I am only an innkeeper, and you may be ashamed of me, but I am so very proud of you. I long for you to fly back home, yet until that day comes, I promise that my letters will continue.' " Edgar sniffled and wiped the back of his hand beneath his nose. " 'Your loving mother, Hattie.' "

As Edgar's voice trailed off, we all sat on the dusty floor, silent, lost in our own thoughts. Elena finally nudged the quiet aside. "So . . . Maxine was the sparrow."

She held up the rest of the envelopes. "And Hattie clearly kept her promise to keep writing."

Each of the remaining envelopes was addressed in the same way as the first one, but all were still sealed. "Maxine must have read the first letter and returned it," I said. "Then she returned all the others without reading them."

This time, even Elena didn't argue for opening them.

Edgar pointed to the date at the top of the first letter. "December 1954. According to the obituary Gina found, Hattie died from unknown causes in 1955. Maybe it was from heartbreak."

I picked up the letter, admiring Hattie's beautiful cursive handwriting. "But why would Maxine be ashamed just because her mother was an innkeeper?" I slid the letter back into its envelope and slipped it inside the front cover of my journal. I could show the letter to Max. See if he knew anything.

Elena shook her head. "Yeah, that's messed up. But maybe that's why we never knew that Maxine was from Grove Park. She didn't mention it in her autobiography or—"

"Hey, guys," Kevin cut in, "Maxine and Hattie can wait. We have other things to worry about."

He pulled a cream-colored envelope from the stack of papers he'd been sorting through. A single word was printed on the front: *GEEKs.*

12

"Open it!" we all shouted.

Kevin peeled back the envelope's flap, pulled a single sheet of paper from inside, and read us the new clue.

At Leonardo's masterpiece
You'll be right where you ought.
Then race headlong into the wind,
And ride your train of thought.

Look beneath the rainbow—
A Steel-Hearted Soul awaits.
Then find its combination,
Where it rests inside the gates.

"That's even more confusing than rivers and poets," Edgar said.

"Anyone have any ideas?" I asked.

The others shook their heads.

"Don't worry. We'll figure it out," Elena said. "But first . . ." She snatched the clue from Kevin's hands and pocketed it. "It's time for another ride in the silver chariot!"

Kevin and Edgar both groaned.

"Oh, toughen up, boys!" Elena bounded to her feet. "Last up, first down. Hop in, Kev, and let's get this chariot rollin'!"

Kevin whimpered but folded himself into the dumbwaiter, and one at a time, we jolted back down to the kitchen.

By the time I came down last, Kevin still looked a little queasy from his ride, and Edgar still looked a bit smooshed. Things didn't improve when we stepped from the inn and discovered a crowd of people waiting on the front lawn. The stringy-haired reporter with the Red Sox beanie crouched at the front of the pack, snapping photos.

Sophina Burkhart stood on the inn's porch, facing the crowd, apparently not realizing we'd emerged behind her. "I know what you all probably think of the GEEKs," she was saying. "I used to think it too–total losers with terrible fashion sense. And, well . . ." She shrugged. "That's mostly true. But they *aren't* liars! One time in fourth grade, Kevin told on *himself* for accidentally seeing someone else's answers on a math test." She held up a large white box. "Now, can I interest anyone in a free cake pop from Burkhart Bakery, conveniently located in the heart of Elmwood?"

"What do you think you're doing?" Elena growled under her breath, stepping up beside Sophina.

Sophina jumped, then quickly recovered. "Oh, here they are now!" She smiled at the crowd, which had begun to press forward and shout questions. "I bet they've already solved the first clue!"

"What *are* you doing here, Sophina?" I asked.

Sophina would make a good ventriloquist. Somehow she managed to keep a toothy smile plastered on her face as she whispered to us: "Smile and pose, GEEKs. Smile and pose."

Edgar, Kevin, and I did our best to follow her instructions, though my mind was busy puzzling over the new clue. Elena just scowled.

The stringy-haired reporter stepped from the crowd and called, "Did you have permission to be inside the inn? Did you vandalize it like you did Van Houten Toys during your first treasure hunt?"

My smile cracked.

Elena stuck out her chin. "This is where the clue sent

us, so we were allowed inside. And"–she glared at the reporter–"we *didn't* vandalize Van Houten Toys. We collected clues left inside the factory by Maxine Van Houten. Yes, we might have climbed on a statue in our search, and yes, we might have picked one little lock. But–"

Before she could finish, Lily Grove appeared, striding up the steps and onto the porch. "Isn't this exciting, everyone? Our very own Finley Brown will be posting a summary of the day's search on the *Grove Park Herald* website later this evening. That will answer all of your questions. Thank you, everyone, for your interest, and have a good evening." She smiled and waved, ignoring the questions still being shouted by the crowd.

Sophina started doing her beauty-queen wave and looped her arm through Elena's elbow, guiding her down the porch steps. "Flip your hair! Look confident!" she said through her smile, leading us toward our jumble of bikes, which now included Sophina's shiny white Diamondback.

As people pressed toward us, we quickly grabbed our bikes and pedaled off, leaving the chaos behind.

After a couple of blocks, Finley said, "I'd better get home for dinner. Then I have to write up my report." He angled off in the direction of the Pink Barn Café. "See you guys tomorrow. Don't go solving the next clue without me!"

After waving goodbye to Finley, we wove our way through Grove Park, heading for Elmgrove Bridge. I really wanted to discuss the new clue as we rode, but . . .

"So what was your little stunt all about back at the inn?" Elena glared over her shoulder at Sophina, who pedaled along in our pack. "We're losers with bad fashion sense?"

"Come on," Sophina said, "you've got to know by now that life is just one big popularity contest. If people like you, they'll believe you. And if they believe you, then maybe I can salvage my reputation, which you GEEKs have totally destroyed."

I rolled my eyes. I should have known it was all about Sophina helping herself, not us. Besides, why couldn't people focus on the facts instead of worrying about popularity?

"She has a point," Kevin grumbled.

"Clearly," Sophina continued, "if you GEEKs are going to have any hope of swaying the public, you'll need help becoming popular. *Lots* of help. That's where I come in. Clothes, hair, attitude. Whatever it takes."

"What's wrong with my hair?" Edgar asked. A sweaty red curl peeked from under his bike helmet, plastered to his forehead.

"We'll talk later." Sophina waved him off. "But don't worry. I'll be there to help every step of the way."

Elena's nostrils flared. "We don't want your help!"

"That doesn't mean you don't *need* it," Sophina retorted.

Elena grunted but didn't push the argument.

I just kept my mouth shut and kept pedaling. But I felt the same as the others—we didn't need Sophina trying to fix us or change us or whatever.

Of course, it was pretty clear Sophina didn't really care what any of *us* thought. She kept biking right alongside us, over the bridge and back into Elmwood. It was going to be a long three days.

Sauce greeted me with a slurp across the kneecap as soon as I got home and stepped into our apartment above the office of the *Elmwood Tribune*. As I knelt to hug him, I noticed my mom.

She sat slumped at the kitchen table in the area that used to be the newspaper's break room way back before she and I were the paper's only employees. "I understand," she said into her phone, giving me a halfhearted wave. "Just temporary." She ended the call.

I stopped hugging Sauce and walked over to the table. "Mom, what's wrong?"

She sighed. "That was the *Boston Globe,* Bean. With all the negative news surrounding Elmwood right now, they're putting my column on hold."

My lips began to tremble. Mom had gotten hired to

write her monthly Letters from Elmwood column because people had wanted to know more about our town after the discovery of the Van Houten fortune. I'd been so focused on how all the lies about Elmwood affected me and my friends that I hadn't stopped to think about how they might affect my mom. I forced my trembling lips into a tight smile. "Don't worry, Mom." I wrapped my arms around her and rested my head against her shoulder. "I'm going to fix this."

Mom stroked my cheek. "Oh, Gina Bean, don't put this on your shoulders. We'll figure it out."

We stayed like that for a long time—me with my arms wrapped around my mom as she sat at the kitchen table, her gently stroking my cheek, neither of us talking. I imagine we were thinking about the same things: Mom losing her monthly column with the *Boston Globe*; whether the other GEEKs and I would succeed in our new treasure hunt; and what would happen if we didn't.

What if, what if, what if . . .

Then Sauce finally reminded us it was time for dinner.

That night, I sat up in bed as Sauce snored beside me. I rubbed his soft head as I read and reread the letter

Hattie Simmons had written to Maxine Van Houten way back in 1954.

During our treasure hunt six months earlier, I'd started to think of Maxine as a hero. She'd been an inventor, an engineer, a businesswoman. She'd done everything she could to save and support the town of Elmwood. Almost a patron saint of geek-hood. But did I have it all wrong?

Family is supposed to support each other through hard times. Like Mom and I had done when it had looked like we'd have to sell the *Elmwood Tribune* and move to Boston. Like we'd done that very evening after Mom's call from the *Boston Globe*.

What I'd started to tell Finley in the turret was true—my mom was my favorite journalist. I was proud of how hard she worked, of how honest and fair she was in her reporting. She was also the strongest person I knew. My dad—Lieutenant Joseph "J. T." Sparks—had died in a Coast Guard helicopter crash before I'd even been born, yet my mom had pushed through her grief and built a life for the two of us. No matter what happened with her *Boston Globe* column or even the *Elmwood Tribune*, I'd be proud of her. No. Matter. What.

So how could Maxine Van Houten have cut off her own mother, just because she wasn't rich or didn't have some amazing job? How could Maxine have been such a snob?

My phone pinged.

A group text from Sophina.

Check this out. It's not bad. STAY ON HIS GOOD SIDE.

Sophina had pasted in a link to Finley's first daily update. I clicked on it.

Along with a pretty cool shot of the blue-tinted sunbeam landing on the wooden chest in the turret of the White Bend Inn, Finley had included a photo he'd snapped of our first clue. Then he summarized all the steps—and missteps—we'd taken in solving it.

Finley was good. Clear sentence structure, solid transitions, and—most important—objective facts. I winced a bit when he mentioned the letter from Hattie to Maxine, which had clearly been sent back. Still, it made me respect Finley that much more. He'd reported the truth. That's a journalist's job—even when the truth is uncomfortable.

I silenced my phone, clicked off my light, and snuggled under my covers, too worn-out from the day to face any more texts.

As I lay there, listening to Sauce's snoring, I hoped Max wasn't mad that we'd allowed Hattie's letter to become public knowledge. But regardless, I was thankful for Finley's reporting. People would read Finley's post. They'd realize the GEEKs weren't fakes—we were real, clue-solving treasure hunters. They'd believe us again.

I drifted off to sleep, convinced things were about to get better.

It wasn't until I awoke the next morning and saw the dozens of missed texts that I realized how wrong I was.

The Fair Valley Tattler

ANONYMOUS • Tuesday, April 12 • 11:02 p.m.

DAY ONE OF GEEK CHALLENGE BRINGS CRIMES & SURPRISES!

On the first day of the Grove Park Challenge, the Elmwood GEEKs proved two things: One, they are undoubtedly criminals. Two, Maxine Van Houten was not the wonderful do-gooder the world has imagined.

Dozens of witnesses were present as the GEEKs fled from a houseboat along the White Bend River this afternoon. The owner of the boat was unavailable for further comment but was overheard screaming "TRESPASSERS!" and "INTERLOPERS!" as he ran the GEEKs off with a frozen yet sizable rainbow trout, pictured below.

The GEEKs' day of CRIMINAL ACTIVITY had only just begun. After fleeing from the scene of their TRESPASSING, the four youths found more than their next clue at the historic White Bend Inn. A witness who was present as the GEEKs left the inn reported that they smuggled additional property from the premises. It is believed that MAIL THEFT may be involved.

As for Maxine Van Houten, the FVT has uncovered new, disturbing facts about her personal history. If you've ever wondered what kind of person would neglect an aging mother and refuse to accept her letters, then look no further than Maxine Van Houten! Then ask yourself:

Would the same woman who was HEARTLESS enough to leave behind an aging parent be kind enough to leave behind a treasure for a town?

If you're like me, you have your DOUBTS.

Now, what's in store for DAY 2 of the GEEKs' treasure hunt? What other CRIMES will they commit? Come back tomorrow to find out. The FVT will be there to help you feel like you're there too!

The Fair Valley Tattler—Finding. Verifying. Truth.

14

"This isn't journalism!" I waved my phone at my friends as we sat on our bikes on the Elmwood side of the bridge. I pointed to the photo the Fair Valley Tattler had included in the blog post—a picture of the four of us plus Finley sprinting away from *The Bard* while the guy on the boat swung a frozen fish over his head like a sword. "This isn't finding and verifying truth. It's falsifying and vilifying it!"

"But who's writing all this garbage?" Elena asked. She reached up to tug her braid, then lowered her hand, fist clenched. Thanks to Sophina, she had no braid to tug. That's because—along with sending us the link to the Tattler's blog post—Sophina had buried us with texts about our lack of fashion sense, along with advice on how to fix it.

We'd wanted to ignore her. But after the Tattler's newest post, Kevin had convinced us we should give Sophina's fashion advice a shot. At this point, changing our images couldn't hurt.

Of course, unlike me, Sophina was all about opinions, not facts.

OPINION #1: "Leave your hair down. It's your best feature!" (Elena's straight black hair lay across her shoulders and flowed down her back.)

OPINION #2: "You have *got* to ditch the polos so you don't look so uptight!" (Kevin wore a T-shirt, though he'd tucked it in, and I'm pretty sure he'd ironed it.)

OPINION #3: "Wear green. It will make your red hair absolutely *pop!*" (Edgar had borrowed a green shirt and pants from his dad, and now looked way more like the world's largest leprechaun than Sophina probably would have liked.)

OPINION #4: "You know, blue would *totally* bring out your eyes." (I wore blue.)

"We need to get to the Pink Barn," Kevin said, reminding us we had a job to do. "Finley's probably already waiting."

We agreed and took off.

I heard the clicking right as we cleared the far end of the bridge and entered Grove Park.

I glanced back just in time to spot the end of a long zoom lens as someone ducked behind the edge of the bridge.

I kept pedaling along with my friends, but my jaw tightened. I thought of the photo in the Fair Valley Tattler blog post. And I thought of the guy I kept spotting in every crowd, always clicking away with his camera.

I suddenly had a pretty good idea who the Tattler was.

We met up with Finley in the back room of the Pink Barn Café. Apparently I hadn't yet unclenched my jaw.

"What's wrong?" Finley asked when he saw me.

"I think I know who the Fair Valley Tattler is."

His eyes widened in surprise. "You do?"

"Spill it, Gee!" Elena ordered.

"The Tattler has to be the guy who's always shouting out the rude, ridiculous questions," I said.

"The one with the Red Sox hat?" Edgar asked.

"Exactly. He's constantly snapping photos, and the Tattler's blog included a picture from the houseboat."

"That makes sense," Kevin said.

"The question is *why*?" My hands balled into fists, my fingernails biting into my palms. "Why does he want to take us down so badly?"

"Just ignore him *and* the blog," Finley said. "It's only clickbait. It's not"—he ducked his head—"like *your* journalism."

My face burned with the compliment. "We need to get started!" I blurted, totally not just trying to change the subject. "We've got to solve our next clue."

Finley coughed nervously. "I'll keep taking notes."

I braced myself for a comment from Elena, sure that she'd noticed my embarrassment around Finley, but all she did was pull out the clue we'd found at the White Bend Inn.

"I thought about it all night," Kevin said, "and I'm pretty sure we need to go to Grove Park Middle. Think about it—a *steel-hearted soul* with a *combination*? Sounds like a school locker to me. And since we're sixth graders, I figured Lily would send us to the middle school, not the high school."

"I thought it might be the theater," Edgar said. "The *beneath the rainbow* line could be a nod to 'Over the Rainbow' from *The Wizard of Oz*. But I suppose that could still be at the school." Edgar turned to Finley. "Does Grove Park Middle have an auditorium?"

Finley made a zipping motion across his lips.

"Oops," Edgar said. "Sorry. I keep forgetting you're not supposed to help."

Elena flopped into one of the folding chairs at the small round table. "What about the *Leonardo's masterpiece* line? How's that fit?"

"I'm pretty sure we won't find the *Mona Lisa* sitting around Grove Park," I said. "But maybe there's a poster of it or something at the school?"

I flipped through the notes about Grove Park in my journal but came up empty, so after a few more minutes of discussion, we decided the locker-theater-*Mona-Lisa*-poster thing was our best lead. We took off toward Grove Park Middle School, which sat at the northern edge of town.

Just like in the neighborhood around the inn where we'd been the day before, every building we saw seemed a bit bigger and in better shape than the ones in Elmwood, probably because of all the good jobs that came to Grove Park thanks to Fair Valley Technology Solutions. We bumped over railroad tracks near a curving, half-circle brick building, which a sign identified as the Fair Valley Transportation Museum. We passed customers bustling in and out of a string of shops that had bright awnings and well-polished windows–Perfect Paint Nail Studio, Lion's Pizza, Madeline's Market. We even passed the church we'd originally wanted to search for our first clue. Compared to Elmwood Community Church, Grove Park United Methodist's steeple rose a little higher, and its white clapboard siding shone a little brighter. And then we got to the school, and I tried really hard not to be jealous.

Even though Elmwood and Grove Park are only separated by the White Bend River, I'd never been to Grove Park Middle before. At the school's entrance, a ten-foot-tall natural rock formation pushed up from the ground. A massive eagle, wings outstretched, had been chiseled from the top, as if it were touching down for a landing. The front of the stone was engraved with:

GROVE PARK
MIDDLE SCHOOL
HOME OF THE EAGLES

I couldn't help but wonder why Grove Park got a cool eagle mascot while Elmwood was stuck with the Fighting Sap Tappers.

The school itself had been designed to blend in with the architecture of the older buildings in town—it was three stories of red brick with arched stonework curving above its windows and doors. Yet it was actually only a few years old, modern, and way bigger than Elmwood Middle. But the biggest surprise was the parking lot–it was packed with cars and minivans and pickup trucks.

"What the what?" Elena said. "It's spring break! On a Wednesday morning! What're all these people doing here?"

"Look." I pointed to a digital sign above the school's entrance. Gold-colored words scrolled slowly across the message board: WELCOME TO THE FAIR VALLEY SPRING BASKET-BALL INVITATIONAL!

"At least the doors will be unlocked," Edgar said. "That means no more accusations of breaking and entering."

Kevin threw up his arms. "But how will we search the school without people following us around and shouting questions and making trouble? This is a disaster!"

"Kevin's got a point," I said. "Think of all the people who showed up at the houseboat and the inn. Just because we're allowed inside doesn't mean we want everyone tailing us through the halls."

"Wait a second." Elena rubbed her chin and studied Edgar. She got the glint in her eyes that is pretty much always worth worrying about. "Hey, Edge, how do you feel about a little Hoopspearean improv?"

"To hoop or not to hoop, that is the question!" Edgar bellowed, standing atop a chair in Grove Park Middle's massive foyer, near the entrance into the gym. We'd found a half-deflated basketball at the top of a garbage can outside, and Edgar now had it smooshed on his head like a helmet. "Whether 'tis nobler to shoot or to pass or to dribble the ball . . ."

Everyone in the foyer—the people in line at the concession stand, the people selling tickets by the gym doors, the fans milling about, *everyone*—turned to look at Edgar. Well, everyone except me, Kevin, Elena, and Finley. We used the distraction to dash down a hallway that led into the heart of the school.

As we scurried out of sight, Edgar's booming

Shakespearean basketball improv carried behind us: "To take the ball against a sea of defenders . . ."

We split up. Elena headed off to the school's auditorium to check the seats and stage and dressing rooms, where Edgar planned to join her once he found a way to slip out from his grand performance in the foyer. Finley came with me and Kevin as we tried classroom doors and checked the hall for unlocked lockers.

We were far from the basketball tournament, so the hallways were unlit, yet even in the dim light I could make out beautiful murals painted on the walls above the lockers. The paintings showed scenes of Fair Valley and children playing and plenty of soaring eagles. I kept an eye out for rainbows or the *Mona Lisa* but spotted neither.

As Kevin and I tried opening locker after locker, our sneakers squeaked quietly on the polished floor. None of the lockers opened. The classrooms were all locked too, but I peered through their windows, spotting things like wall-mounted digital smartboards and shelves of laptops. I turned to Finley, who trailed behind us, taking notes. "You must love it here. Everything's brand-new!"

Finley shrugged. "It's okay, I guess. It's just . . ." He shrugged again, like his shoulders could complete the sentence.

"What?"

"Never mind."

"No, really. What is it?"

Finley ran a hand through his hair and stared at his feet. "School's lonely sometimes. People here don't really *get* me." He gestured to me and Kevin. "You GEEKs are lucky you found each other. I'd love to have friends like you."

I thought of how right Finley was. Of how lost I'd feel without the other GEEKs. I reached out and gently rested my hand on his forearm. "It's okay. We're right here. So you *do* have friends like us."

The half-sad, half-happy smile Finley gave me made my heart pound.

An hour later, Kevin, Finley, and I met up with Elena and Edgar outside the auditorium. I had no idea how Edgar had managed to sneak away after his performance in the foyer, but I was sure he'd pulled it off with flair.

"Nothing!" Kevin said. "No rainbows, no Leonardo's masterpiece, no nothing."

Elena sniffed. "You know, this school stinks."

I nudged her and cut my eyes toward Finley. "He goes here," I whispered. "Be nice."

"No," Elena said. "I mean it literally stinks." She

sniffed again. "It stinks like sweaty basketball players. It stinks like a gym *locker* room."

Kevin gasped. "I get it—the gym lockers. We can still find a steel-hearted soul with a combination."

"You betcha, Kev!" Elena gave him a high five.

"To hoop or not to hoop, that really *is* the question!" Edgar said.

We stood in an empty hallway on the back side of the gym. The muffled sounds of the game made their way through the walls—the pounding of basketballs and squeak of sneakers on the gym floor, the chant of cheerleaders stirring up the crowd, a coach shouting.

"No way we're starting with the boys' locker room." Elena put her hands to her throat and gagged. "The funk in there might be deadly."

Edgar and Kevin both eyed the door to the girls' locker room and frowned.

Kevin shuffled his feet. "We can just wait out here."

Edgar bobbed his head. "Yeah, we'll be the lookouts."

"Oh, get a grip, boys!" Elena rolled her eyes. "Don't you hear the game? Nobody's in the locker room. They're all on the court. This is the perfect time to sneak in and find the clue." She pushed the door open, shoved Edgar through, and then dragged Kevin in after him. Finley and I hustled in behind them. We smacked right up against their backs.

"In the second half, we need *hustle*! We need *passion*!"

The shouting coach wasn't in the gym.

A tall woman with short, spiky brown hair stood in the middle of a group of kneeling players. She smacked her fist into her palm with each emphasized word. "We need–" The coach's eyes cut to us, and she froze mid-rant, her fist still raised. "Who are *you*?"

Edgar adjusted the half-deflated basketball on his head. "Um . . . big fans?"

A blond girl stood up. Her white uniform had thick navy-blue stripes running down the sides and EAGLES printed on the front of her jersey above the number thirteen. She stabbed a finger toward us. "It's those kids from Elmwood!"

I took a step back, bumping against the locker room door, which had swung shut behind us.

"This could be going better," Elena muttered.

The coach put her hands on her hips. Her eyes narrowed. "Trying to spy on the competition during half-time? Planning to steal our plays?"

"We can explain," Kevin said. "We didn't realize that–"

"No time for explaining, Kev," said Elena.

The coach took a step toward us. Her players stood, tightening in around us.

Edgar and Kevin and Elena pressed back into me and Finley. Finley and I pressed back against the closed door. There was no room to swing it open. We were trapped!

Edgar put his hands to his chest and burst into song. "Oom-pah-pah! Oom-pah-pah! That's how it goes. . . ."

The Grove Park players and the spiky-haired coach stopped and stared at Edgar, obviously caught off guard by his halftime performance of *Oliver!*

Elena was the first of us to react. "Oom-pah-pah!" she shouted. She charged into the press of players, who instinctively stepped aside. Elena shot toward a second door on the far side of the locker room.

The rest of us knew enough to follow her lead. "Oom-pah-pah!"

We burst from the locker room into the gym like a herd of stampeding cattle. Edgar—who had one hand clamped to the deflated ball still on his head—collided with a rack of basketballs. The rack crashed over, sending a dozen balls bouncing across the gym floor. The Elmwood Middle School varsity girls were practicing layups at one end of the court while the Grove Park cheerleaders led the home crowd in a chant, along with the help of someone dressed in an oversized eagle costume, complete with a jersey that had EGGY printed across the back.

As Eggy hopped around, flapping his wings, pumping

up the crowd, one of the loose basketballs rolled toward him.

He never saw it coming.

Eggy made a backward hop and landed right on top of the ball. His feet shot into the air. His wings flapped helplessly. The crowd gasped. Eggy *thump*ed onto his back. His eagle head popped off.

"They killed Eggy!" someone in the crowd shouted.

Kevin groaned.

"Come on," I said. "Let's make sure Eggy's all right!" I ran across the gym toward the fallen mascot.

Reeeet!

A referee in a black-and-white-striped shirt cut me off, blowing his whistle. "Stay clear of the mascot."

"But–"

"Stay clear," the referee repeated.

I could hear Eggy groaning, "My ankle! My ankle!" but the referee blocked my path.

Boos and jeers rained down from the Grove Park side of the gym. The fans from Elmwood–parents and friends of our classmates–sat in shocked silence.

Kevin raised his hands, trying to quiet the crowd. "We're sorry! As Elmwood Middle School's sixth-grade co-president, I can assure you that we never meant for this to happen!"

The booing grew louder.

"Come on." Elena tugged Kevin's sleeve, then mine.

I looked at the angry fans, the injured Eggy. "They have to realize this was an accident!" I pointed back toward the locker room. "And what about the clue?"

"It's more of Elmwood's dirty tricks!" someone roared.

"We gotta go *now*, GEEKs!" Elena urged.

Edgar's half-deflated basketball dropped from his head as we bolted from the gym.

I heard the clicking as soon as we burst out the school doors.

The stringy-haired reporter lowered one of his cameras and called out, "Can you confirm that you were responsible for an injury inside the gymnasium?"

The Tattler! How in the world did he get his scoops so quickly?

We veered to the right, where we'd stashed our bikes behind some bushes.

"Was it assault?" the guy yelled after us.

We strapped on our helmets, leapt onto our bikes, and shot away from Grove Park Middle, leaving the Tattler behind. Again.

"You guys should have let me handle that!" Kevin

called to the rest of us. "I could have explained, and everything would have been fine. It's called diplomacy."

"We were scared for our lives!" Elena called back. "We had to get out of there!"

I couldn't help but think, though, that Kevin had a point.

A few minutes later, we finally slowed our pedaling as we came to the strip of shops with the bright awnings. I cruised up beside Elena at the front of the pack. "Let's get to a side street, stop, and make a plan," I told her.

"On it, Gee." Elena cut around the corner at the end of the row of shops. "Oh, sweet Einstein!"

A white-haired woman had just stepped from the curb, directly into our path.

I swerved left. Elena swerved right.

"Ahhh!" The woman dropped the two canvas grocery sacks she'd been carrying. Her hands flew up. She stumbled backward.

I passed by in front of her. Elena bounced up and over the curb, barely avoiding the woman from behind. I heard the sounds of Kevin, Edgar, and Finley smashing their brakes. We all skittered to stops.

"We're sorry!" I dumped my bike up onto the sidewalk and rushed to make sure the woman was okay.

The woman's canvas bags lay in the street. A bag of Doritos, a box of Twinkies, and other groceries had spilled across the asphalt. Her pale, veiny hands trembled.

"Are you all right?" Elena asked, gently taking the woman's elbow and guiding her back up the curb. "I should've looked before I turned!"

"I-I'm fine," the woman said. A knob of a chin gave her lined face a heart shape. "You just gave me a fright, is all."

Kevin, Edgar, and Finley gathered her spilled groceries. Then Edgar hefted the repacked bags. "We can carry these for you," he said. "They're pretty heavy."

"Oh, I don't want to be a bother," the woman said.

"It would be our pleasure to be of assistance," Kevin said.

The woman laughed. "Well, since you put it that way." She waved a hand toward the other side of the street. "I only live a half block down."

Kevin and Edgar each looped a bag of groceries over their handlebars and pushed their bikes. The rest of us walked slowly along, pushing our bikes too.

"My name's Elizabeth, by the way," the woman said as we moved down the sidewalk. "Elizabeth Baldoni."

We all introduced ourselves too.

Elizabeth gestured toward the bags hanging from Kevin's and Edgar's handlebars. "Please don't think too poorly of my eating habits. My grandnephew, Tommy, was supposed to come down from college for a visit this weekend, so I stocked up on his favorite snacks."

Kevin eyed the box of Twinkies sticking out of the bag on his handlebars, and licked his lips.

"Unfortunately," Elizabeth continued, "Tommy called right as I left Madeline's Market. He had to cancel." She sighed, and her heart-shaped face seemed to sag in on itself. "College keeps him so busy. That's the third time he's canceled this month."

"I'm sure he'll make it for a visit soon," I said. I didn't have any facts to back up my claim, but I could tell she needed some cheering up.

"Of course, once he comes, Tommy will probably empty my cupboards in the first hour and then tell me he's starving." Elizabeth laughed. "That boy could eat a horse and still be hungry! The last time he visited . . ." Elizabeth launched into a tale about her grandnephew and egg rolls and an all-you-can-eat Chinese buffet, and chattered until she stopped by a white picket fence and swung open the gate. "Here we are!" White, purple, and yellow crocuses lined the front walk, which led to a cozy, gray-shingled house with a bright blue door. Elizabeth looked at the five of us, her face brightening. "I just realized—since Tommy can't come this weekend, there's no one to eat all this food. How about you children come inside for a quick snack instead? I can practice my hostessing."

Clearly Elizabeth was lonely. I felt bad for her, but we had a clue to solve, a treasure hunt to complete, a

Bolt to find. We'd already wasted an entire morning! I exchanged glances with the others.

Kevin stepped forward. "Thank you, Ms. Baldoni, but—"

"Of course! We would love to come in," Elena said quickly. "Thank you. Though, are you sure it's no trouble?"

Elizabeth's eyes sparkled with happiness. "Oh, it's no trouble at all!"

As we wheeled our bikes through the gate and followed Elizabeth toward her home, Kevin whispered, "Elena, we don't have time for this!"

"Well, I say we *do*," Elena said, keeping her voice low. "If that was my abuela who was lonely and sad and missing her family, I'd want someone to take the time to talk to her. So that's what I'm going to do."

Kevin sighed. "I guess you're right."

The five of us followed Elizabeth Baldoni into her house.

In Elizabeth's living room, I got squeezed in between Kevin and Elena in the middle of a flowery, pale yellow sofa, with Edgar on one end and Finley on the other. We left the only chair for Elizabeth, who bustled about, serving us Doritos, Twinkies, and tall glasses of cold lemonade. She chattered away about the weather and spring flowers and how Grove Park had changed over the years.

"Have you lived in Grove Park your whole life?" I asked.

"Indeed I have. I still have some family in town as well." Elizabeth picked up a framed photo from an end table and held it out. In the photo, Elizabeth stood beside a round-bellied, middle-aged guy outside the pizzeria right down the street. The guy wore a red, flour-caked apron. "It's Tommy's father, my nephew, the proud owner of Lion's Pizza."

We all perked up at the mention of pizza, except for Edgar, who was too busy staring at a photo of a slightly younger Elizabeth with her arm around a tall man with salt-and-pepper hair as they stood outside a well-lit theater. A large sign behind them read MAMMA MIA! THE SMASH HIT MUSICAL.

Edgar's voice barely squeaked out. "You saw *Mamma Mia!*? On *Broadway*?" He picked up the photo, his eyes wide and dreamy.

Shhk.

The back slipped off the frame.

Elena—with the reflexes of a cat—whipped her hand out. She caught the back of the frame right before it fell to the floor. But not before a second photo dropped from behind the first and fluttered to the carpet.

Elizabeth gasped.

"I'm sorry, Ms. Baldoni," Edgar said. "I should have been more careful."

Elizabeth waved him off, her eyes still locked on the photo on the floor. "Could . . ." She blinked a few times. "Could you hand me that photo, please? I'd nearly forgotten."

As Edgar bent to pick up the photo, Kevin nudged me. He pointed to the time on his phone and mouthed, *We need to go.*

I knew Kevin was right, but . . . I looked at the photo as Edgar handed it to Elizabeth. The picture was grainy. It showed Elizabeth again—at least it still looked like her, with the same heart-shaped face. She was only a teenager or maybe in her twenties. Just below her throat, a pendant on a necklace flashed green in the sunlight. She stood on a dock, smiling up at a guy with shaggy blond hair and deep-set eyes crinkled with laughter.

I could tell Elizabeth was overcome with emotion, and I didn't think we should leave her. I shook my head at Kevin and mouthed back, *Not yet.* Then I turned to Elizabeth and pointed to the photo, which she held in trembling hands. "I recognize you. Who's the other person?"

A smile curled onto Elizabeth's lips. "Why, it's my first love."

Elizabeth set the photo down. "It was the summer of 1968. He even proposed to me. Jon was twenty-three, but I was only nineteen. My father said I was too young and forced me to end the relationship." A wistful smile passed across Elizabeth's face. "Five years later, I ended up with Angelo–a wonderful husband who laughed with me and loved me and gave me a beautiful life." She took the *Mamma Mia!* photo from Edgar. "And of course who took me to musicals on Broadway." She winked at Edgar. "I have no regrets. Though, I'll confess to once in a while wondering, What if?"

Elizabeth shifted in her seat, and I noticed a flash of green near her shirt collar. I pointed. "Is that the necklace in the photo?"

Elizabeth gazed down at her necklace, which was a silver chain with a small turtle pendant hanging from it. The turtle's shell was studded with tiny emeralds.

"That's right. Jon gave it to me. You see, on our first date, we saw a turtle crossing the road, and I made Jon stop the car so I could carry the turtle to safety."

Elena leaned forward excitedly. "What kind of turtle was it? A Blanding's turtle? An eastern box turtle?"

Elizabeth chuckled. "Oh, I don't know enough about turtles to tell you that. All I know is that Jon told me that when I made him stop to help a turtle, that's when he knew he loved me." She cupped her hand loosely around the pendant. "That's why he bought me this necklace. There's nothing like a first love."

For some reason, I glanced toward Finley. For a split second, his dark eyes caught mine. We both quickly turned our heads.

Kevin took a bite of a Twinkie. "I'm sorry, Ms. Baldoni," he said, "but we've got a clue to solve and really must get going. Unless you also dated someone called Leonardo."

He laughed a little at his own silly joke, but Elizabeth tilted her head to the side, her forehead crinkling.

"Leonardo?" she said. "Why, that's the name of my *nephew*!"

17

"I can't believe we were looking for the wrong Leonardo!" I said as we backtracked toward where we'd met Elizabeth. "Though, it totally makes sense that her nephew would name his restaurant Lion's Pizza. *Leonardo* is an Italian name that comes from a word meaning *lion*."

Elena zoomed past me, her legs churning. "That's cool, Gee. But how about a word that means *super-duper-rocket-fast*? Because that's how we need to be pedaling!"

I pumped my pedals extra hard to keep up.

In no time, we were there, our bikes clattering to the sidewalk. I grabbed my journal and pencil from my bike basket, then pressed my face against the large front window, studying the menu inside. The pizzas listed on a large chalkboard above the counter had names like the Last Supper, Vitruvian Man, and . . . "The Mona Lisa! It's the name of one of the pizzas!"

"Leonardo's masterpiece, here we come!" Elena yanked open the door and charged inside.

Kevin held the door for the rest of us as we followed on Elena's heels.

The first thing I noticed was the tangy aroma of pizza sauce and melted cheese that hung in the air like the scent of heaven. A country song twanged from a jukebox in one corner, and most of the booths and tables were full of people chatting and chowing down on their lunches. A mass of people wearing Red Sox gear huddled at a bar area, watching a game on a wall-mounted TV. A hodgepodge of framed photos blanketed the walls.

A waiter stepped up, holding a stack of plastic-covered menus. "A table for five?"

"Actually," Edgar said, "we were only–"

"Yes!" Elena said. "For five!" When Edgar turned and looked at her, Elena shrugged. "What? We have to eat lunch *somewhere*, don't we?"

As the waiter led us between the tightly packed tables, fingers started pointing. Hands covered mouths, hiding whispered conversations. Phones emerged from pockets and purses and began snapping photos. I overheard a few mutters of "It's them" and "The Elmwood

GEEKs," but I didn't react. We couldn't afford more bad press.

The waiter stopped beside a booth on the far side of the dining room. Edgar and Kevin slid onto the red vinyl bench on one side, while Elena and Finley settled on the other. When I went to follow Finley, someone bumped into me. I stumbled sideways. A girl wearing massive white-framed sunglasses and a paisley head-scarf slipped in next to Finley.

"Hey, what do you–?" I stopped. A wisp of blond hair peeked from beneath the girl's headscarf. *"Sophina?"*

"Shhh. Keep your voice down and have a seat." Sophina tucked the stray strand of hair back under her scarf.

I scowled at her but slid in next to Kevin. "What are you doing here?"

"And how did you find us?" Elena asked, adding a scowl of her own.

Sophina brushed away the questions with a brief wave of her hand. "Obviously I've been tracking Kevin's phone since we were voted sixth-grade co-presidents. I need to be able to find him at all times."

Kevin's eyes widened. "Hey, you can't–"

"And what were you thinking with your stunt at Grove Park Middle?" Sophina lowered her sunglasses just enough to glare around the table at all of us. "Aren't things bad enough already?"

131

Edgar lowered the menu he'd been studying. "That was all just an accident. We—"

"Eggy the Eagle is at Fair Valley Hospital getting X-rays on his ankle and may be out for the school year. #JusticeForEggy is trending on Twitter." Sophina ground her teeth. "This is *not* what I meant when I told you to get people on your side!"

Elena pointed her menu at Sophina. "We don't *need* people on our side. We just have to find the Bolt."

"What good is the Bolt if everyone still thinks the worst of you? I'm trying hard to clear your names, but you GEEKs insist on making my job nearly impossible." Sophina turned to Finley, and her voice softened from a growl to a purr. "At least *your* first report covered them fairly." She took off her sunglasses and smiled. "And has anyone ever told you that you have amazing hair?"

Finley blushed.

My shoulders tightened and my neck grew warm. Sophina was right about Finley's hair. But did she have to *say* it?

An awkward silence draped itself over the table for only an instant before Elena tossed up some jazz hands. "All ten of my fingers vote for eating. Let's order!"

Edgar tapped his menu. "How about the Mona Lisa?"

Elena bobbed her head. "Colosseum-sized! Extra cheese!"

Finley gave a thumbs-up. "Good choice. I don't think

I'm giving any clues away when I tell you it's the best pizza in New Hampshire."

The rest of us quickly agreed on the pizza order, and the waiter reappeared at our table, order pad in hand. As soon as he left, Elena pulled out the clue.

"So we're supposed to find a *steel-hearted soul* beneath a rainbow," I said. "Does anyone see a rainbow around here? Or a steel-hearted soul?"

Kevin pointed to a reproduction of an oil painting hanging by our booth. "Look at the tag beneath that picture. It says it's Thomas Grove, the founder of Grove Park, along with his sons, George and Louis." He gestured around at all the other framed pictures hanging around the dining room. "Maybe the clue's in one of those."

"Good idea, Kev." Elena tucked the clue back into her pocket. "We can check the pictures while we wait for our pizza." Elena nudged Finley. "Bamboozle Bolt hunter coming through."

Finley and Sophina slid from the booth so Elena could get out. I slid from the other side, followed by Kevin and Edgar.

We spread out, weaving through the tables, examining the walls. I tried to ignore the stares and whispers of the other customers as I studied all the photos of people and places around Grove Park. Some of the photos looked recent, like the one of the Grove Park

High School boys' basketball team celebrating inside Lion's Pizza, a tall golden trophy sitting beside a half-eaten pizza in the middle of one of the tables. Other photos looked old, like the black-and-white photo of an old-fashioned paddle-wheel riverboat cruising down the White Bend River. I even spotted a duplicate of the photo Elizabeth had of her and her nephew standing outside the restaurant.

"*Ahhh!*" someone shrieked.

I spun.

Sophina stood, trembling, pointing at the wall above one of the booths. The family sitting at the booth scooted away from her. The man and woman pressed themselves against the wall, wrapping their arms protectively around their two children.

Sophina didn't seem to notice. She pulled out her phone and leaned across the table, snapping a picture of whatever she'd found.

Was it a photo of a rainbow? A steel-hearted soul?

The rest of us hurried toward her through the maze of tables.

Sophina's voice came out in a wobbly shriek: "Did you know that BTS ate here? BTS! *The* BTS! Look! Their picture is on the wall! With a pizza!"

Elena rolled her eyes. "A boy band? Seriously, Sophina? We're kind of on a mission here, you know."

Sophina clicked her tongue. "I can't help it if your

musical taste is as poorly developed as your fashion sense."

Elena stepped toward Sophina, glaring.

Sophina stepped back.

"Come on," I said, quickly wedging myself between them. "We're on the same team here. We need to focus and–" I cut off when I spotted something else on the wall beside the photo of BTS. Something that wasn't just an ordinary photo. "You know what? I think Sophina is onto something. . . ."

18

As soon as the others saw what I was pointing at, Sophina plastered on a smile and turned to the family still huddled at the far end of the booth. "Sorry. Official treasure-hunting business. Out you come." She waved them forward, signaling for them to slide out of the way. "I'm afraid we need to swap booths."

The man adjusted his glasses. "We're nearly finished eating. Can't you–"

Sophina stomped her foot. "Hustle, people, hustle!"

The two young children's eyes went wide, and one of them whispered, "Mommy, why's that girl so rude?"

I grimaced. Wasn't Sophina supposed to be *helping* us? "We know it's inconvenient and we're sorry," I said, trying to salvage our reputation. "Could we buy you some milkshakes for the trouble?"

The man muttered something, but he and his partner herded their children out of the booth and across to where we'd been sitting.

Edgar and Kevin helped bus the family's plates and remaining food over to their new table, while I went and ordered four milkshakes.

But nearly every person in the restaurant was scowling at us now. The damage had already been done. We slunk into our new booth and examined the item on the wall, while Finley snapped pictures and recorded notes on his phone.

Instead of a framed photo, the item I'd spotted was an old album cover. It'd been autographed by the musician—some guy I'd never heard of named Oakley Seasons—and it had a picture of him, tall and trim, standing in the bed of a red Chevy pickup. He faced away from the camera, blond hair falling over the collar of his flannel shirt, a guitar slung across his back. The name of the album was *Steel-Hearted Soul*.

Kevin held up his phone. "I Googled 'Oakley Seasons.' There's not much about him, but there's a Wikipedia page that includes a scan of a newspaper article from the sixties that called him 'the next big thing in blues.'"

"As if," Sophina said. "He clearly wasn't the next big *anything*, because I've never heard of him."

Elena cocked an eyebrow. "What blues musicians *have* you heard of?"

Sophina chewed her bottom lip. "Whatever. Never mind."

"Wait," Kevin said, scrolling through the article. "Oakley Seasons was from Grove Park."

"That's cool," Edgar said. "But there's no rainbow on the album cover."

"And the clue said something about *find its combination*," I said. "That doesn't fit the album cover either."

Before we could discuss things further, the waiter showed up with a stack of plates and the biggest pizza I'd ever seen. "One Colosseum-sized Mona Lisa, extra cheese. Anything else for you today?"

Edgar licked his lips. "This masterpiece should be plenty." He started humming "Food, Glorious Food," a song from *Oliver!*

The steaming pizza was nearly two feet across, and pepperoni and sausage were piled on top. The cheese stretched as Edgar started dishing out slices.

Edgar slid a slice in front of me, and its warm, spicy scent drifted to my nose. But . . .

"I can't eat." I pushed the plate away. "I'm too worried about the clue. The thought of pizza makes me queasy right now."

"Suit yourself, Gee." Elena snatched my slice of pizza and plunked it onto her own plate. "*I* treasure-hunt better on a full stomach."

My mind churned along with my stomach. We'd found Leonardo's masterpiece and the steel-hearted soul, but that wasn't enough. What were we missing? Where was the next clue?

My thoughts were accompanied by the sounds of pizza being chewed, another twangy country song starting up on the jukebox, and an eruption of cheers from the Red Sox fans watching the game by the bar.

Sophina wiped her lips with a napkin. "This music is almost enough to ruin my appetite."

I looked toward the jukebox in the corner. *Holy cow.* "That's it!" I cried. "Look!" I pointed to the jukebox.

Everyone turned. Eyes widened.

Edgar dropped his slice of pizza back onto his plate. "Are you thinking what I'm thinking?"

"Yes!" Sophina said. "That's perfect. We can play some BTS!"

Kevin smacked his forehead.

Elena groaned. "Not the music, Sophina. The *jukebox.*"

The jukebox looked like an old-fashioned spaceship, ready for takeoff. Probably about five feet tall, it squatted on round legs and was built from dark wood with chrome highlights. Pages of song choices sat behind a half circle of glass above a panel of buttons used to pick the song you wanted. Multicolored tubes of lights ran up the sides and arced over the top.

They formed a rainbow.

We blasted from our booth and raced to the jukebox.

Elena started flipping through the song choices. "'Steel-Hearted Soul' *has* to be one of the songs."

"Right there!" Kevin practically punched his finger through the glass.

The card for the song selection read:

"Steel-Hearted Soul"
Oakley Seasons

"Look at the code to play the song," Edgar said. "*W*-forty-eight. That must be what the clue meant by *find its combination!*"

"We've gotta play it." Elena started digging through her pockets. "Who's got a quarter?"

We all came up empty until Finley stopped taking notes and dug a quarter from his jeans. "Here."

Elena snatched the quarter and jammed it into the coin slot.

Kevin punched in the song's code.

I held my breath. And . . .

The twangy country song kept playing.

Elena thumped the jukebox with the palm of her hand. "Where's my song?"

"I think you have to wait for the other song to end," Kevin said.

Elena crossed her arms and started tapping her foot.

Eventually the other song faded out. The jukebox clicked and whirred. And then the song opened with the hum of a harmonica.

An acoustic guitar joined in. Then a gravelly voice launched straight into a chorus:

> She's a steel-hearted soul, racin' the wind.
>
> Can't stay put—gotta keep goin' on without end.
>
> I may try to catch her, but I know she can't be tamed.
>
> Rollin' on, rollin' on, day after day.
>
> A steel-hearted soul, whistlin' on by—
>
> Gone in a puff of smoke, fadin' in the sky . . .

Edgar pretended to wipe a tear from his eye. "It's a love song."

I shook my head. "It's a *train*."

"Huh?"

"Racing the wind? Rolling on day after day? Whistling on by, then gone in a puff of smoke? I think the *steel-hearted soul* is an old train engine."

Kevin started bobbing his head. "That might just make sense."

"And we rode over some railroad tracks earlier," Elena said.

"So what about the combination W-forty-eight?" Edgar asked. "Was that just to help us find the song?"

I shrugged. "I guess."

Sophina snorted. "Try the engine number." We all stopped and stared at Sophina, who blushed and adjusted her headscarf. "What? My dad has model trains, so he used to teach me stuff. Not now, of course. You know—totally a long time ago. When I was a little kid. We used to visit the Fair Valley Transportation Museum a lot. It's right here in Grove Park."

"Yeah," Elena said. "Of course." She grinned and faked a sneeze that sounded an awful lot like a train: *"Achoo-CHOOOO!"*

Sophina's face grew even redder, but for once, I was glad she was there. Sure, she got on my nerves sometimes—okay, pretty much *all* the time—but none of the rest of us knew anything about trains. Maybe there was another GEEK in Elmwood after all.

"Sophina, can you lead us to the transportation museum?" Kevin asked. "Maybe someone there can help us find the W-forty-eight."

"Normally I'd agree because I know we're in a

hurry, but . . ." My eyes flicked toward our table and the half-eaten Mona Lisa pizza. "Now that we figured out part of the clue, my appetite's making a comeback. So don't you guys think maybe we should finish our masterpiece first?"

After we polished off and paid for our pizza, the GEEKs plus Finley followed Sophina along the short ride to the Fair Valley Transportation Museum.

When we stepped through the double doors of the half-circle brick building, I looked around the large open area. In one section, a coal-powered steam engine sat beside a more modern model. In another section, an old railway dining car had a sign above it that read WALK INSIDE TO TRAVEL BACK IN TIME. A third section contained a miniature train chugging through a landscape that looked like it might be a model of the Fair Valley. Sprinkled throughout the entire museum were various displays and miscellaneous railway artifacts. It seemed like we were the only visitors.

"Welcome!" A smiling woman bustled from a side room. She was dressed like a long-ago train engineer— brown leather work boots, a red handkerchief tied around her neck, overalls with narrow blue and white pinstripes, and a matching floppy cap perched on her head. An oval badge sewn to the front pocket of the overalls identified her as Florence. A cloud of red hair puffed from under her cap. "Would you like a tour?"

Elena stepped forward. "No thanks! We just need to see train W-forty-eight. Is it here?"

"*Engine*," Sophina corrected her. "W-forty-eight is the engine, which pulls the train."

Florence tilted her head and studied Sophina a moment. "That's right. The W-forty-eight *is* an engine." Her smile turned a bit sad. "Or . . . it was. This old roundhouse is where train cars and engines used to be serviced and repaired for the New Northern Rail Company, but I'm afraid that seeing the W-forty-eight's impossible."

"Why?" Kevin asked, stepping up beside Elena.

I pulled out my notebook and pencil as Finley continued to record his observations on his phone.

Florence sighed and told her story. I recorded the facts.

FACT #1: Engine W-48 had been one of the last steam engines ever made.

FACT #2: Florence's father was the last engineer to drive Grove Park's engine W-48.

FACT #3: Florence's father had almost been killed when the engine got wiped out by a mudslide just across the White Bend River, near the current location of Bamboozleland.

"Wait a second." I looked up from my notes. "There were railroad tracks near Bamboozleland?"

Florence nodded. "The tracks led to the original theme park—the one that was there before Bamboozleland."

I wasn't the only GEEK whose mouth dropped open.

"What do you mean 'before Bamboozleland'?" Edgar asked.

"The Fair Valley Fun Park," Florence said. "Back in the early 1900s, people often took 'pleasure trains' to get to amusement parks. They would come here from the cities and ride the train to the amusement park for the day. Then the mudslide happened in the 1950s, right around the time the highway was being expanded. The railway decided not to rebuild the tracks, since more people would be using the highway anyhow."

"But what about the park?" Elena asked, jumping back into the conversation.

Florence stuffed her hands into her overalls. "It was too small an attraction for the modern era. It closed and sat abandoned until Maxine Van Houten bought it and turned it into Bamboozleland. She changed the whole thing, except for a single ride." Florence paused. "Now that I think about it, it's kind of a coincidence that you were asking about the W-forty-eight."

My breath caught. My pencil hovered over my notebook. "Why?" I asked.

Florence smiled. "The only ride Maxine Van Houten kept from the Fair Valley Fun Park was the Old-Time Express—the child-sized train that circles the park's perimeter. It's carried along by a scaled-down model of the W-forty-eight."

I looked at each of the other GEEKs. Their lips all curled into goofy grins that must've matched my own. The Old-Time Express had to be where we'd find the next clue!

Edgar swept down into a grand bow. "Thank you"–he paused and looked up at the name tag on Florence's overalls–"Florence. We are most appreciative of your assistance on this fine day."

Florence laughed. "I'm not sure what I've done to deserve a bow. I certainly don't feel like I've been much help."

"You've been more help than you know!" Kevin said.

"Wait a second." Florence adjusted the floppy cap on her head, studying each of our faces before her eyes came to rest on Sophina. "My goodness. Sophina

Burkhart! I *thought* there was something familiar about you when you started talking train engines."

Sophina drew in her shoulders like she hoped she could disappear.

"I hardly recognized you with your headscarf and those sunglasses. It is so good to see you here again! I always look forward to your and your father's monthly visits. Please tell him I said hello."

"I will," Sophina said quietly, her face reddening.

The rest of us exchanged glances. *Sophina comes to the museum every month with her dad?* So she was a serious train geek. I almost felt sorry for her. Was she a GEEK trapped in cool kids' clothing, denying her true self?

Florence looked back over the rest of us. "Wait, you're those kids doing the treasure hunt, aren't you?"

"Yes, ma'am, we are," Kevin replied.

I braced for Florence's face to turn angry, which seemed to be a popular reaction whenever we were recognized in Grove Park, but she only smiled. "I hope you'll consider putting in a word with the park developer to keep the model train. It would mean a lot to the people here in town."

"We will," we all promised, heading toward the doors.

Deep down, though, I wondered if we'd get the chance to keep our word. After all, we had less than forty-eight hours left to complete the search, and so far we'd only solved a single clue. If we failed to hunt down the Bolt, Bamboozleland would continue to rot and rust and crumble until there was no model W-48 engine left to keep.

It was all just one more reminder: We couldn't afford to fail.

As we raced toward Bamboozleland, my friends stayed busy sharing what we remembered of the park before it had closed, though all our memories were limited—when it shut down, we hadn't even been in first grade yet, so we hadn't been big enough to go on rides like the Log Mill Run roller coaster. Still, we'd enjoyed the Ferris wheel, the carousel, and the Bump-a-Saurus Wrecks bumper cars. And—of course—the Old-Time Express, which Elena remembered riding.

"I kept tugging my braid and howling, '*Toot-tooooot!*'" she said. "I totally rocked as a train whistle."

I just hoped we somehow managed to complete our quest. *Then* maybe we could convince Mr. Schoozer to rebuild the park the way it was—not tear it apart.

As we crossed the Elmgrove Bridge, Sophina drifted in beside me. "You like Finley, don't you?"

My face grew warmer than an overused printing press. "I—I don't know what you're talking about."

"Chill," Sophina said. "I'll keep your secret." She kept her voice low, though the others were chattering in front of us and I didn't think they would hear. "I was just thinking it could work to our advantage. You know—you can cozy up to him. Get him on our side."

Was she serious? I snorted. "I'm not going to use Finley to get good press!"

Sophina heaved an exaggerated sigh. "Fine. Have it your way. I'm only trying to help."

I shook my head, pedaling on. What was she thinking? Just then a loud *Dun, dun, DUN!* sounded from Edgar's pocket. He skidded his bike to a halt and fished out his phone. "Uh-oh. That's the notification I set for news alerts that mention us!"

We all pulled off to the side of the road and huddled around him.

"What is it?" Elena demanded.

Edgar held out his phone. "The Tattler's at it again!"

The Fair Valley Tattler

ANONYMOUS • *Wednesday, April 13* • *1:03 p.m.*

GEEKS CHEAT CHALLENGE WHILE
HARASSING LOCAL DINERS!

The Elmwood GEEKs invaded Lion's Pizza this afternoon, but they had a lot more on their minds than eating lunch.

HARASSMENT? Yes.

CHEATING? Yes.

SHAME? *No.*

The GEEKs began their assault by TERRORIZING a family with two young children, FORCIBLY REMOVING the family from a dining booth simply because the GEEKs were unhappy with their own assigned seating in the crowded restaurant. One of the GEEKs then went on to mock the beloved local pizzeria, going so far as to say the thought of the food made her "queasy."

However, while the GEEKs were busy acting nauseated by the terrific Grove Park cuisine, they should have been nauseated by their own behavior, especially once their CHEATING began.

After HARASSING the innocent family and MOCKING the best pizza in New Hampshire, the GEEKs were overheard consulting with an outsider in an attempt to solve their latest clue. Clearly the GEEKs can't find the Bamboozle Bolt on their own, so they have resorted to letting others do the work for them. Now only one question remains:

WHAT WILL THEY TRY NEXT???

The Fair Valley Tattler—Finding. Verifying. Truth.

20

Kevin jabbed a finger at Sophina. "This is all your fault! Why did you have to kick that family out of their booth?"

"And why'd you butt in and solve part of our clue?" Elena demanded.

Sophina clicked her tongue. "I was only trying to help!"

Elena snatched Edgar's phone and shook it in Sophina's face. "Well, you're clearly not helping!"

"You know what—*GEEKs*—if you don't want my help, then fine. I'll let you fail on your own." Sophina tried to do a pouty, beauty-queen toss of her hair, but apparently she'd forgotten she was wearing both a head-scarf and a bike helmet, so it mostly just looked like a nervous twitch. She took off on her bike and called back over her shoulder: "Good luck getting the public on your side without me!"

As Sophina pedaled away, part of me was happy to see her go, but I also realized we might not have gotten as far as we had without her help. After all, she *was* the only one who'd known about the W-48 being a train engine. But she'd also created extra trouble for us.

I pictured all the people at Lion's Pizza who'd witnessed the things posted in the Tattler's new blog post. And that's when it dawned on me.

The Tattler! I turned to the others. "I was so caught up in looking for the clue in Lion's Pizza that I didn't pay enough attention to the people. I should have known better! Remember the Boston fans by the bar?"

Edgar frowned. "With his Red Sox hat, the Tattler would've blended right in!"

"Exactly," I said. "But I still can't figure out why he's so caught up in smearing our reputations."

My friends muttered their agreement, while Finley scuffed a foot across the grass, looking thoughtful.

Finally he said, "Sometimes people like that reporter guy don't really have a reason. They're in it for the money or whatever, and they give all journalists a bad name."

Elena gripped her handlebars, her jaw set. "Well, I say forget the Tattler. If we let him distract us, we'll lose, which is obviously what he wants. Come on, GEEKs." She took back off toward Bamboozleland, her unbraided hair streaming behind her. "Let's ride!"

The previous fall, Edgar had cut a hole through the fence along the back side of the park during our search for the Van Houten fortune. This time, there was no way we'd reuse that as our entry point. We'd already faced too many accusations of breaking and entering; we didn't need to add another to the list. We rolled right up to the park's front gate.

And there stood Cy Porter, the security guard from Van Houten Toys. The same person we'd tricked in order to get inside the toy factory during our first treasure hunt. Twice.

Fortunately, he wasn't the sort of person to hold a grudge.

"Cy!" I said. "What are *you* doing here?"

"Picked up a little side job for the week," Cy said. "Can I help you kids?"

Finley tugged his helmet over his eyes and scooted into the shade, where he could see his phone screen better while he took notes.

Elena hopped off her bike. "We need in to Bamboozleland!"

Cy arched one of his bushy white eyebrows. "Know the password?"

"*Password?*" Elena threw up her hands. "You can't be serious. We're here for the treasure hunt!"

Cy shrugged. "Gotta have the password."

"*W*-forty-eight?" Kevin guessed.

"Nope."

"*Steel-hearted soul?*" Edgar asked.

"Still nope."

"Oh, come on, Cy. It's *us*," Elena said.

"Sorry." Cy shook his head. "No password, no entry."

"*Please,*" I begged.

Cy chuckled, his eyes twinkling. "Yep, that's the password." And he swung open the gate into Bamboozleland. "You're on your own now, though–I'm not allowed to help!"

Once inside the gates, we followed the miniature train tracks toward where the ride began. The train was even smaller than I remembered. The miniature model of a W-48 steam engine sat on rusty wheels, its black paint peeling. Three tiny train cars were hooked behind it, each with a pair of cramped seats designed for small children.

"Anyone find anything?" Kevin asked, peering under the seats of one of the train cars.

"Nothing here," I said, inspecting the track beneath the train.

Elena sat perched in the engine, pretending to be the engineer. "I found the cord for the whistle, but it totally doesn't work anymore." She ran her fingers through her hair instead. *"Toot-tooooot!"*

"Um, guys . . ." Edgar cleared his throat. "I think we have to ride it."

Kevin looked from Edgar to the cramped seats of the train cars. "Are you kidding? We're way too big."

"But think of the clue," Edgar said. *"Ride your train of thought.* Remember?"

"That can't be what it means. The train's been shut off for years," I said. "It won't go anywhere unless we can get the electricity running."

Elena rubbed her hands together, swung herself out of the engine, and grinned. "Ten bucks says I can find a way to kick in the juice!"

None of us took the wager. We'd all learned a long time ago not to bet against Elena, especially when it had anything to do with science or engineering. She disappeared into a control booth off to the side of the ride.

We waited.

After a minute, there was a *whunk.* A *thunk.* Then a short buzz followed by an electrical hum.

Elena popped out of the control booth. "The juice is jiving like moths at a dance party!" She vaulted back into the engine. "I call engineer. All aboard the Elena Express!"

The rest of us crawled on. Edgar wedged himself into the first train car, his knees mashed up under his chin. Finley smooshed in beside me in the second car.

Kevin hesitated before folding himself into the third car and snapping the seat belt across his lap.

"Buckle up, kiddies! Prepare for the ride of a lifetime!" Elena pulled the cord for the train whistle, which worked now that the train had power.

Toot-tooooot!

Elena yanked back a lever along the side of the engine, and–*ka-chunk!*–the Old-Time Express lurched into motion, its rusty wheels squawking in protest.

It moved about as fast as a snail in a tar pit.

"Woo-hoo!" Elena thrust her fists into the air. "Feel the power!"

Even Kevin laughed, relaxing.

I tried not to think about the way Finley's shoulder pressed against mine. The train crept along, and we scanned for signs of the next clue. We passed Bump-a-Saurus Wrecks, where only a single dinosaur-shaped bumper car still sat under the ride's sagging roof. We crawled by the skeletal remains of the Ferris wheel. And we wound around a man-made pond that used to hold lily pads and fish but now lay stagnant, filled with dead leaves and a scummy blanket of green algae.

"Come on, old girl." Elena patted the side of the

engine as it strained up a hill toward a tunnel at the top. "You can make it, *W*-forty-eight!"

I had my doubts.

The whole train groaned and shuddered with the effort. Then it was there. We entered the dim tunnel, our route lit only by the sunlight coming from the ends of the tunnel and through occasional gaps and cracks in the roof. The train began to chug more easily as the tracks sloped slightly downward.

"Watch for signs of the clue!" Kevin called, though it wasn't like we needed reminding.

We pulled out our phones and shone their lights on the tunnel walls. I spotted cobwebs and a few wet patches where water had seeped in through cracks in the roof. No clue.

The downward slope of the tunnel steepened.

"Elena," I called, "are we speeding up?"

"On it, Gee," Elena said. She grabbed the brake lever on the side of the engine and pushed.

The lever didn't budge.

The *click* and *clack* of the wheels on the track tightened their beat. I felt Finley tense beside me. We were definitely moving faster.

"Elena?" Kevin's voice came out in a wobbly squeak.

"Don't bug the engineer when she's busy!" Elena barked. She shoved at the lever again.

The engine cleared the mouth of the tunnel, and the wind blew Elena's hair back. Had the downslope at the end always been so steep?

"There!" Edgar pointed above his head, right as his car passed back into daylight.

I looked up. An envelope dangled from the top of the tunnel. *The clue!* As Finley's and my car passed beneath it, I lunged, but my seat belt jerked me back. It was too high to reach. "Kevin!" I shouted.

I twisted in the car in time to see Kevin unfastening his seat belt just as the envelope passed over his head. He jumped onto his seat and sprang up for the clue in the nick of time. I let out a cheer.

"GO, KEV!" Elena shouted as Kevin folded himself back into his seat. His eyes were wide, like even he couldn't believe what he'd just done.

Was I just imagining it, or were we picking up steam? I faced forward again. Elena was still working on the lever. She punched it harder. Kicked it. The lever snapped off. It dropped with a *clang* onto some rocks beside the track.

At the bottom of the hill, a rusted metal pole from a railway signal had fallen across the tracks. And we had no brakes.

The *click-clack* beat of the train's wheels transformed into a drumroll—*clickety-clickety-clickety-clickety.*

"Is there a way to stop the train?" I yelled to Elena.

"I'm checking! I'm checking!" Elena's head swiveled and swooped. Her hands groped and grabbed. She checked the engine's cockpit, looking for something. *Anything.*

The Old-Time Express had become a runaway roller coaster rather than a ride for preschoolers! As we plummeted toward the bottom of the hill, I let out a scream.

"Abort mission!" Elena called as Finley and Kevin let out screams of their own. "I repeat, *abort!*"

"How?" Edgar shrieked.

"JUMP!" Elena flung off her seat belt, dove from the train, and tumbled head over heels.

As I unbuckled my own seat belt, I heard a thump behind me. Kevin must have ejected too.

Finley sat frozen, his eyes wide. In front of us, Edgar struggled, his knees folded too tightly to his chin.

Forty feet until impact. . . .

Thirty . . .

Edgar's body uncurled like a jack-in-the-box. "For Ollie!" He took flight.

Twenty feet . . .

I unsnapped Finley's seat belt.

Ten . . .

"Together," I said, grabbing his hand.

Five . . .

"Now!"

CRUNCH!

Finley and I leapt from the train car, hand in hand, right as the train hit the end of its run. Our hands tore apart as we struck the ground.

I somersaulted, tumbling, flipping. I heard the screech of crumpling metal. The shriek and judder of train cars leaping from their tracks. Weeds and over-grown grass whipped my face, my legs, my arms. I felt a stab in my left knee. The world spun.

And then it was over.

I lay facedown in slimy, half-rotted leaves, their musky smell filling my nose. I rolled over and sat up. Something had gashed a hole in the left leg of my jeans. Warm blood trickled from my kneecap.

"You okay, Gee?" Elena rushed over. She looked all right, just a little muddy.

"Yeah," I said, letting her help me to my feet. "I'll be fine."

"Can't say the same for this." Elena bent and plucked something from the ground.

I groaned when I realized it was my phone, shat-tered beyond repair.

Edgar and Kevin knelt beside Finley, who sat dazed about ten feet away. His gaze was aimed at the tracks, his mouth hanging open.

I forced myself to look at the train. I gasped. The W-48 lay crumpled on its side. A single wheel still spun, squealing, sparks shooting out as it rubbed against a piece of the engine's carcass.

"We killed the pride of Grove Park!" I moaned.

Edgar shook his head. "If they didn't hate us before, they sure will now."

"Maybe Mr. Schoozer's engineers can fix it. I sure hope so. In the meantime, at least we got this." Kevin held up the envelope.

"Thanks to you!" Elena said admiringly. "I didn't know you had it in you, Kev."

Kevin smiled.

"Gotcha!" a voice called.

We all spun our heads and looked up the hill we'd plummeted down only moments before.

My heart sank. Not only had we destroyed the Old-Time Express but we'd been caught doing it.

I could just make out the smirk on the Tattler's face as he lowered his camera and disappeared back into the tunnel.

21

Mom rushed over as soon as I hobbled into our apartment. "Gina Bean!" She spotted the bloodstained gash in my jeans and knelt to look at my knee. "Are you okay?"

"I'm fine." I shuffled to the kitchen table and flopped into a chair. "It's only a scrape."

Sauce, who'd been asleep under the table, woke up and snuffled my leg.

"Only a scrape?" Mom echoed. "I just saw the video of what happened. It got posted to Twitter a few minutes ago. What if you hadn't jumped in time? I've been worried sick. You haven't answered any of my texts. I was just about to come looking for you."

I grimaced. "There's kind of a reason for that." I set my shattered phone on the table.

Mom massaged her temples. "Bean, someone could have been seriously hurt today." She sat down and took my hand. "Maybe this hunt has gone far enough. Maybe we should call it off."

"No!" I yanked my hand away. "Mom, we can't do that! We have to show everyone we're not liars. It's about more than just saving Bamboozleland. The whole town's at risk. Who'll want to come see plays or visit the Van Houten Museum if they think Elmwood's full of fraudsters and fakes?"

"Bean, I'm sure we can–"

"And what about *your* reputation?" I asked. "All the lies are affecting you too. It's not fair. You're an honest journalist!"

Mom sighed. "We can discuss this more later. Right now"–she glanced at her watch–"we'll have a visitor any minute."

Before I could ask what–or *who*–she was talking about, I heard the ting of footsteps on the metal stairs that led up from the newspaper's printing room to our apartment. A moment later, there was a knock on our door.

"Come on in," my mom called. "We're both here."

The door swung open, and in walked Max Van Houten. "Hi, Christina. Hey, Gina," Max said. "Thanks for letting me swing by."

"No problem." My mom gestured toward an empty chair. "Join us."

I bit the inside of my cheek. We hadn't talked to Max in a few days. Was he there because of the letters we'd found in the turret? Because of what had been published about Maxine and her mother, Hattie?

Max settled in at the table and looked toward me. "Gina, I want to talk about Maxine."

I gulped. *Uh-oh.* "You're upset, aren't you?" I asked. "You didn't know that Maxine abandoned her mother?"

"Sure, I'm upset. But not for the reason you think." Max adjusted his glasses. "You see, I'm upset about what's been reported, but that's because I know it's not true. Maxine didn't leave her mother out of shame."

I blinked. "But the letter."

"It's true that Maxine and her mother had a disagreement," Max said. "Maxine wanted to go to engineering school, and her mother didn't think it was an appropriate occupation for a woman. It was Maxine's mother who cut off the relationship, not the other way around."

I bit my lower lip. I couldn't imagine my mom telling me that a newsroom was no place for a woman to work. So if Maxine wanted to be an engineer, it must have been terrible not to have her mother's support. It helped me kind of understand how it would have been hard for her to forgive her mother for not supporting her.

"Maybe Hattie had a change of heart later in life when she wrote those letters," Max continued. "But if she did, my grandmother never knew about it. Otherwise,

I know she would have done her best to reconcile their relationship."

Sauce nuzzled my leg. I robotically reached down and scratched his head. Thanks to the Tattler's blog, Max knew the rumor about a letter Maxine had refused to accept from her mother. But he hadn't *read* the desperate letter. And he didn't know about the stack of other unopened letters, which were stamped and addressed, with nothing on them that said they were undeliverable. Maybe Max was right that Maxine hadn't been the one who'd originally cut off the relationship with her mother, but the facts didn't back up his claim that she'd have done her best to fix the relationship, even though I wished they did.

Max took off his glasses and polished them on the hem of his shirt. "I admit I was young when my grandmother died, Gina. Still, I knew her long enough to remember that she was a kind, caring woman from head to heart to heel."

I wanted Max to be right, but I couldn't shake the image of those unopened letters from my mind. I looked up, ready to tell Max about them, but when I saw the earnest look in his hazel eyes, I hesitated. Max didn't need to have that information weighing him down. He didn't need to have his image of his grandmother tarnished even more. Sometimes a journalist finds a fact she has to keep to herself.

I offered a smile I hoped looked sincere. "Yeah, Max, I guess you're right."

A few hours later, I sat on my bed, stroking Sauce's flowing ears. After a long debate with Mom—and after we'd read Finley's latest update together—she'd agreed to let me keep hunting down the Bamboozle Bolt. Still, she'd given me a warning: "You have to use better judgment than what you showed today at Bamboozleland. Got it, Bean?"

I'd nodded. What choice did I have but to agree?

Finley's daily post about our search was fair and objective once again. He avoided identifying Sophina by name, but he provided plenty of facts to combat the lies and half-truths being spread by the Tattler.

FACT #1: It hadn't been the GEEKs who'd asked the family to switch booths at Lion's Pizza. (It had been Sophina.)

FACT #2: The GEEKs also hadn't asked "their source" (Sophina) for help—it wasn't our fault she'd made the W-48 connection for us.

FACT #3: Finley had even interviewed Lily Grove, who said: "I can't believe those children nearly got hurt on my watch. I never dreamed they would actually find a way to *ride* that old train! I meant that line of their clue figuratively, so I certainly bear my share of responsibility for the accident."

As I reread Finley's report for about the tenth time, a message popped up in the corner of my computer screen. Finley! It was like thinking about him had made him text me! With my phone broken, I was glad my laptop still let me read and respond to messages.

> Today was . . . a lot. Hope you get this message since your phone broke. You OK?

> Fine. Just a sore knee. Texting from laptop now.

> Bummer. I know I'm only supposed to observe, but I was worried about you. Not very professional of me, huh? 😉

A winking emoji? Finley sent me a winking emoji? Was it a hey-I-was-worried-about-you-because-I'm-your-friend winking emoji? Or was it a hey-I-was-worried-about-you-because-I-*like*-you winking emoji?

I hated that there was so much room for interpretation. I messaged Finley back:

> What are you up to?

I held my breath, staring at my laptop, waiting for his answer.

And I waited.

And waited.

And waited.

I closed my eyes. I also stopped holding my breath before I passed out. *Please, please, please.*

My computer chimed. My eyes popped open. *A message!*

Only, it wasn't Finley.

I groaned when I saw the link from Elena.

The Fair Valley Tattler

ANONYMOUS • Wednesday, April 13 • 9:31 p.m.

CAN VICTIMIZED VALLEY SURVIVE
MORE VIOLENCE AND VANDALISM?

Grove Park community members have grown understandably angered by the Elmwood GEEKs' ongoing patterns of VIOLENCE and VANDALISM. To begin the second day of the GEEKs' treasure hunt, a VICTIM was seriously injured. (Get well soon, Eggy!) Later in the day, the GEEKs continued their ASSAULT on Grove Park by destroying a chapter of the town's history—the model W-48 train engine that had been the only surviving artifact from the Fair Valley Fun Park.

As the Fair Valley Tattler has recently uncovered, the GEEKs are continuing a pattern of VICTIMIZATION by Elmwood that goes back generations. As local resident Wilton Snivley so astutely observed, "This is history repeating itself! Back in 1956, Elmwood overlogged land near the railroad tracks. This caused the mudslide that DERAILED and DESTROYED the Grove Park W-48 engine. Now the GEEKs have also destroyed the model that honored the original."

Of course, the GEEKs weren't content with

simply DEMOLISHING the historic and irreplaceable W-48 model engine. Photographic evidence was collected, showing that Kevin Robinson, who is facing growing pressure to resign from his post on Elmwood Middle's student council, was SHAMELESS enough to celebrate their VICIOUS vandalism. (See photo below.)

How much longer will Grove Park be forced to tolerate this REIGN OF TERROR?

The Fair Valley Tattler—Finding. Verifying. Truth.

22

I lay in bed, unable to sleep. I messaged the other GEEKs to let them know about the visit from Max, but my brain spun around Finley and the fact that he'd never replied to my last message. It turned over and over with the new clue Kevin had plucked from the train tunnel; Kevin had opened it before we'd left Bamboozleland, and it had been the most confusing clue so far. And finally my brain whirled with the photo from the FVT blog.

Kevin had been holding up the envelope with our new clue, not celebrating the destruction of the Old-Time Express. But that's not what it looked like in the photo.

The Tattler had snapped the picture from just the right angle, making it so Kevin's arm blocked the view of the envelope. Instead of the photo showing Kevin holding up a clue, it looked like he was thrusting his fist triumphantly into the air, while the Old-Time Express lay mangled and sparking in the background.

Elena, Edgar, Kevin, and I were trying so hard to help Elmwood, but it seemed like all we did was make things worse. For ourselves. For the entire town.

I rolled over and buried my face in my pillow.

The only useful thing to come from what had happened was, I now knew that the stringy-haired reporter was definitely the person behind the FVT blog. I'd already been pretty sure of the blogger's identity. Still, I liked having facts to back it up. I knew he'd been the one to take the photo, and then he'd used the photo in his blog. But even with those facts in place, my mind spun with another question: *Why does the Tattler hate us so much?*

I rolled over again and stared up at nothing.

If I could figure out why the Tattler was out to get us, maybe I could find a way to discredit him. But where would I find the time?

I looked at the glowing red digits of the alarm clock beside my bed. It was already past midnight. We had under thirty-six hours left to succeed. Or to fail. We still had three clues to solve. We didn't have time to worry about the Tattler, too!

Then I realized that even if *I* didn't have the time,

maybe someone else did. I just hoped she was still on our side.

Bleary-eyed and exhausted, I rolled out of bed in the morning and messaged Sophina from my laptop:

> Still want to help us?

A few minutes after that, she and I were on a video chat.

And a few minutes after *that*, I was on my bike, headed to the Maple Leaf for breakfast and clue-solving with the other GEEKs.

The only thing better than the dinnertime smells of burgers and fresh-baked apple pie at the Maple Leaf is the *breakfast*-time smells. As soon as I walked through the door, I inhaled the fragrance of bacon, eggs, and Mrs. Dupree's fresh-baked cinnamon rolls.

Cy Porter sat perched on one of the stools at the counter, cradling a steaming mug of coffee and eating a cinnamon roll. When he heard the bell jingle above the door, he turned. He saluted with his coffee mug. "Keep that chin up, Gina. I let you kids into Bamboozleland fair and square yesterday, and I know you ain't trying to destroy anything. Don't matter *what* that blogger person says."

Mrs. Dupree topped up Cy's coffee. "Cy's right, sweetie. You children can't get down on yourselves."

I gave a half smile. The encouragement from Cy and Mrs. Dupree melted away at least a little of my stress from the past couple of days. "Thanks," I said, settling in at an empty table to wait for my friends. "Good to know somebody's still on our side."

Before I could order my own breakfast, the other GEEKs arrived.

Elena's eyes widened when she spotted me. "Wow, Gee. You turn into a zombie overnight?"

"That obvious, huh?" I rubbed my eyes. "I had a tough time getting to sleep."

Edgar sat down across from me. "Don't let that stupid Tattler get into your head."

Kevin plopped into one of the other seats. "It's not just the Tattler." He pinched the bridge of his nose. "Did you see how many likes his post got last night? And that photo." He banged his fists on the table, rattling the silverware. "I wasn't celebrating! I was holding up the clue, and I was smiling because Elena had just complimented me. Not that it matters. The only way to beat the Tattler is to solve the clues and find the Bolt.

Otherwise I'm going to be forced to resign. My political career will be over before it began."

"Not if I have anything to say about it," said Elena.

Kevin perked up a little as Elena began trash-talking the Tattler. I was glad they didn't know that the Tattler's article wasn't the *only* reason I'd been up all night. Since I'd barely slept, I should have at least been figuring out our new clue. Instead my mind had spent the night continually drifting toward Finley. Even though I'd kept my laptop open, he'd never messaged me back. What did that mean? After all, *he'd* been the one to text first. And where was he, anyway? He was supposed to meet us at the Maple Leaf so he could report about our work on the new clue.

Finley finally walked in right as Mrs. Dupree delivered our breakfasts—her famous Maple Leaf Sunshine Platters—each one piled with three eggs, three slices of crispy bacon, and a stack of buttermilk pancakes.

"About time, Fin!" Elena said. She stuffed a strip of bacon into her mouth as Finley sat down, his Grove Park Middle School hoodie replaced by a baggy white windbreaker with large pockets. "Thought we'd have to solve the entire treasure hunt without you."

"Sorry. I stayed up late last night and overslept."

If Finley had stayed up late, couldn't he at least have taken a minute to message me back? I did my best to push down my hurt feelings and waited for him to look my way, but he never met my eyes.

"Well, we'd better get started. We have three clues left and twenty-seven hours to solve them." Kevin scooted his plate to the side, pulled out our latest clue, and unfolded it on the table. "Any ideas?"

We'd all looked at the clue the night before, but we hadn't taken time to really talk about it. This was our chance.

Winter, spring, and summer, fall—
For your next clue, go find them all,
At rest upon a hidden bed,
While nighttime light shines overhead.

Climb up toward the starry skies.
Find the eagle where it flies.
Its perch is found off to the west
And holds the next step in your quest.

Elena huffed out a breath. "This clue had better not be talking about Eggy. I don't think he's gonna be fly-ing anywhere anytime soon. Plus, this first part doesn't make sense." She snitched a piece of bacon off Kevin's plate and used it to point at the first stanza. "The winter solstice could be considered a time when fall and winter meet, and the summer solstice could be when spring and summer meet. But c'mon, people. This totally lacks scientific accuracy." She tapped the bacon against the clue's second line, leaving a small grease stain on the paper. "All four seasons at once?"

Kevin snorted. "You mean you didn't figure that part out yet? I cracked those first two lines before I even got home yesterday."

Elena's eyes narrowed. "You'd better not be messing with us, Kev."

"I'm serious. Besides, you already said the answer, Elena." Kevin tried to take a bite of his scrambled eggs, but Elena used her bacon to block Kevin's fork before it reached his mouth.

"Dramatic pauses are Edge's specialty. Out with it."

"We aren't looking for a single season. Don't you see?" Kevin lowered his fork to his plate. "We're looking for *Seasons.*"

For a second, we were all trying to figure out Kevin's point. Then Edgar smacked his forehead. "Of course! I get it!"

My eyes widened in understanding. "As in . . ."

"Oakley Seasons!" we all said at once.

23

Winter, spring, summer, fall–the four seasons . . . *Oakley Seasons*. How could I have missed it? I really needed to get my head back into the hunt. I couldn't let myself be distracted by anything. Or by *anyone*.

I glanced toward Finley, who still avoided my gaze.

"Okay, Kev," Elena said, grinning at Kevin. "Gotta give you credit–you nailed that one. So we need to find Oakley Seasons. But where? The clue talks about *nighttime light shines overhead*, but I doubt he's hanging out on the Grove Park High School football field with the lights on."

"How about the information Kevin found yesterday?" I asked. "There was that old article about Oakley being 'the next big thing' as a blues musician. Did it have any clues that might help us find him?"

Kevin pulled Oakley Seasons's Wikipedia page back up on his phone and scrolled down to the scanned article.

Edgar leaned over to look, nearly planting his elbow in Kevin's stack of half-eaten pancakes. "It's from the *Grove Park Herald,* Friday, October 18, 1968," Edgar said. "But . . ."

"But it's not all here!" Kevin wailed. He turned his phone so Elena and I could see the screen.

I looked. Whoever had added the article to Oakley Seasons's Wikipedia page had clipped it and scanned it and included a caption that told when and where it was from. But the article itself was only a couple of paragraphs that ended abruptly with a single line:

Continued on page 8.

"I'm not sure how far back the library's archives go," I said. "But we could go to the *Grove Park Herald* office. I bet the archives include *all* the old papers."

"Plus, I bet you wouldn't mind a chance to scope out the competition," Elena said with a wink. "Let's finish eating and hit the road." She folded an entire pancake into her mouth. Her next words were garbled by her mouthful of food. "We gotta go find the next big thing in the blues."

I hated to admit it, but the *Grove Park Herald* office was way nicer than the *Tribune*'s. Our two-story building was crumbling red brick, and THE ELMWOOD TRIBUNE stenciled on the front window in black-and-gold paint was chipped and peeling. The *Herald*'s office was also a two-story brick building, but that's pretty much where the similarities ended.

The *Herald*'s brown bricks were clean, and the freshly painted dark red double doors were flanked by a white pillar-like doorframe. An American flag flapped gently in the cool morning breeze. A decorative arch spanned the top of the doors, with THE GROVE PARK HERALD carved into it, along with an engraving of an eagle in flight.

I would have been excited by the flying eagle, since that was part of the clue, except there were eagles all over Grove Park. The eagle was pretty much the town's symbol—from the school mascot to the newspaper's masthead. So how would we ever know which eagle was the one we were looking for?

We were greeted as soon as we walked through the doors. Well, at least *one* of us was greeted.

"Finley Brown!" A balding, smiling man with horn-rimmed glasses waved from behind a dark mahogany desk that was a jumble of paper and scattered pencils. He leaned back and patted his rounded stomach. "You'd better not be here to steal my doughnuts."

"You wouldn't want Nigel's doughnuts anyway," a woman at a second—much more organized—desk said.

"Yeah," a short, stocky man called from a long, waist-high layout table on the other side of the newsroom. "They look like glazed, but that's only because Nigel already licked the chocolate off."

They all laughed.

A thin woman with salt-and-pepper hair trimmed into a chin-length bob stepped from the editor's office and walked over. "Finley, you know you're still too young for me to hire, right?"

Finley grinned. "I'll be twelve in a few months."

The woman turned to the rest of us. "I recognize the four of you, since you've been in the news quite a bit lately. And, Ms. Sparks"–she smiled at me–"I'll confess that I went to the New England Youth Journalist ceremony to root for Finley, but congratulations on your well-earned victory."

"Thanks," I said. I nodded toward Finley, who looked away. "He gave me a run for my money."

The woman reached out and shook my hand. "I'm Leslie Frazier, editor of the *Herald.*"

After we all introduced ourselves, we met the other staff. The balding, doughnut-eating man was Nigel Weaver, the *Herald*'s secretary, advertising manager, and all-around do-whatever-needs-doing guy. The other two people were the *Herald*'s main reporters–Nicholas Grinsler and Amy Chan.

"So," Ms. Frazier said, "since you're in the middle

of a treasure hunt, I'm guessing this isn't a social call. What can we do for you today?"

I was thankful she was smiling; it reminded me that not everyone in Grove Park automatically believed the Tattler's rumors and lies about the GEEKs.

"We need to scope your archives," Elena said.

"What Elena's trying to say," I added, "is that we're searching for an article from the October 18, 1968, edition of the *Herald*."

Elena put her hand on her hip. "I was getting to that, Gee!"

Ms. Frazier laughed. "Of course. Our archives are all digitally preserved, so your search should be simple and fast."

I surveyed the newsroom. "And maybe I can peek around a little . . . just for fun?"

"Certainly, Ms. Sparks. Feel free. However"–Ms. Frazier winked at me–"you're not allowed to scoop any of our stories."

Ms. Frazier took Elena, Edgar, and Kevin over to a computer to pull up the paper's digital archives while Finley observed. Meanwhile, I wandered around the newsroom, soaking in the familiar fragrance of printer's ink and newsprint while jealously noting the new-looking computers on every desk. The chatter of the staff contrasted with the quiet of the *Tribune*, where my mom was forced to be editor, secretary, ad manager, and reporter, because our paper still didn't make enough money to hire other staff.

As I strolled past the long table on the far side of the newsroom, I stopped and looked at the dummy sheets being put together for the paper's next edition. The dummy sheets were used to make a mini-version of the newspaper to figure out the layout for the articles, headlines, ads, and so on. The headline for Friday's front page caught my eye:

FAREWELL, FAIR VALLEY TECH

Fair Valley Technology Solutions was moving? That was huge! I couldn't help but wonder why the town's largest employer was shutting down, but this was the *Herald*'s scoop, not mine. Regardless, it was no wonder Lily Grove had organized our treasure hunt! Grove Park would soon need Bamboozleland to survive just as much as Elmwood did—maybe even more.

"Hey, Gina." Edgar's voice snapped me away from Friday's headline. He waved me over. "We found something."

Kevin pointed over Elena's shoulder. "It's another name."

I scanned the part of the article Kevin was pointing at. It included a quote from an interview with Oakley Seasons's best friend and backup guitarist, Jerry Smokes.

"So who's Jerry Smokes? Does he live around here?"

Kevin shrugged. "We don't know yet. But at least it's a lead."

"Actually," Elena said, "this would be a good time for all of you to bow to Elena the Googling Guru. Because I *do* know who Jerry Smokes is." Elena held up her phone. "And, boy, are you guys in for a surprise!"

We all leaned forward and looked at her phone. A photo filled the screen.

I blinked. "Is that . . . ?"

Edgar groaned. "No, no, no."

"We're not going back there, are we?" Kevin asked. "Please, tell me we're not going back."

"No choice," Elena said. "It's our only lead."

I looked again at the photo. Jerry Smokes's eyes weren't wild like they'd been the only other time I'd seen them, but the bristly white beard and gray stocking cap were the same. Really, the only thing missing was a frozen fish.

The Bard still sat along the dock, all rust and peeling paint, bobbing in the gentle current of the White Bend River. It also still looked abandoned, but that's what we'd thought the first time too. We kept our distance.

Edgar cupped his hands around his mouth and called, "Mr. Smokes, sir? Are you there? We come in peace!"

When nothing happened, Elena nudged Kevin.

"What?" he asked.

"You're the one who's always going on about diplomacy. Well, now's your shot to strut your stuff."

She made a shooing gesture toward the boat. Kevin gulped, then inched forward onto the deck, where he knocked gingerly at the door. No sooner had he taken a wary step back than–

Bang!

The houseboat's door crashed open. The white-bearded man–Jerry Smokes–stomped out. "I told you kids not to come back!" He scowled at us, but something about his look told me that even though he didn't *want* to see us, he wasn't all that surprised by our arrival.

Kevin offered a smile to Jerry Smokes that would have made any politician proud. "Mr. Smokes, we respect your privacy and wanted to come apologize for trespassing on Tuesday. We're on a treasure hunt and–"

"I know about your treasure hunt," Jerry Smokes growled.

"Oh. Um . . . good?" Kevin shuffled his feet, trying to get back on track. "As I was saying, we thought we were supposed to be here, but we never would have gone aboard your boat if we'd known we were in the wrong spot. We're very sorry."

Jerry Smokes stared at Kevin a minute. Then he said, "Yeah, I kinda figured you being on my boat was an accident." He scratched the back of his neck and stared at the deck. "I might've overreacted a bit with the fish. The rest of you might as well come aboard."

When we were all on deck, Elena put one arm around Edgar's shoulders and the other around Kevin's. "These two tend to deserve overreaction. They're complete pains in the butt." She grinned. "Me and Gee, on the other hand? Totally innocent young ladies. Anyway, we *are* sorry for the other day, but since we're here, do you think we could chat a bit about something else?"

Jerry laughed, which made him at least a little less scary-looking. "You kids are pretty persistent trespassers, huh?" He chewed his bottom lip, then sighed. "Okay. I suppose a quick chat can't hurt. But . . ." He glanced around, looking nervous about having guests. "We should go inside. I'll pour you some coffee."

As Jerry turned back toward the door, Finley met my eyes for one of the first times that morning, and I mouthed, *Coffee?*

Instead of looking away, he gave a half smile and whispered, "Better drink it. You want to stay on his good side."

And then we followed Jerry Smokes—onetime best friend and bandmate of Oakley Seasons—into *The Bard.*

It was no wonder Jerry had looked nervous about having guests. The inside of the houseboat was a single, narrow room that was dimly lit by the snatches of daylight sneaking through the cracked, dusty windows. At one end, a built-in, U-shaped couch ran along the wall, and a jumble of blankets on top suggested it also served as Jerry's bed. A few cabinets lined one of the longer walls, their red paint chipped, revealing older layers of green and white hiding underneath. A small kitchenette had a sink piled with dirty dishes, and the countertop held a few empty cans of beef stew and an open box of saltines. On the wall opposite the kitchenette were two chairs with cracked backs, and a small square table covered with papers and books and even a box of Mrs. Dupree's maple leaf cookies. A cast-iron woodstove, its black stovepipe rising through the roof, radiated heat, taking the chill from the early spring air.

We all huddled in the cramped space, unsure what to do.

"Sorry for the mess." Jerry shoved the jumble of things on the table to one side and set down a half dozen mismatched coffee mugs. He gestured toward the two chairs and the couch-bed. "Find a seat if you'd like."

"Um, thanks, Mr. Smokes," Kevin said, sitting down at the table, along with Edgar. Elena, Finley, and I sat on the couch-bed.

"Just call me Jerry." Jerry picked up a pot from the top of the woodstove, poured steaming coffee into the mugs, and handed one to each of us. If he thought there was anything weird about serving coffee to a bunch of sixth graders, he gave no indication. "I feel old enough without you calling me *Mr. Smokes*."

"Yes, sir," Kevin replied. "Sorry."

I sniffed my coffee, the warm steam bathing my cheeks. I wasn't exactly a coffee drinker, but it didn't smell too awful. I took a sip. *Pfff.* The bitter taste smacked against my tongue. I gagged, nearly spitting the coffee back into the mug. My eyes watered.

Finley took a sip of his coffee too. His cheeks puffed out, and he squeezed his eyes shut before finally swallowing and setting his mug to the side.

Kevin and Elena must have noticed our reactions. They cradled their mugs but never raised them to their lips.

Only Edgar seemed immune. He took a big slug of coffee, smacked his lips, and said, "Ah, delicious! You make a good, strong brew!"

"Glad you approve." Jerry picked up the box of maple leaf cookies and handed it to Edgar. "Help yourself to some of these too. Eat all you want. Don't really like them much anyway."

"Thanks!" Edgar took a cookie and dunked it into his coffee as Jerry passed the box of cookies around. I raised my eyebrows at Elena. Edgar was up early all the time to tend to the animals on the farm—maybe he'd developed a taste for coffee while milking the cows?

I opened my notebook. I didn't want to be distracted by bitter coffee or even by Mrs. Dupree's cookies. We were there because we needed to find Oakley Seasons, and Jerry Smokes was our only lead. "So," I said, turning to Jerry, "we were—"

"What's this for?" Elena snatched up a textbook

that had been half-buried beneath the blankets on the couch-bed. "*Introduction to Organic Chemistry*? Are you a chemist?"

Jerry frowned, took the book, and tossed it to the side. "It's nothing. Just a silly idea from a silly old man. Thought I could go back to school. Become a science teacher or something. Signed up for online classes and everything but can't even get the Wi-Fi to work. Some scientist, huh?"

Elena straightened her glasses. "If there's one thing the world needs, it's more science teachers. You know the network and password?"

"Sure, it's from the marina. Supposed to be a good strong signal. But–"

"Gimme your laptop, Jer." Elena stuck her hand out. "They don't call me Elena the Wi-Fi Princess of Tech for nothing."

Fact: No one had ever called Elena "the Wi-Fi Princess of Tech" before in her life, and most likely no one ever would. But that wasn't about to stop her.

Jerry Smokes must have realized that it's usually best to do what Elena says. He grabbed an old laptop from a nearby shelf and handed it to her.

As Elena's fingers flew over the keys, Kevin cleared his throat. "So, Mr.–Jerry–sir . . . we–"

"I know who you kids are," Jerry said. "I don't get out

much, but I know about your treasure-hunt thing. I'm guessing that's why you're here."

"You're right." I held my pencil poised above my notebook. "We were hoping you might have some information about an old friend of yours, Oakley–"

"Seasons!" Edgar grabbed something from the pile of things on the table and waved it in the air. "You have mail for Jonathan Seasons! Is he related to Oakley Seasons?"

Elena the Wi-Fi Princess was busy messing with Jerry's laptop, but Finley and I hopped up to see what Edgar was talking about. Sure enough, there was an entire stack of mail addressed to a PO box for a Jonathan Seasons.

Jerry snorted. "Jonathan *is* Oakley. *Oakley* is his middle name, but I convinced him it was a better stage name. No one's called him Jonathan for ages."

"Oakley Seasons is who we're looking for!" I said. "Why do you have his mail?"

"I . . ." Jerry scratched at his beard. "Well, we both have PO boxes. When I pick up my mail, I get his too. Deliver it to him a couple times a week."

Kevin's eyes sparkled. "And where exactly do you deliver it?"

Jerry turned away and poured himself another cup of coffee. "I'm not supposed to help you. Probably said too much already."

I wanted to scream. *Not help us?* I thought of the upcoming headline I'd seen at the *Herald,* announcing that Fair Valley Tech was leaving Grove Park. Thought about how important Bamboozleland was for all of Fair Valley, not just for Elmwood. How could we make Jerry Smokes understand how badly we needed his help? We hadn't shared any of our clue with him, so it wasn't against the rules. How could we—

"*Boom!* Wi-Fi Princess rocks the tech!" Elena bounded up from the couch-bed and handed Jerry his laptop. "You see, Jer, cached IP information was causing network connectivity issues. Just had to access the configuration, do a quick release and renewal of the IP address, and *whizzle-sizzle-poof!* Fixed it. As simple as stealing bacon from a baby."

Jerry stared at his laptop, eyes blinking rapidly. "Um, thanks?" I couldn't tell if he was trying to understand Elena's Wi-Fi explanation or her bacon-and-baby analogy.

"Now let's get you logged in for school." Elena snapped her fingers. "Chop, chop! The world needs more science teachers!"

I sighed as Jerry slowly poked at his laptop with one-fingered typing. I was glad Elena could help him, but that wasn't going to get us through our treasure hunt. I stared at the pile of mail addressed to Jonathan Seasons. It reminded me of the letters Maxine

Van Houten's mother had written, but there was something different. . . .

I massaged my forehead. *Think, Gina!*

It felt like my reporter radar was pinging, but–unlike the Wi-Fi on Jerry's laptop–I couldn't quite pick up the signal. I glanced toward Finley. I wished I could talk to him about it as a fellow journalist, but I knew he wasn't allowed to help. There was just something about Oakley's letters compared to Maxine's. Obviously the addresses were different–a PO box in Grove Park versus Maxine's address on Scrubstone Lane in Elmwood. But that wasn't it. There was something more.

"Earth to Gina!" Kevin tapped my shoulder. "You still here?"

I blinked. "Huh?"

"As I was just saying to you and Edgar, why would Oakley need someone to deliver his mail? Why not get it himself? Even if he lived out of town, the post office would still deliver his mail."

Edgar wound one of his loopy red curls around his finger. "What if he lived someplace where only Jerry could reach him?"

My heart skipped a beat. I felt the gentle but constant rocking of Jerry's houseboat on the river. I smiled and patted the wall. "You mean like somewhere only accessible by boat?"

Kevin's eyes lit up. "How about an island?"

"Think of the clue!" Edgar said. "The *hidden bed*, the *nighttime light*. What if it's an island . . . on top of a *river*-bed? Under the light of the moon?"

"But where's there an island on the White Bend River?" I asked.

Kevin pulled out his phone. He scrolled through the map of Grove Park, following the path upriver from the Elmgrove Bridge and up and around the town.

"There." Edgar pointed to where the river curved around the northeastern edge of Grove Park. "Zoom in."

Kevin did. And sure enough . . .

"An island," Kevin murmured.

"It's at the farthest point of Grove Park from the Elmgrove Bridge," I said. "No wonder I've never seen it."

"Elena!" Kevin said. "Come on. We need to go."

Elena and Jerry both looked up from the laptop.

"What's up, Kev?" Elena asked.

"We know where the next clue is," Kevin said.

"On an island in the river!" Edgar added.

"One little problem." I waved my pencil in the air like a flag. "How are we supposed to get there? We don't have a boat."

Elena adjusted her glasses. Grinned. Patted Jerry Smokes on the shoulder. "*Soooo*, Jer, ol' buddy. I know you're not supposed to help us figure out the clues, but now that we've got it . . . think you might be ready to return a teensy personal favor to the Wi-Fi Princess?"

25

It was a slow journey. We chugged along in Jerry's rickety houseboat, battling the river's current, munching sack lunches from Mrs. Dupree that I'd been toting around in my bike basket but that we'd been too busy to eat until then. Eventually we made it around the horseshoe bend in the river, looping from the western side of Grove Park up to the northeast corner. A small island sat plopped right in the middle of the White Bend River, dotted by a few scraggly trees. In the center, a small cottage with white shingle siding and a green metal roof sat at the base of a tall, round tower that looked like a lighthouse. Though, that didn't make sense. Weren't lighthouses for coastlines and oceans, not rivers?

A short pier jutted out from the island and had a motorboat tied up along one side. Jerry drifted expertly along the other side of the pier and hopped ashore even before his boat had stopped moving. To keep the boat from floating away, he quickly looped a rope around a post that had a rusty mailbox perched on top.

"I don't think I told you anything that would mean you cheated on your treasure hunt," Jerry said, sliding Oakley's mail into the mailbox. "And I don't think the rules said I couldn't give you a lift on my boat. But . . ." Jerry looked around, studying the banks of the river, which were thick with trees. "I'd better hit the road . . . well, the river. You know—before someone sees. Oakley'll have to give you kids a ride back."

We stepped out onto the pier and offered Jerry our thanks. Then—the next thing we knew—Jerry Smokes was navigating back downriver, leaving us by ourselves on the rocky island.

Kevin watched the houseboat disappear around a bend in the river and gulped. "I sure hope we're right about the clue. Otherwise, we might be stuck."

I pointed to the round tower. "That looks like a lighthouse. But why's there a lighthouse on a river?"

"It is strange," Elena said. "But it fits the clue. *Night-time light shines overhead . . . climb up toward the starry skies.* It's perfect!" She looked ready to sprint toward the tower, but that's when Finley moaned, hunched forward, and clutched his stomach.

I rested my hand on his back. "Finley, are you okay?"

Finley stayed bent over, so I couldn't see his face, but he groaned and mumbled, "I don't do so well on boats. I get kind of seasi—"

Finley never finished talking. He lurched. Gagged. Stumbled to the end of the pier.

"No! Noooo!" a man shouted at the same time Finley knelt and started retching into the river.

I whipped around. Was someone yelling at Finley for getting sick on the pier?

Another wail: *"Noooo!"*

Wait. The voice had come from the cottage. Was it angry? Terrified? I couldn't tell, but the shouting didn't seem to have anything to do with Finley.

"That must be Oakley. We have to make sure he's okay!" Elena tore off toward the cottage.

"Proceed with caution!" Kevin cried, chasing after her.

I hesitated, then took a half step toward Finley instead.

"Come on." Edgar tugged at my sleeve. "Give poor Finley some privacy. We need to help check on Oakley."

"But . . ."

Finley raised his hand and waved us off, signaling his agreement with Edgar.

"Ahhhh!" The shriek from the cottage seemed charged with pain.

Edgar and I bolted off the pier.

When we barged through the cottage door, we nearly ran over Kevin and Elena, who stood, frozen and staring. A tall, lean man with a horseshoe of shaggy white hair surrounding his otherwise bald head stomped back and forth in front of a massive wall-mounted TV. White stubble shadowed his cheeks and chin, and a wireless headset covered his ears, a built-in microphone curving around in front of his mouth. He pounded at a video game controller, and the TV flashed with laser blasts and explosions.

"Die, Twinkle Toes Four-Seven-Nine! Die!" the man screamed. Purple laser blasts pulsed from the weapon of some spacesuit-wearing guy on the screen identified as DEATHSEASONS1. Each of his blasts deflected off a glowing blue sphere that surrounded a female character identified as TWINKLETOES479. I couldn't tell for sure, but the character inside the blue sphere seemed to be grinning.

Then two things happened at once. First, the man noticed us standing in his living room. Second, in the video game, one of the purple laser blasts ricocheted off the blue sphere and bounced straight back toward DeathSeasons1.

The character's vaporization was instantaneous and spectacular.

Five words stamped themselves onto the screen:

"Noooo!" the man wailed. He tore off his headset and flung it to the floor. "I had her!"

Kevin stepped forward. "Um, Oakley? Mr. Seasons?"

The man scowled. "Where did you come from? Can't you see I'm busy here?"

"But you're Oakley Seasons, right?"

He sighed deeply. "I knew there might be folks wandering around my island this week, and I can't stop you because it's technically town property. But this house is mine, and I didn't agree to be some happy host. Now leave me in peace."

"But—"

"I'm going to beat Twinkle Toes Four-Seven-Nine if it's the last thing I do!"

And before Kevin could say anything else, Oakley Seasons snatched his headphones off the floor, jammed them back over his ears, and clicked restart.

As DeathSeasons1 and TwinkleToes479 began blasting away at each other again on the screen, Finley staggered into the cottage. Sweat dripped down his forehead, and his hands were dirty from being pressed against the pier while he'd been heaving into the river. "What did I miss?" he asked, his voice shaky and weak.

I pointed to Kevin, Elena, and Edgar, who were

trying to get Oakley's attention, saying things like "Jerry Smokes brought us!" and "We only want to ask a few questions!" and "Use your ectoplasmic-Martian-milker!"

Oakley didn't pay them any attention. He was too busy screaming into his headset as he battled Twinkle-Toes479 in hand-to-hand combat. At least he *was* busy. Until Twinkle Toes backed Oakley's character against a metal crate that had LIVESTOCK stamped on the side. Suddenly a half dozen slimy black tentacles burst from the sides of the crate, wrapped themselves around Death-Seasons1, and crushed him. The character's demise looked a lot more painful than when he'd been vaporized by the laser.

"Argh!" Oakley growled. "Not again!" He banged his controller against his forehead. Then he seemed to notice he still had strangers standing in his living room. He locked his deep-set eyes on us. "What are you kids still doing here? I told you to leave me in peace. Now scram!"

Edgar tilted his head to one side. "Do you want to get rid of *us*, or would you rather get rid of Twinkle Toes Four-Seven-Nine?"

Oakley pinched the bridge of his nose. "How am I supposed to concentrate on Space Farm Defenders when I have five kids breaking into my house?"

Edgar squared his shoulders. "Well, you *are* talking

to a Space Farm Defenders player who's earned fifty thousand Colonial Space Credits and reached Black Hole Farmer status. And if that player were to stay, then he could explain exactly when to hit X-Y-X-X-up-left-up on the controller in order to create a Space Warp Mass Exchange, which would cause Twinkle Toes Four-Seven-Nine to vaporize herself. But . . ." Edgar shrugged and turned toward the door. "You're right. We should leave you alone."

"Wait!" Oakley Seasons stumbled toward Edgar, hand outstretched. "Don't go!"

"Don't go?" Edgar turned slowly back and placed his hands over his heart with dramatic flair. "Me?"

"Please!" Oakley folded his hands around his game controller like he was praying. "What's a Space Warp Mass Exchange?"

Elena crossed her arms. "If Edge helps you win, then we talk."

"And then we'll leave you alone," I piped up.

"We promise!" Kevin added.

Oakley nodded. "Deal."

Edgar rubbed his hands together. "Okay, now the first thing to remember is . . ."

A moment later, Edgar was coaching Oakley Seasons through an epic laser-blaster shoot-out at a farm on the surface of Mars.

As I watched Edgar and Oakley play the game, I

studied Oakley's beard-stubbled face. Something about him looked familiar, but it was like when I'd been on Jerry's houseboat—my reporter radar was pinging, but the signal was muddled. I couldn't quite put it together. Had Oakley been at the Grove Park Challenge kickoff ceremony? Or had I seen him at the Maple Leaf before? Or had Mom done an article about him for the newspaper?

I still hadn't figured it out before Edgar shouted, "Now!"

Oakley punched at his controller, fingers flying. The screen flashed once. Twice. Suddenly the Death-Seasons1 character crouched behind a space barn where TwinkleToes479 had been only moments before. Poor Twinkle Toes stood where DeathSeasons1 had stood—right in the path of her own laser blast.

Foomp!

Her vaporization was instantaneous.

"Take that, Twinkie!" Elena cried. "Taste the wrath of Edge's Space Warp Mass Exchange!"

Oakley whooped and dropped his controller. He grabbed Edgar's hands and started dancing in circles. "I won! I won!" When he stopped to catch his breath, he looked admiringly at Edgar. "Where'd you learn to play like that, kid?"

Edgar offered a lopsided grin. "I like farming."

"And where did *you* learn to play, Mr. Seasons?" Kevin asked.

"Yeah," I said. "Aren't you supposed to be a musician, not a gamer?"

"And why live on this weirdo island?" Elena added.

The seventy-something-year-old former blues musician sighed again, but then he sat down and began talking. And the answers to our questions were *way* more interesting than I could have imagined.

Finley didn't look as pale as he had earlier, but he didn't bother taking notes on his phone. Of course, I couldn't resist pulling my pencil from my hair bun and getting to work on notes of my own.

Thursday, April 14

Observations & COGITATIONS

(Grove Park Challenge, Day 3, Oakley Seasons)

— Edgar knows more about playing Space Farm Defenders than Oakley does

> ↳ WHEN DOES EDGAR FIND TIME TO MASTER VIDEO GAMES, WHEN HE'S ALREADY SUPER BUSY WITH ACTING & WORKING ON HIS FAMILY'S FARM?

— Right as Oakley Seasons's musical career began to take off, he had his heart broken by the woman he loved; he lost his passion for music and quit writing songs

— After quitting music, Oakley decided to live in isolation, where no one could cause him further heartache, so he bought the cottage over 50 years ago

> ↳ ISN'T LIVING AS A HERMIT FOR OVER 50 YEARS ON A ROCKY ISLAND IN THE MIDDLE OF A RIVER KIND OF EXTREME?

— The round tower attached to the cottage really is an old, decommissioned lighthouse, which Oakley has kept in working condition

→ IS THE LIGHTHOUSE THE KEY TO SOLVING OUR LATEST CLUE? (WE HAVE LESS THAN **24** HOURS TO FINISH THE CHALLENGE!!!)

26

After talking for a few minutes, Oakley leaned back and said, "Now I know you kids didn't come here to hear my life story. So what is it you *really* want to know?"

Kevin explained about our treasure hunt, and I told Oakley about our latest clue leading us to his island.

"It was pretty much like we got help from Shakespeare, because Jerry gave us a ride on *The Bard*," claimed Edgar.

Then Elena capped it off by saying: "And you see, Oak, our clue talks about a *nighttime light shines overhead* and climbing *up toward the starry skies*. So . . . we're gonna take a look in that lighthouse if it's all the same to you."

Oakley tugged his bottom lip. "Like I said, I can't stop you."

"Still," Kevin said, "we appreciate the opportunity to investigate. You could join us if you wanted. You might be able to be of assistance."

I thought for sure Oakley would say no, so I was surprised when he shrugged and stood up. He glanced back at the screen. "Guess I should quit while I'm ahead, for now, at least. Come on, let's go."

Even though the cottage was built right against the base of the lighthouse, we had to go back outside to get to the lighthouse entrance. As Oakley led us around the side of the cottage, Kevin stumbled over something. He looked down and gasped. "A gravestone?"

"Sorry," Oakley said. "I should've told you to watch your step. I'm so used to walking around that, I forget it's there. It's not a gravestone, though. It's a memorial."

I bent and brushed dirt from the top of the rectangular stone, which was a few inches thick and lay flat on the ground. Weather-worn words were engraved on its face.

IN MEMORY OF
CAPTAIN JOSHUA TEMPLETON
AND THE RIVER PRINCESS
1949

I turned to Oakley. "Does this have something to do with why there's a lighthouse here?"

"In a way." Oakley swung open a thick wooden door and started up a long set of spiral stairs. "You see, back in the 1920s, Grove Park built a riverboat–the *River Princess*–to take people for pleasure cruises. It was big business. Brought lots of money into Grove Park. They built this lighthouse to make sure the boat would never run aground on the island after dark. But then, one night . . ." Oakley's voice trailed off. The echo of his words seemed to fill the tower.

"One night *what*?" Elena said. "Don't leave us hanging, Oak!"

For a moment, there was only the sound of our six sets of footsteps marching up the spiral staircase toward the top of the lighthouse. Then Oakley continued: "Well, the *River Princess* crashed into the island. As the boat broke apart, the passengers had to swim for it. Some made it onto the island. Others were swept downriver but eventually made it to shore. In the end, they all survived. All of them *except* the riverboat's captain–Joshua Templeton. A guy whose family had lived in Grove Park since the town's founding in 1758."

"So why'd it crash?" Edgar asked.

"Wasn't the lighthouse working?" Kevin said.

Oakley scratched his stubbly chin. "Well, now, that's a mystery. The lighthouse keeper swore the light had been working properly, but the townspeople accused him of lying. Said there was no way the captain would've crashed into the island if Elijah Sánchez had been doing his light-keeping job properly."

"Wait," I said. "Did you say *Elijah Sánchez*?"

"Yep."

"Could he be related to Mrs. Sánchez?" I asked. "The Elmwood librarian?"

"Don't know." Oakley stopped as he reached a platform at the top of the spiral staircase. The rest of us crowded around him. "All I know is that even though Elijah only lived across the bridge in Elmwood, rumor has it that he never stepped foot in Grove Park again because the townspeople here never forgave him." Oakley patted a ladder that was bolted to the wall. It rose up from the platform, leading to a trapdoor in the ceiling. "This here's the only way up to the lantern room. Hope you kids like climbing."

"Do pandas like cream cheese?" Elena said. "Let me at it!" She slipped past Oakley, scurried up the ladder, and disappeared through the trapdoor.

Oakley chuckled. "Not sure I understood the cream cheese business, but I guess she likes climbing. Who's next?"

"Finley's our observer," Kevin said, making room for him to get to the ladder. "He can go."

"Okay," Finley said, though his voice sounded weak.

I hoped heights didn't affect him the same way the boat ride had.

Once Finley had made it up the ladder, the rest of us–including Oakley–followed.

Elena barely noticed our arrival. She was busy admiring the light that sat in the center of the room and looked kind of like a three-foot-tall Easter egg made from copper and glass. I heard her murmuring something about "a Fresnel lens" and "reflection *and* refraction for increased light intensity and focus."

"According to the clue, we have to *find the eagle where it flies,*" Edgar said. He looked around the room, then peered through a glass door that led outside to a platform that circled the lantern room's perimeter. "Does an eagle roost up here or something?"

Oakley shook his head. "Had plenty of birds poop on my lighthouse. No eagles, though."

"What if we got the clue wrong somehow?" Kevin asked. "What if we're not actually supposed to be here?"

We walked out onto the platform, inspecting the top of the lighthouse and peering down over the platform's metal railing. Nothing.

"We have to be in the right spot. We just *have* to be." I scrubbed my hands over my eyes. "Everything fits too perfectly. And why else would Oakley have been warned people might show up on the island?"

"Fine," Kevin said. "But if you're right, then why

would we be brought here? What's so special about this place?"

"Isn't that the easy part?" Elena pointed back inside the lantern room at the giant Easter-egg-shaped light.

"You mean . . . ?" said Kevin.

Edgar snapped his fingers. "Maybe the clue isn't here. Maybe we have to use the light to *find* the clue."

"Nice work, Edge!" Elena clapped him on the shoulder.

"So if we aim the light westward, we'll find the eagle." I shielded my eyes and pointed toward the sun. "Though *that*'s a problem."

"Just great," Kevin huffed. "We still have two clues left to find before tomorrow, and now we have to wait until sunset?"

"Technically, Kev, we're gonna have to wait until thirty or forty minutes *after* sunset," Elena said. "It'll take time for it to get dark enough for the beam from the lighthouse to do any good."

Kevin put his face into his hands and groaned.

Elena checked the time on her phone. "Sunset's around seven-thirty, which is still over an hour away. That means we have at least an hour and a half until it'll be dark enough."

I turned to Oakley. "Is it okay if we stick around until then?"

"Sure." Oakley nodded. "What would you kids like to do while you wait?"

Edgar cleared his throat. "Well, you know . . ." He scratched behind his ear. "I sure wouldn't mind my own shot at Twinkle Toes Four-Seven-Nine."

27

The other GEEKs and Finley all texted their parents, letting them know we were safe but had to stay out late because we needed darkness to locate the next clue. Elena also sent a text to my mom, since I no longer had a working phone of my own. Then Kevin and Elena helped Oakley put together some sandwiches, while Edgar logged himself into Space Farm Defenders. Finley and I settled down on opposite ends of the couch and watched as Edgar taught countless opponents that they never should have challenged Ollie4Ever.

But I was only half watching Edgar's gaming domination. My eyes kept drifting to Finley, who still seemed a little pale from his ride on the river. "Are you feeling okay?" I finally asked.

Finley stuffed his hands into his windbreaker and rattled something in one of the pockets. "Yeah, I'm okay." His voice was quiet, and he stared blankly toward the TV. "Thanks."

I wanted to say something more. Wanted to probe deeper, just like any other journalist would. But . . .

I sighed. Things had felt off between Finley and me ever since we'd messaged back and forth the night before. Why had he stopped messaging me? Had I done or said something wrong?

I was saved from the awkward silence when Oakley called out "Grub time!" and set a platter of ham sandwiches on the coffee table. Kevin and Elena followed with a bowl of carrot sticks, ranch dip, and a six-pack of root beer.

As we all dug into the food, Oakley said, "Been a while since I've shared a meal with anyone other than Jerry."

Edgar popped open a can of root beer. "So have you really been here by yourself for over fifty years because of an old girlfriend?"

Oakley picked at his fingernails. "Well, to me, she was a lot more than just a girlfriend."

Elena swiped a carrot stick through the ranch dip and pointed it at Oakley. "Then it's time for you to spill the beans about your long-lost love."

Oakley pursed his lips. "I don't know."

"It might help if you talked about her," Kevin prod-ded. "We're good listeners."

Oakley took a sip of root beer and gazed off across the room. "Well . . ." And then—even though Oakley had given up music so long before—his story began flowing out like a song.

The rest of us sat there, caught up in the melody of his memories. Even Elena stayed quiet.

Eventually Oakley's voice trailed off. He sniffled, his eyes glistening with recollections and regrets. "Really, I suppose all you need to know about Betty is that she was the type of gal who couldn't even let a turtle get hit crossing the road."

A turtle crossing the road.

I gasped. "Betty? As in *Elizabeth*?"

Suddenly I knew why my reporter radar had pinged when I'd watched Oakley playing video games earlier. Now I knew why he looked so familiar. He was decades older, but the deep-set eyes were the same. *Jonathan Oakley Seasons.* "You're Jon—the guy we saw in the photo at Elizabeth's!"

Oakley scratched at his stubbly beard. "You know Betty?"

"I nearly ran her down with my bike!" Elena offered.

The rest of us chimed in too, and we told Oakley all about our chance meeting and visit with Elizabeth the day before.

Oakley sighed. "I always felt like she broke our relationship off before we really got our chance."

"But you could still have a chance," I said. "Elizabeth's a widow now, and she's been thinking about you too."

"You should go see her," Kevin said.

"She still wears the turtle necklace!" Edgar added.

Oakley's face lit up at the mention of Elizabeth's necklace, but then the spark faded from his eyes. "It's too late for us. I . . ." He swallowed. "I couldn't take another heartbreak."

I reached out and rested my hand on Oakley's knee. "You should at least think about it." My gaze flitted over to Finley, then came back to settle on Oakley's weathered face. "Maybe it's not as late as you think."

"Agreed. Now enough mush." Elena hopped to her feet. "It's getting dark. We gonna find that eagle or what?"

I looked out the cottage window and realized the sky *had* grown dark. We all stood. Oakley grabbed a pair of binoculars, and we retraced our spiraling journey to the top of the lighthouse.

In the lantern room, Oakley said, "I sure hope this'll help you kids." And he flipped a switch.

The light blazed to life. A low hum filled the room. That's when I realized that the Easter-egg-shaped thing wasn't actually the light—the light sat inside it, shining upward, and the copper-and-glass egg was the lens, which rotated around the light, focusing and directing the beam.

As the lens began to rotate, Elena plucked the binoculars from Oakley's hand. "Eagle-hunting time!" She went to the outside platform and focused to the west. The rest of us joined her, leaning against the railing, searching, hoping.

The lens made a slow and steady rotation, offering a brief glimpse of Grove Park when it spun around to shine westward about every ten seconds.

After the third or fourth pass, Elena slowly shook her head. "Nothing."

"Here." Kevin grabbed for the binoculars. "Let me have a turn."

Elena reluctantly surrendered the binoculars to Kevin.

It was a cool night, and the air held the scent of coming rain. High up in the lighthouse, there was nothing to block the wind, and I shivered as I continued to stare west, waiting for the light to come back around and give us another peek at the town. Once it did . . .

"There!" Kevin jumped up and down, the binoculars still pressed to his eyes. "At the church! On the roof!"

"Let me see." Elena snatched the binoculars back, waited for the light. "It's a golden *Aquila chrysaetos*–a golden golden eagle!" Elena thrust the binoculars toward me. "Check it out, Gee!"

The first time the light spun around, I missed the eagle. But then, "I see it too!"

The golden statue perched in a nook of the cross-topped steeple of Grove Park United Methodist Church. In the daytime, it would have been in the shadows and difficult to see from the ground. But at night—and from our high vantage point—it flashed every time the beam from the lighthouse passed by.

After me, Edgar took a turn, followed by Finley and Oakley, who were also curious.

We all high-fived Kevin for spotting the statue, and we thanked Oakley for letting us borrow his lighthouse.

"You're welcome," Oakley said. "Can't say I minded the company. You're welcome to come back and visit." He turned off the light, and the lantern room went dark.

My eyes adjusted slowly to the night. Oakley's face was hidden by the shadows, but I remembered the look of longing in his eyes when he'd talked about his lost love. "You'd better promise to keep in mind what I said about Elizabeth," I told him.

"Fine," he grumbled, though I could hear a touch of a smile in his voice. "I promise to think about it."

"It's a true love story." Edgar sounded ready to weep. "Like *Romeo and Juliet*."

"Um, Edge?" Elena said. "Didn't Romeo and Juliet both end up dead?"

Oakley barked a laugh, then coughed in an unsuccessful attempt to hide it.

"Well, maybe that wasn't a perfect comparison," Edgar admitted.

"Oakley said he'll think about it," Kevin said. He turned to Oakley. "In the meantime, well, any chance you can get us back to Jerry Smokes's? We left our bikes there, and it's time to go to church."

We piled into Oakley's motorboat, which bobbed beside the pier.

Finley already looked like he might throw up again, but Elena's knees bounced up and down excitedly. "Hey, Oak. How fast can this baby go?"

"Guess you're about to find out," Oakley said. He stuck the key into the ignition and gave it a twist.

Click.

"Is something wrong?" Edgar asked.

Oakley twisted the key back and forth.

Click, click, click.

The night was filled with the sounds of the river flowing past, the ribbits and chitters of frogs and insects, the far-off hoot of an owl. No engine roaring to life. Not even a sputtering attempt.

"Strange." Oakley held the key in front of his face like it might have the answers. "I was just out on the river this afternoon. Engine fired right up, no problem."

I glanced around at the GEEKs. "That *is* strange. Do you think it might have been tampered with?"

Oakley let out a disbelieving laugh. "Tampered with? Out here?"

"There are loads of ways to disable a battery, you know," Elena said. "I even did one of my YouTube videos on it. Slip a little baking soda or Tums into the battery and voilà!" Elena smacked the side of the boat for emphasis, and Finley jumped so high that he nearly dropped into the river. "Battery's kaput."

Kevin palmed his forehead. "Elena, you are the only one who would even know something like that. Or actually try it."

"What about the Tattler?" I asked. Both banks of the river were dark with silhouetted trees, though on the Grove Park side, lights reflected off the water from a couple of houses farther upriver. Overhead, thick clouds had rolled in, blotting out the moon and stars. I scanned for any Tattler-sized shadows or the glint of a zoom lens. "Maybe he isn't just snapping photos and blogging anymore. Maybe now he's actually sabotaging us."

"It's possible," Edgar said. "But the battery also could have just died on its own. That happens sometimes with our tractors on the farm."

"Could be Tums. Could be bad timing," Elena said. "Either way, we gotta get across to find the next clue."

"Do you kids have someone you could call?" Oakley asked.

I held up my hands in surrender. "My phone's broken. And even if it weren't, there's no way I'd tell my mom I got myself stranded on an island in the middle of the river. She was already about to make me quit the hunt after what happened *last* night."

Elena snorted. "I've had enough rides in my dad's police car to last a lifetime. I'm not calling home."

"My parents would flip too," Kevin said. "They still haven't recovered from the shock of our *first* treasure hunt."

When we looked to Edgar, he held up his hands. "And risk extra milking duty? No way. What about Jerry Smokes? Can't we call him?"

Oakley shook his head. "Jerry is the earliest sleeper I know. He'll be dead to the world by now."

We turned to our final hope.

"Well." Finley shifted uncomfortably in his seat. His voice was weak and unsteady, probably from the thought of another boat ride. "I can think of *one* person I could call."

It took nearly an hour before we heard the roar of an engine and the sound of a boat skipping across the river's surface. As the vessel approached, a bright light mounted on the front reflected off the water. Right before it would have collided with the pier, the boat cut hard, sending up a spray of water and sliding expertly up to the end of Oakley's pier.

"Sorry it took so long, kids!" Lily Grove shouted over the rumble of the engine, her hair swept this way and that from her ride. "I had trouble finding a boat to borrow. I got here as quickly as I could." She waved us aboard. "Climb in and grab life jackets."

"Thanks, Ms. Grove," Kevin said. Oakley helped steady him as he carefully stepped from the pier to the boat.

"Yeah, you rock!" Elena ignored Oakley's helping hand, leapt onto the boat, and flopped a life jacket over her head.

Edgar, Finley, and I followed, with me taking the seat in front, next to Lily.

"I'm so glad Finley chose to call me," Lily said. She looked back his way, but he'd already settled into a seat, head in his hands, obviously not looking forward to another ride on the river. "I could understand if you didn't quite trust me anymore! First, there was the trouble with the train at Bamboozleland. Now this–I got you stuck on an island. Honestly, though, I thought you would rent canoes and–" Lily stopped herself. "Sorry. I'm not supposed to say anything about whether you're on the right track."

"It's okay," I said. "You couldn't have known we'd get a ride from Jerry, or that Oakley's engine would die."

She smiled at me. "Now, I knew you children would be cold after standing out here waiting for so long, so I brought hot chocolate and maple leaf cookies." Lily passed out paper cups, then handed us a thermos of cocoa and a box of Mrs. Dupree's cookies.

I was glad she was being so nice and that she didn't mind Finley calling her to help us out. Still.

"Ms. Grove?" Kevin said. "It's getting late. Can we get going? We're still hoping to find the next clue tonight."

Lily twitched. "Oh. Yes. Of course." She turned to

Oakley. "Have a good night, Mr. Seasons. I hope this wasn't too much trouble."

Oakley waved off Lily's concerns. "No trouble at all. Quite enjoyable, actually."

And then we were off.

With all of us on board, Lily drove the boat more slowly than when she'd zoomed up to get us, but it was still a faster journey than it had been on Jerry Smokes's houseboat. As we motored downriver, I turned to Lily. "I'm sure you've read the Tattler's posts, but I hope you don't think we've actually shown patterns of violence or vandalism."

"Of course not," Lily said, speaking loudly enough to be heard over the boat's engine. "The media have a way of blowing things out of proportion." She laughed. "That's certainly happened to me a time or two during my years as mayor of Grove Park."

Despite Lily's assurances, I couldn't help but wonder if—in some way—the GEEKs *were* acting like the Tattler said. It seemed like Elmwood had been causing trouble for Grove Park for a long time. Were we just more of the same?

Lily must have sensed my mood. "What's wrong, Gina?"

"I don't know." I stared ahead as the boat's light illuminated the river. "We've been learning things this week, and it sure seems like Elmwood has caused Grove

Park a lot of harm. The mudslide that wiped out the train. The crash of the riverboat on the island."

There was a pause before Lily said, "The riverboat crash?"

I told Lily everything we'd learned from Oakley about the *River Princess,* Captain Joshua Templeton, and lighthouse keeper Elijah Sánchez.

"Naturally I'm familiar with the story," Lily said. "But I didn't know Elijah Sánchez was from Elmwood." She drummed her fingers on the steering wheel, her back straight, her focus on the river. "That's all history, though. Nothing to worry about."

I worried anyway. Because the further we got into our hunt, the more I saw the pattern of Elmwoodians doing things that hurt Grove Park. Even Maxine had played a role, by leaving her mother all alone. And even though Elena was the scientist and Kevin was the mathematician, I'd learned enough in both subjects to know that patterns are hardly ever random.

So, what if Elijah Sánchez had sabotaged the riverboat on purpose? What if the people of Elmwood had known they were putting Grove Park's train at risk by cutting down too many trees along the tracks? And even though Max Van Houten was convinced his grandmother wasn't the thoughtless woman revealed by the long-lost letters, what if he was wrong? And what if

Elmwood–like Maxine Van Houten–wasn't as good as I had always thought?

The doubts skipped across my mind like the boat skipped across the surface of the river, and I turned to look back at my friends. Kevin and Elena were arguing about something, though the noise of the boat's engine made it so I couldn't tell what they were saying. Edgar stared off across the river, twirling a finger in his curly hair, lost in thought like me.

I hoped his thoughts weren't as depressing as mine.

"We're here," Lily said, snapping me from my trance.

I turned and saw the marina silhouetted against the night. A few slivers of light snuck between the curtains on Jerry's houseboat, and I could just make out our bikes still piled on the shore.

Lily throttled down the boat and coasted expertly alongside one of the docks. "Good luck tonight, kids. I'm looking forward to seeing you at the finish line tomorrow."

We thanked Lily and quickly climbed out. She zoomed off to return the boat to whomever she had borrowed it from.

As we strapped on our bike helmets, Edgar was still staring out at the river.

"What're you thinking about?" I asked him.

"Isn't it kind of strange that Lily didn't know about Elijah Sánchez being from Elmwood?" he asked. "She put this whole treasure hunt together because she's from the family that founded Grove Park, and she knows everything about the town's history. So it seems like she'd know every detail of that story, especially since Elijah was never allowed back into Grove Park."

I shrugged. "It's a pretty small detail. Maybe it's something Lily heard before but just forgot about."

"Speaking of stuff I wish *I* could forget about"—Elena pulled out her phone—"I wonder if there are any new and nasty posts from the Tattler."

The other GEEKs pulled out their phones to check the FVT blog too. Since I didn't have a phone, I used the opportunity to try to make things feel more normal between me and Finley, who was acting a bit sluggish after the boat ride.

"Mind if I check the blog with you?" I asked, stepping up beside Finley.

"Oh." Finley blinked. "Sure."

Finley pulled out his phone, hurriedly swiped some open apps from the screen, and pulled up the Tattler's blog just as Elena said, "There's nothing new."

"Maybe we finally gave him the slip," Edgar said. "I haven't seen him today."

"He's probably just waiting to sneak attack us again," Kevin said, always the optimist.

I stayed quiet but thought of Sophina and our video chat early that morning. Had she come through already? Had she found a way to stop the Tattler?

29

By the time we neared Grove Park United Methodist, it was already after nine-thirty. Just as we rolled up, a man was locking the doors, his back to us.

"Wait!" Elena cried.

"Ah!" The man spun around, dropping his keys, which jangled onto the sidewalk.

"Sorry!" Edgar said. "We weren't trying to scare you."

The man put a hand to his chest. "Well, at least I know my heart still works." He smiled. "I'm Pastor Bailey. I believe I recognize the lot of you as our local contingent of treasure-hunting youths."

"Yes, sir." Kevin laid his bike in the grass and stepped forward to shake Pastor Bailey's hand. "We were hoping you might allow us a brief opportunity to inspect your church's steeple."

Pastor Bailey scratched his neatly trimmed goatee. "Part of your treasure-hunting challenge, I presume?"

Kevin nodded. "Yes, sir."

"Well, God must be on your side. Our midweek Bible study class couldn't get enough of Genesis this evening. I'd normally be long gone by this hour, but Noah's ark kept our discussion *afloat* quite late tonight."

I snorted. "Nice pun, Pastor."

Pastor Bailey winked. "I do try." He retrieved his keys from the sidewalk and reopened the doors. "Right this way."

As Pastor Bailey led us inside, I peeked back over my shoulder, searching for any sign of the Tattler, but I saw no camera flashes or mysterious shadows. Maybe we really *had* finally given him the slip.

Our sneakers padded softly on the thick carpet of the church's foyer.

"How do we get up into the steeple?" I asked.

Pastor Bailey flipped on some lights and pointed toward a doorway to our left. "That will lead you straight there. There's a nice view from the top, even at night."

"Thank you again," Kevin said. "We appreciate—"

"Race ya!" Elena took off.

I glanced at Pastor Bailey, hoping he wasn't angry at Elena for running inside the church. He just laughed and made a shooing motion at the rest of us. "You'll never catch her if you just stand there."

That was all the permission we needed. The rest of us took off, feet pounding as we wound our way up a few flights of stairs. The stairs ended in a small, square room that was just large enough for the five of us. Each wall had a tall window that looked out over Grove Park.

"Which window would the eagle be above?" Edgar asked.

"We saw it by looking west," Elena said. "So we were seeing the *east* side of the steeple." She spun slowly, her finger pointing like a compass. *"There!"*

We crowded around the window Elena was pointing at, smooshing together like Edgar's cows at feeding time. We scanned the window, the wall. Where was the clue?

"Look up." I pointed. The outline of a small, square hatch was visible in the ceiling at least ten feet above the floor.

"Oh, man," Kevin said. "How are we going to get up there?"

"There's probably a ladder here at the church," Edgar said. "If Lily hid the next clue in the ceiling, she had to get up there somehow. Let's go ask the pastor."

"Ladder-schmadder." Elena flopped her arm across Edgar's shoulders. "Come on, Edge. Who needs a ladder when we've got *you*?"

I shook my head. "Elena, a ladder's safer. I think we should–"

"Do you see a ladder?" Elena swept her arm out, gesturing around the room. "I sure don't. But Edge's shoulders are right here. All I've gotta do is climb aboard, and–*boom!*–I'm up." She clapped Edgar's broad shoulders. "Now the clock's tick-tocking, so let's get rocking!"

I still didn't like the idea, but once Elena has made up her mind, she's pretty much unstoppable.

Edgar must have reached the same conclusion. He sighed and squatted down.

"That's what I'm talking about!" Elena said. She grinned and climbed into a crouch on his shoulders.

Kevin and I helped steady them as Edgar gripped Elena's ankles and stood back up.

"Be careful," Finley said.

"Stop worrying, Fin." Elena rose from her crouch, wobbling slightly as she stood on Edgar's shoulders. "They don't call me Elena the Ninja Scientist for nothing."

I snorted. "Elena, nobody actually calls you that."

"Don't distract me with minor details, Gee." Elena reached for the hatch in the ceiling. "A ninja scientist's gotta be allowed to concentrate."

I stayed quiet as she opened the hatch.

When the door swung upward, the light from inside

the steeple spilled over the golden eagle. Its outstretched wings flashed. Elena reached through the opening.

"Anything?" Kevin asked.

Elena felt around above her head. "Wait for it. . . . Wait for it. . . ."

Edgar gritted his teeth. "Try to hurry." He shifted his feet a little, and Elena swayed, then grabbed the edge of the hatch opening for balance.

I heard Finley suck in a breath behind me, but I kept my gaze on Elena and the eagle.

"Got it!" Elena pulled an envelope from behind one of the eagle's wings. "Edgar the Elevator may now lower Elena the Ninja Scientist!"

Edgar grunted but didn't say anything. His legs trembled as he slowly crouched back down.

"We've got you," Kevin said as he and I continued to steady both Edgar and Elena.

I held my breath. *Don't fall. Don't fall.*

And then Elena was safely back to the floor. "No ladder, no matter!" she shouted. "All-GEEKs victory hug!" She slung her arms around me and Kevin, and Kevin and I pulled in Edgar.

Finley shuffled backward, trying to give us space.

"Hold it," Edgar said. "Even a traveling journalist is part of the team." He reached out and hauled Finley into our circle.

"Leave no GEEK behind!" Elena declared, her braid

bouncing up and down on her shoulder as she danced and hugged and danced some more.

And right there in the steeple of the Grove Park United Methodist Church–despite himself–Finley let us pull him into our celebration. For the first time that night, he smiled.

The Grove Park Challenge Daily Update

FINLEY BROWN • Thursday, April 14 • 11:03 p.m.

GEEKS CONTINUE TO CONQUER CLUES

On day three of the Grove Park Challenge, Gina Sparks, Elena Hernández, Edgar Feingarten, and Kevin Robinson—the so-called Elmwood GEEKs— successfully solved yet another clue. They visited musicians and Methodists, lighthouses and steeples, demonstrating both teamwork and determination throughout the day. However, only about twelve hours remain for them to solve the final two clues and locate the Bamboozle Bolt.

It is not a journalist's job to say whether the GEEKs told the truth about their discovery of the Van Houten fortune six months ago. All that can be done is to report observations and events during their current quest. Yet even an objective reporter must give credit where credit is due, and so far, the GEEKs have proven to be both genuine and skilled treasure hunters.

The summary below contains highlights of the GEEKs' day three efforts. Read on to determine for yourself what credit you feel their efforts deserve. . . .

30

My special treasure-hunting curfew was ten o'clock, and I was fifteen minutes late. Luckily, Mom had fallen asleep on the couch waiting for me, which saved me from being scolded as I crept to my room.

After getting ready for bed, I read Finley's daily update, with Sauce licking my feet. The rain I'd smelled on the air earlier that evening finally arrived. First, it came as a soft pattering, then as a downpour that smacked against the roof. Gusts of wind rattled the window. I watched my clock flip to midnight. Day four had arrived. We had until noon—twelve more hours. Then we'd either prove to the world that we were the *genuine and skilled treasure hunters* Finley had mentioned. Or we'd fail, and Mr. Schoozer and the Deepsight board would abandon their plans to restore Bamboozleland.

The problem was, we'd spent all of Thursday solving a single clue, starting during breakfast at the Maple Leaf and ending late that night at Grove Park United Methodist. How could we possibly solve two more clues by noon? And what if the Tattler showed up again?

With worries of the Tattler rattling through my mind, I jotted some observations and cogitations that I should have started the first day the Tattler's blog appeared—places where we'd seen him and questions I had. Even a list of people who had a reason to dislike Elmwood and the GEEKs, and who might have put him up to it. I couldn't think of any reason for a stranger to want to take us down so badly. But I got nowhere with my notes. Finally I reminded myself that Sophina was working to dig up information on the Tattler, and I had to trust she'd find some. I needed to focus on finishing the treasure hunt.

I pulled my laptop out, opened the photo Elena had sent of our new clue, and flipped to a fresh page in my journal. I spent the rest of the night listening to the storm outside and trying to figure out what the clue could possibly mean.

Your time is running out,
Yet it's time that you should seek.
Now in the present you must search
The past and its mystique.

One time a rightful owner
Had a treasure that was taken,
Hidden then beneath the ground,
Both stolen and forsaken.

The past? Stolen treasure? The entire clue was so vague, I didn't know where to start. Then, as the night's storm finally ended and the rising sun began to peek through my window, I realized there was one person in Elmwood who might be able to help—the one person who'd been working with both treasure *and* things from the past.

I immediately messaged Finley and the GEEKs.

Elmwood library, 8:30. Be there.
Mrs. Sánchez might be our only hope.

Fortunately, there was nothing in the rules of our challenge that said we couldn't ask local experts for information, and I figured a librarian would probably be most knowledgeable about Fair Valley history. Plus, thanks to all the work Mrs. Sánchez had done to prepare the artifacts from the Van Houten fortune, she might have ideas about the treasure the clue talked about. And, of course, the journalist in me wanted to ask if she was related to the lighthouse keeper Elijah Sánchez. If so, maybe she would know something more about what had happened.

As I got ready to leave, my computer chimed with a message. The sound woke up Sauce, who nuzzled his snout into my arm. I scratched between his ears and glanced at my laptop, expecting to see a reply from Finley or one of the GEEKs. But the message was from Sophina.

> Closing in on the Tattler. Chasing down a lead. More info soon.

I admit that Sophina's message made me a bit jealous. *I* was the one used to chasing down leads. *I* wanted to be the one who got the scoop on the Tattler's full identity and motives. I also wondered why–if Sophina hadn't already stopped him–we hadn't seen any signs of the Tattler the day before.

But . . .

I had a clue to solve. I sent Sophina a quick reply:

> Thanks! Hunting down the final clues. Only a few hours left! Keep us posted.

As I stood, Sauce barked "Rah-oo!" and bounded off my bed, then spun in excited circles as if he knew how close we were to the end.

"Sorry, boy," I told him. "You have to stay home for now."

He whimpered. His long, floppy ears drooped in disappointment.

I crouched and kissed his head and added a promise I hoped I could keep: "I'll see you at the finish line at noon."

Sauce sighed and plopped to the floor like a spilled pudding cup. But I didn't have time to worry about his pouting. Because right then a *ding* announced another message from Sophina.

> One more thing. Check your front door.
> I left you something for today. WEAR IT.
> IMAGE IS EVERYTHING!

Wear it? Image is everything? I swallowed. With Sophina, those types of statements tended to worry me. But she *was* helping us by tracking down the Tattler, so maybe I could go ahead and wear whatever she'd left for me. After all, how bad could it be?

31

If you've ever pedaled a bike on rain-slicked roads in high-heeled boots and a jumpsuit, you know it's not easy. And if you haven't? Well, I don't recommend trying. Especially if you have a long, shimmering scarf flapping from your neck, making it feel like you're being strangled by a glitter-covered boa constrictor.

I will never understand Sophina's sense of fashion.

When I rolled up to the library a little before eight-thirty, Elena was the only one there. She barked a laugh as soon as she saw me. "Lookin' snazzy, Gee!"

"You're one to talk." I eyeballed her outfit and slowly shook my head. "Though, it looks like you made a few non-Sophina-approved alterations."

"I'm not really sure why I humored her at all, but . . ."

Elena grinned and pirouetted. "This seemed like a good compromise."

Her white, long-sleeved top glittered with sequins down the sleeves, but she'd pulled a rumpled pink T-shirt over it that read IF HISTORY REPEATS ITSELF, I'M GETTING A WOOLLY MAMMOTH. Instead of a scarf like mine, she'd been given some kind of shawl with dangly fuzzy bits. She'd duct-taped a large, Superwoman-like *S* onto the shawl, then flipped it backward so it looked like a cape.

"Makes me wonder what Kevin and Edgar will be wearing," I said, climbing off my bike and sliding it into the bike rack on the sidewalk. "Hopefully, they hurry up and get here."

"I'll do a status check." Elena thumbed a quick text into her phone. It chimed with a reply a few seconds later. She read the message and ground her teeth. "Seriously?"

"What?" I peered over Elena's shoulder and read the text, which came from Kevin.

E and I following another lead. Meet at bridge at 9?

Elena scowled. "We're supposed to be a team."

I didn't like Kevin and Edgar keeping us out of the

loop on a different lead, but we *were* running out of time. "Maybe it's better this way," I said. "We can cover ground more quickly."

"Well, Kev and Edge better not do something dangerous without me!"

"Where *are* Kevin and Edgar?" Finley asked, pulling up and hopping from his bike.

Elena only grunted, so I said, "They're following another lead. Looks like you only get to observe me and Elena this morning."

"Well, um." Finley scanned me, from my silvery high-heeled boots to my shimmering scarf. He took off his helmet and ran a hand through his hair. His wavy swoop of bangs dropped perfectly into place across his forehead. His eyes dropped toward the sidewalk. "You look . . . different today."

Elena saved me before I could figure out how to respond.

"Don't hold Gee's current style against her, Fin. We owed Sophina a favor, so we accepted her fashion choices." Elena fluffed her cape. "Though, in my case, there were a few changes." She hopped up the library steps and started knocking on the door. "Now let's see if Mrs. S is here!"

A moment later, Mrs. Sánchez bustled over and opened the door. "Good morning! I'm not officially open yet, but let me guess–last-minute treasure hunting?"

I nodded as she ushered us inside. The rules of our treasure hunt wouldn't allow us to show Mrs. Sánchez our latest clue, but we could still ask about details it contained. "I figured you know a lot about the history of this area, so I was wondering . . . do you know anything about a treasure that was stolen from around here?"

Mrs. Sánchez frowned and shook her head. "The only treasure I know about is the one you children found last fall. But those things all belonged to Maxine Van Houten—they weren't stolen." She took off her glasses—which matched her turquoise pants that day—and polished them on the edge of her shirt. "I'm so sorry I'm no help."

"That's okay." I tried to keep the disappointment from my voice. "Thanks for listening."

"Yeah," Elena said. "Thanks for trying, Mrs. S."

The weight of our treasure hunt pressed against my heart. I'd been so hopeful that Mrs. Sánchez would have some answers for us, and now it was just a dead end. I looked at the clock on the wall behind the front desk. Eight-forty-two. Three hours and eighteen minutes left before we had to be at Bamboozleland with the Bolt, but I had no ideas, no leads. Only an indecipherable clue. Hopefully, whatever lead Edgar and Kevin were chasing proved more useful.

As we turned to go, I remembered that maybe I could get *something* from our trip to the library, even if it was only to resolve my fears about Elmwood. I turned back. "Mrs. Sánchez, this isn't about our treasure hunt, but there was something we learned yesterday." I picked at the edge of my notebook with a fingernail. "This question is a bit more personal, and I hope you don't mind me asking, but are you related to the Elijah Sánchez who worked at the Grove Park lighthouse a long time ago?"

Mrs. Sánchez's usually smiling face grew serious, and a touch of sorrow shadowed her eyes. "Elijah was my husband's grandfather. I'm guessing you learned about the riverboat? The accident?"

I nodded, a lump forming in my throat. "I'm sorry. I shouldn't have asked."

"That accident has haunted my husband's family. The guilt. The questions." Mrs. Sánchez gave a deep, sad sigh. "It was a terrible tragedy, but the cause was a mystery. I only ever heard Elijah speak about it once, soon after Mr. Sánchez and I were married. He swore the lighthouse lamp was working, and the only solace he took was the realization that it could have been so much worse. He said the first cold front of the year had just swept in, but the river was still warm from summer. If it had been colder, the people who were carried downriver might have gotten hypothermia and died."

"Hold up." Elena held out a hand like she was stopping traffic. "Roll that back."

"Well," Mrs. Sánchez said, "hypothermia is—"

"No, no, no. The deal about the weather."

Finley and I exchanged a glance. Where was Elena headed with this?

Mrs. Sánchez looked up, thinking. "My grandfather-in-law said it was the first cold front and—"

"I know why the riverboat crashed!" Elena blurted.

We all stared at her.

Elena started bouncing up and down. "When cold air moves over warm water, it forms a type of fog. Actually, there are *lots* of types of fog. I learned about them at science camp." Elena began ticking them off on her fingers. "Freezing fog. Advection fog. Radiation fog. Anyway, you get the idea. But what matters here is *steam* fog."

Mrs. Sánchez arched an eyebrow but didn't interrupt, which is usually the best policy when Elena gets rolling about science or technology.

"So," Elena continued, "with steam fog, a mass of cold, dry air moves over a body of warmer water—in this case, the White Bend River. Then—thanks to the second law of thermodynamics—as the warm, moist air above the river water contacted the cold, dry air above it . . . *WHAM!* Steam fog."

I glanced at the clock above the desk again. A couple more minutes had passed. But we couldn't leave now.

"Elijah would have seen the fog," Mrs. Sánchez protested.

"Not necessarily," Elena replied. "Steam fog can appear quickly but stays low to the surface. The fog could've been thick enough to keep Captain Templeton from seeing the light from the lighthouse, but your husband's abuelo might not have noticed it from his high perch. For him, the night would've looked clear unless he was looking down at the river."

Mrs. Sánchez rested her hands over her heart. "That explains everything. Elijah was so honest, so responsible. He never would have left the light off, and if he had, he wouldn't have lied about it." She sniffled. "I wish he were still around to hear this, but it will mean so much for my husband to hear."

Despite the fact that Elena and I needed to get to the bridge and continue our treasure hunt, I felt my heart lighten with Elena's news. "So it *wasn't* sabotage," I murmured.

Elena and Mrs. Sánchez both stared at me. "Um, why would it have been sabotage, Gee?" Elena asked.

"Oh, nothing." I hadn't meant to mention sabotage out loud. "It's just . . ." I riffled the pages of my notebook. "We learned about the mudslide that wiped out the train, then about Elijah and the riverboat. It felt like a pattern. Like Elmwood was out to get Grove Park or something."

Mrs. Sánchez looked thoughtful. "I heard about the train accident growing up," she said. "The whole town of Elmwood felt terrible about it. In fact, memories of that accident were a major part of the push to create the nature preserve. The preserve would keep the surrounding forest intact, making sure nothing like the tragedy of the mudslide ever happened here again. And, of course, Maxine Van Houten was the one who stepped in and financed the project, making the preserve a reality."

Despite the pressure of our treasure hunt still hanging over us, I felt my lips curl into a smile. *That* sounded like the Elmwood I knew. And the Maxine. I thought of Max's assurances about his grandmother and the type of person she was—good and honest, just like Elijah Sánchez. "Thanks, Mrs. Sánchez. That's good to know."

Finley stuffed his hands into his pockets, listening but not interrupting.

"Enough chitchat, Gee." Elena tapped her wrist, even though she doesn't wear a watch. "We gotta get to the bridge."

I didn't bother pointing out that *Elena* had been the one doing most of the talking, lecturing about fog. Still, she was right—we'd already stayed at the library longer than we should have. I turned to Mrs. Sánchez. "Thanks again."

"I know you children are in a hurry, but may I ask

one quick favor?" Mrs. Sánchez picked up an envelope off the counter. "I was mistakenly delivered a letter for the Maple Leaf Diner this morning. Would you drop it through the slot on their door on your way?"

"Do wild ferrets enjoy barbecue pizza?" Elena took the envelope and used it to salute Mrs. Sánchez. "We got ya covered, Mrs. S!"

We hurried from the library. And there—beside the bike rack—sat yet another unexpected addition to our morning.

32

"Sauce!" Elena called. "What are you doing here?"

"Rah-oo!" Sauce bounded over and licked Elena's kneecap.

Elena laughed, tossed the envelope from Mrs. Sánchez into the basket on my bike, and ruffled Sauce's ears. Finley reached down to pet him too. He must have gotten out somehow and followed my scent.

"Bad dog, Sauce," I scolded through my smile. "I told you to stay home."

Sauce showed how sorry he was by chugging in excited circles around the bike rack, ears flapping.

I sighed. "I guess we have an extra treasure hunter this morning." I scooped Sauce up and wedged him into the bike basket beside my journal, the letter for the

Maple Leaf, and the spare leash I keep on hand just in case.

When we got to the town square, we paused at the Maple Leaf. I had the envelope halfway through the mail slot when I froze. I gasped, my eyes locked on the envelope's stamp. My mind flashed to the letter written by Maxine's mother, which I still had tucked into my notebook. I thought of the mail on Jerry Smokes's table, which had made my reporter radar ping the day before.

"Earth to Gee." Elena knocked on my helmet. "Drop the mail. We gotta roll."

I pulled the letter back from the Maple Leaf's mail slot, too stunned to respond.

How could I have missed that?

"Look at this!" I took out the envelope addressed by Maxine's mother and held it up next to the letter for the Maple Leaf.

Finley squinted at the envelopes, studying them.

"So?" Elena asked. "Different people. Different handwriting."

"No," I said. "Look at the stamps. The Maple Leaf's letter went through the mail, so it has a postmark." I tapped the stamp on the bright white business-sized envelope, surrounded by a series of lines and a stamp that said BOSTON, MA. Then I waved around the old, yellowed envelope addressed to Maxine Van Houten. It held an old stamp, but . . . "There's no postmark here. Maxine's mom wrote letters, *but she never sent them.* In the end, she must have been too proud or too scared to put them in the mail."

That meant Maxine hadn't ignored her mother's attempts to repair their relationship. She hadn't even known her mother *wanted* to repair it. I felt relieved, but I was still mad at myself for not noticing the missing postmarks from the start. As a journalist, those are the types of details I'm supposed to spot.

Finley seemed dazed. "So the Tattler had it all wrong?"

"Exactly." I dropped the letter we'd gotten from Mrs. Sánchez through the slot and tucked the old letter to Maxine back into my notebook beside Sauce. "Will you put this in your daily update? Plus, what Mrs. Sánchez told us about the nature preserve protecting against more mudslides? That could really help prove how unfair the Tattler's posts have been."

Finley nodded, still looking shaken by our discovery.

The Elmwood Community Church's bell tower began its hourly tolling. "C'mon, Gee." Elena tugged my arm. "It's nine. We're supposed to be at the bridge."

"Right." I pushed away the thoughts of Maxine and her mother and the missing postmarks. "I just hope Edgar and Kevin had better luck than us."

"You're late," Kevin said as soon as we pedaled up to him and Edgar on the bridge. The usually lazy river rushed beneath us, swollen by the overnight storm. "And why do you have Sauce? We can't waste time when we have less than three hours to find the Bolt and get to Bamboozleland."

Sauce gave an indignant "Yip!"

"Never mind Sauce," Elena said. "But speaking of wasting time . . ." She tilted her head and studied Kevin and Edgar. "Did the two of you spend the morning doing a safari-disco photo shoot?"

I heard Finley stifle a laugh. Clearly Sophina had given outfits to all of us, not just me and Elena. Kevin had on round-framed mirrored sunglasses, polished black boots, and a blue silk shirt with a wide, open collar. Edgar sported more of an Indiana Jones look–khakis with a wide brown belt, plus a brown leather jacket and matching fedora.

Kevin frowned and tugged on the collar of his shirt. "It was faster to put on the stupid clothes than to argue with Sophina." He gestured toward me and Elena. "Besides, it looks like you guys had the same problem."

"Point taken," Elena said. "Anyway, you'd better not have had too much fun without us. Where were you? Did you find anything?"

Kevin and Edgar glanced at each other. Then Edgar said, "Nothing. Dead end. What about you guys?"

"Mrs. Sánchez didn't have any information on a sto-len treasure," I said, "but we *did* learn a couple of inter-esting things." I quickly explained what we'd learned from Mrs. Sánchez and what we'd figured out about the letters written by Maxine's mom.

"That's all well and good," Kevin said, "but it doesn't put us any closer to figuring out the clue."

"I know." My shoulders slumped. "This clue seems like the vaguest one yet. Where should we start?"

Edgar laughed. "Well, that's the one thing the clue *does* tell us—we're supposed to begin in the present to search the past. The starting point seems pretty obvi-ous, doesn't it?" He paused dramatically, making sure he had our full attention.

"Spit it out, Edge," Elena said.

"A museum!" Edgar said. "Living history! In the pres-ent, searching the past!"

"Maybe the train museum?" Kevin asked.

"No way." Elena shook her head. "Lily wouldn't have two clues about trains."

"You're probably right," Kevin grumbled. He pulled out his phone and did a quick search. "Got it!" He showed us his phone and pointed to a red dot near the south-ern edge of Grove Park. "There's one other museum in Grove Park—the Grove Manor History Museum."

"Let's roll like fat puppies down a sand dune!" Elena said.

And we took off, hoping to solve our next-to-last clue.

The Grove Manor History Museum was tucked away down a winding, tree-lined drive. The house itself was a mini-mansion of brown fieldstone with arched windows and doors. Ivy climbed the walls outside, and a half dozen stone chimneys sprouted from the red tile roof. A bronze plaque hanging by the front door taught me some basic facts:

FACT #1: After founding Grove Park in 1758, Thomas Grove had the home built in 1769, on the site of his family's cabin, which had burned down in a fire.

FACT #2: Thomas Grove lived in the manor with his wife, Charlotte, and their two sons, George and Louis.

FACT #3: Thomas Grove's descendants continued to live in the manor house for the next two hundred years.

With Sauce on a leash looped around my wrist, I jotted information from the plaque into my notebook, recalling the reproduction of the oil painting we'd seen by our booth at Lion's Pizza. It had shown George and Louis sitting in chairs in front of a large stone fireplace, their father standing behind them, a hand on each boy's shoulder. All three of them had worn knee-length breeches, long suit coats, and serious expressions.

I was still writing in my notebook when Elena knocked on the door, which swung open immediately.

"Ah! There you are!" a woman exclaimed. She looked like she'd arrived in a time machine from the 1700s. She wore a dark green dress with a subtle, lighter green floral pattern. A white, frilly shawl covered her shoulders, and the long sleeves of the dress were cuffed in the same white fabric. "You're a bit late, but you must be my nine o'clock tour!"

"Actually," Kevin said, "we're—"

"Come, come. No time to dally." The woman held open the door and ushered us inside. She hesitated when she saw Sauce. "We usually don't allow dogs, but I suppose since you're a special tour group . . ."

"We aren't here for a tour." I held up my notebook. "We need to—"

"Good morrow, children." The woman curtsied. "My name is Annabelle Bradstreet, and I have been working for the Grove family since Thomas Grove had this home constructed thirteen years ago. Mrs. Charlotte Grove is so pleased to have you as guests today."

Elena leaned toward me and whispered. "Wasn't this home built in seventeen-something-or-other?"

"*Shhh.*" Edgar put his finger to his lips. "It's living history. Annabelle's an actor."

Annabelle Bradstreet—or whoever the woman actually was when she wasn't playing a role from the 1700s—didn't miss a beat. She guided us down a hall, chattering away. "I must say that your breeches and petticoats are not what I am accustomed to seeing here in 1782, nor is your hunting dog. You children must have traveled quite a fair distance for today's visit. Please rest assured that your journey will not have been in vain."

As we followed the woman through the house, Kevin groaned. "We don't have time for this."

"We also don't know what we're looking for," I pointed out, coaxing Sauce to keep moving as he sniffed and snuffled everything in his path. "Maybe this tour will help."

"I may even learn something for my next acting role," Edgar said. "Annabelle's great at staying in character!"

Elena gave a silent, frustrated tug on her braid, but she followed along, trailed by Finley.

I kept my journal open, pencil in hand, hoping for a scoop that would solve our next-to-last clue.

33

Annabelle guided us from room to room through Grove
Manor, presenting plenty of interesting facts–from telling us how many cords of wood were required to keep
fires burning in the manor's six fireplaces during the
winter, to showing us the copper tub where laundry was
soaked in a process called *bucking*. But nothing Annabelle showed us or told us seemed to have anything to
do with the clue.

As Annabelle led us into yet another room, Kevin
whispered, "We're wasting our time. It's already ten-
twenty. We've got to figure out this clue and get out of
here!"

"This room," Annabelle said, sweeping her arm
wide, "was Thomas Grove's study and is now used by
his widow."

A large desk sat near a stone fireplace, which was flanked by built-in floor-to-ceiling bookshelves. The wooden mantel above the fireplace was empty, but what hung above it instantly caught my eye—the actual painting we'd seen a copy of at Lion's Pizza.

"As you may be aware," Annabelle continued, "before the family difficulties, Thomas Grove owned all the land on which Grove Park and Elmwood now sit."

My friends and I exchanged looks. What did Annabelle mean by *family difficulties*? And about Thomas Grove owning Elmwood? We hadn't even heard of Thomas Grove or his family until a couple of days ago!

Annabelle smiled, as if she were recalling a fond memory. "Aye, I remember well the days when the young twins—George and Louis—were inseparable, playing together and getting into mischief from sunrise to sunset." She gazed at the painting hanging above the fireplace. "When they weren't sneaking into the kitchen and pilfering food, those two lads loved coming up with codes and puzzles, hiding things for each other to find."

I thought of Maxine Van Houten. Her love of puzzles had led her to invent the Bamboozler, which had become popular all around the world. Puzzle-making seemed to be as much a part of the Fair Valley as the air and the trees.

Annabelle's smile faded. "But, alas, those days of innocence and puzzle-making did not last."

Edgar leaned over to Finley and whispered, "Isn't Annabelle good at staying in character? Look at her eyes–actual *tears!*"

Sauce seemed less impressed. He lay flopped across my feet, snoring, his drool pooling on the toe of one of my high-heeled boots. But whether it was Annabelle's acting ability or the story itself, I found myself intrigued by her words. *Could this have something to do with our clue?*

Annabelle gestured toward the painting. "Although the lads were twins, George was the firstborn, having come into the world fourteen minutes sooner than Louis. As a result, George was set to inherit all of the family's land. Then, in 1776, both Thomas Grove and his son George joined the Continental Army to help fight for America's independence from Britain. Louis was unable to join them due to lingering problems with his health. Tragically, Thomas died from smallpox in March 1778 while encamped at Valley Forge, and this drove an unexpected wedge between his sons."

"What happened?" I asked.

"Immediately upon their father's death, Louis staked a false claim to the land across the White Bend River, saying it had been their father's will to split the land between his sons. This angered George, who was still off fighting in the war. He felt betrayed by his brother, who not only took land that was rightfully George's but also divided the community their father had created."

"That's why I'm glad I'm an only child," Elena said. "So much easier."

Annabelle arched an eyebrow. "Indeed, miss, it may be. In the last letter George ever sent to Louis, he wrote, 'Our fortunes, Brother, have always been at odds with one another. Now, so too shall those of Elmwood and Grove Park be.'"

Those final words sent a shiver slithering up my spine. I thought of the mudslide and train wreck, the fog and the riverboat, even Maxine leaving Grove Park to settle in Elmwood and make her fortune there. Had all this trouble really started way back in the 1700s? Even if Elmwood hadn't meant for any of those things to go wrong, what if George Grove was right? What if the words he'd written to his twin brother had become some kind of self-fulfilling prophecy?

These thoughts were still wandering through my mind—and Annabelle was still telling about the Grove family's history—when I realized Kevin was talking too.

"So if the land was all supposed to be George's," Kevin said to me, Elena, and Edgar, "then Louis stole it? Like in the clue? *One time a rightful owner had a treasure that was taken.*" Kevin grinned. "What if *Elmwood* is the treasure?"

Elena groaned. "So we're already almost out of time,

and now we're supposed to search for something buried somewhere in Elmwood? That's all we get? That's
ridiculous!"

Elena's voice had risen as she'd said this, and Annabelle paused in her storytelling, her forehead wrinkling
in concern. "Is everything all right, miss?"

"Oh, sweet Einstein, no! Of course everything's not
all right! We have—"

"We have a question." Edgar stepped forward. "In
addition to the land, I don't suppose Louis stole anything else from George, did he?"

"Actually . . ." Annabelle leaned on the empty mantel
and motioned toward the painting. "This portrait was
completed in this very room. Notice anything missing?"

As we studied the painting, Finley stuffed his hands
into his pockets and joined us. Edgar began humming
"The Room Where It Happens" from *Hamilton*.

In the painting, Thomas Grove and his sons were po-
sitioned in front of the same fireplace above which the
painting now hung, and there—just visible over Thomas
Grove's left shoulder—sat the missing object.

"The old clock on the mantel?" I pointed to the
painting.

Annabelle nodded. "That's right!"

Something about the clock looked familiar, but I
couldn't figure out what, and its details were difficult
to make out in the painting's background. All I could

tell was that the clock was square and made of wood with gold accents, and it had something carved on top, though I couldn't make out exactly what it was.

Annabelle pointed to the clock in the painting. "When Thomas Grove founded Grove Park in 1758, he commissioned Isaac Ashford—one of the premier clockmakers in the world—to make that clock. It was one of Thomas Grove's prized possessions, but the priceless heirloom went missing in 1779, shortly after Louis founded Elmwood, and it has long been rumored that he is the one who took it." She sighed. "Unfortunately, the clock's disappearance was soon overshadowed by further tragedy, and the clock has long since been lost to–"

"*Time!*" Kevin blurted. "Thank you so much, Annabelle, for your time. We need to go!"

"But you paid for the full ninety-minute immersive experience," Annabelle said, finally breaking character. Her entire face wilted. "I haven't told you the rest of the story about George and Louis. Don't you want to–"

"No time!" Kevin started dragging Elena and Edgar from the study. I scooped a still-snoring Sauce into my arms and followed after them, along with Finley.

"The clue. The clock," Elena said, stumbling to keep up as Kevin pulled her toward the front door.

Kevin bounded from the manor, Elena and Edgar still in tow. "Exactly! It's time that we should seek!"

Edgar nodded. "We're seeking *time*–so we have to find the missing clock."

Elena buckled on her bike helmet and threw her shawl-cape over one shoulder. "But it's not like we can cruise all over Grove Park and Elmwood, randomly looking for a clock that was stolen over two hundred years ago."

I was about to agree, but as I set Sauce into the basket of my bike, his floppy ears flashed a memory through my mind. A clock. A table. A disobedient dog sliding across a slick granite floor.

Our search for the clock didn't need to be random.

"Actually, guys . . ." A grin stretched my face. "I know *exactly* where to find it."

34

The clue said time was running out, and it was right. We had an hour and a half to find the final clue, figure it out, retrieve the Bolt, and then—somehow—get to Bamboozleland by the noon deadline. We flew through the streets of Grove Park, our legs spinning like tornadoes as we pedaled back toward Elmwood and our town's not-yet-opened museum.

Elena's Superwoman shawl-cape flapped in the wind. Sauce—now awake—howled happily from my bike basket, his nose in the air, his ears streaming behind him like wind socks in a hurricane.

On the way, I explained to everyone how Sauce had bumped into a table when he'd gotten loose in the Van Houten Museum, and how I'd then barely managed to save an old, square clock from smashing on the floor. Like the clue said, the clock had been *hidden then beneath the ground, both stolen and forsaken* when Maxine Van Houten's fortune had been stored away in its underground treasure vault. And *we'd* been the ones to unbury it six months earlier.

Fortunately, Max had gotten the emergency text Elena had sent before we'd left Grove Manor. He was already waiting outside the Van Houten Museum when we skidded to a stop, leapt from our bikes, and dashed up the steps.

Max waved. "Hey, I got your–"

"Max!" I gasped his name as I struggled to catch my breath from our bike ride. "Did you give Lily Grove a tour of the museum?"

Max scratched his head. "Sure. Just last week she–"

"We need to see the antique clock from the Van Houten fortune," Kevin said.

"Pronto!" Elena blurted.

Max didn't bother to ask why. He knew we were on a treasure hunt. And he knew it ended at noon, which was only a little more than an hour away. He yanked out a ring of keys and unlocked the front doors. "Follow me!"

He didn't need to say that last part. Elena was already halfway across the lobby, her sneakers slapping

267

against the granite floor. Edgar, Kevin, Finley, and I were hot on her heels, Sauce pulling me along on his leash, which I held in a gorilla grip.

We flew into the back room, which was still filled with artifacts waiting to be researched and cataloged. The clock sat on the same table as before, and we huddled around, examining it.

It was definitely the clock from the painting, the gold accents highlighting its square wooden case. Now I paid attention to the finer details. Flowers and vines had been engraved on the front of the clock's casing, and thin decorative designs were etched into the gold encircling the clock's face. But the most stunning aspect was the elaborate carving. It looked as if an elm tree grew straight from the top of the clock, and an eagle perched high in its branches.

Max's phone rang. He pulled it from his pocket and checked the screen. "Sorry, kids, I have to take this call. Be careful with the clock. It's got to be very, very old."

"No need to worry about us," Elena said, reaching for the clock. "We'll be as careful as grass in a lawn mower factory!"

Fortunately for Max, he was already talking into his phone and walking toward the hall, so he was saved from trying to figure out Elena's analogy.

As Elena lifted the clock, I spotted the envelope beneath it. Seconds later, we were reading our final clue.

Where the alpine trees blaze red,
The path will guide you straight ahead.
Higher up and up you'll climb
To find a place that is sublime.

When a sorcerer you meet,
The treasure lies beneath your feet.
Hurry now and excavate—
Your deadline nears. It will not wait!

Hope drained from me like ink from a broken printing press. The final clue was simple and straightforward. I knew exactly where to go. But . . .

"There's no way," Kevin mumbled.

"You must be kidding me." Elena massaged her temples.

"Um." Edgar was the only one who looked more confused than hopeless. Even Finley looked like he understood what the clue meant. How impossible it would be. Edgar glanced from me to Kevin to Elena. "What am I missing?"

Elena set the clock gently back onto the table. "Did you already forget our end-of-year fifth-grade field trip?"

"I was absent, remember? I had a morning milking

accident with Ollie that day. You guys got a field trip. I got a trip to Dr. Byer's and ten stitches."

"Oh yeah," Elena said. "Anyway, so you know that big ol' hill on the far side of Grove Park?"

"Cloud Tapper Hill?"

"Yeah. That one." Elena nodded. "The trail to the top is marked with little red rectangles painted on trees—the markings are called *blazes*."

"Okay, so that explains the *alpine trees blaze red* part. But what about sorcerers or wizards or whatever?"

"At the top of the hill," Kevin said, "there's a huge boulder that looks like an old, stooped-over man, called Wizard Rock."

"The problem is," I said, "even once we bike to the far side of Grove Park, recross the river, and get to the hill, it's still a nearly two-mile hike to the top."

Edgar's face drooped further and further as each of us spoke, his understanding catching up with everyone else's. His usually booming actor's voice was quiet as he said, "So it's the easiest clue to solve but the hardest one to get to."

"Exactly." Kevin ground his teeth. "I don't think we can make it."

"C'mon, Kev. Is that any way for the sixth-grade co-president to talk?" Elena bounced around, punching the air like a boxer warming up. "We've gotta fight to the end!"

"But we'll never get all the way there and back to Bamboozleland by noon," said Kevin.

"Sure, it'll be tight. But if we leave now and get Max to drive us to the bottom of Cloud Tapper Hill, then we can sprint up the trail and nab the Bolt. We just might do it!"

"To the Bolt for victory!" Edgar shouted, caught up in Elena's enthusiasm. He turned for the door.

"Wait!" I called. Kevin still looked skeptical, and I had my doubts too. But Elena was right—we couldn't quit. Not with so much at stake. But there was something else we needed to do too. I picked up the clock. "We should take this."

Kevin's mouth dropped open. "No way! That thing's fragile. Do you want to be responsible for wrecking another Grove Park treasure?"

"It doesn't feel right leaving it here," I argued. "Not when it belongs to Grove Park. Especially after everything we've learned that's happened between the two towns. If we take it with us, we can present it to Lily Grove during the ceremony at Bamboozleland." I turned to Finley. "Don't you think Lily would like that?"

Finley scraped a hand through his hair and stared at the floor. "Yeah," he said flatly. "Sure."

I'd thought Finley would show a little more enthusiasm for my idea, but at least he'd agreed with me.

Kevin still didn't. He shook his head. "I really don't think–"

"It's like Sophina is always saying," I said. "Image matters. Well, imagine us arriving at the ceremony with this clock. We can make up for all the stuff we've done. Injuring Eggy, wrecking the Old-Time Express. We can get people back on our side!"

"GEEKs!" Elena stomped her foot. "Stop wasting time! We'll take it with us and ask Max." She grabbed Sauce's leash and pointed at me. "Gee, don't drop the clock." She swung her finger around to point at Kevin. "Kev, get over it." Finally she swung her finger toward the door. "Now let's roll!"

We rolled.

Unfortunately, our entire plan fell apart as soon as we got outside.

"Where's Max?" Edgar asked.

As if in answer, the others' phones all chimed. A text from Max:

> Sorry I disappeared. Forgot I'd promised Ms. Kaminski a ride to the ceremony. Good luck and see you at Bamboozleland!

"That answers the question about Max," Kevin said. "But where's *anyone*?"

Even on a good day, downtown Elmwood is never very busy—some people wandering around the shops, others hanging out in Van Houten Park, that sort of thing. But I'd never seen it so deserted. The reason *why* Elmwood was so empty got announced by the Elmwood Community Church's bell tower.

BONG!

"It's eleven o'clock!" Elena snatched up Finley's bike helmet and tossed it to him. "Fin, I hope you can keep up!"

BONG!

"Everyone's on their way to Bamboozleland for the start of the final ceremony," I said. I whipped off my scarf and wrapped it protectively around the antique clock.

BONG!

"They'll expect us in an hour!" Edgar cried. He handed me his leather jacket to use for extra clock padding. I wrapped it around the clock and knotted the sleeves together. One shimmering end of the scarf stuck from the bundle like a tag on a birthday gift. I settled the entire clock-jacket-scarf bundle into the basket on my bike.

"I'm going to have to resign!" Kevin cried.

BONG!

"Don't give up, Kev." Elena pushed the glittery, sequined sleeves of her shirt up above her elbows and leaned down to lift Sauce onto the front of her bike, so that he was hanging over the handlebars. He settled into the nook her body made and barked, eager to get going. "We'll start out on our bikes and flag down the first car we see. Let's ride!"

We rode.

As we shot down the street toward the Elmgrove Bridge, the squeak of bike chains and whir of tires on asphalt were joined by the final chimes of the church bell tolling behind us. Each peal seemed to echo through all of Fair Valley, pushing us, prodding us, warning us.

Time . . . time . . . time . . .

We were just about to blast across the Elmgrove Bridge when we got cut off.

Sophina Burkhart shot from a side street and skidded to a halt in the middle of the road. We all braked. Sophina's finger stabbed toward us, her shriek cutting the air like the screech of an angry owl. *"You!"*

I flinched. Then I realized her finger wasn't pointing at me. Or at any of the other GEEKs.

"You!" Sophina repeated, hopping from her bike and letting it clatter onto the road. She stomped toward Finley, her face red, her finger still pointing.

Finley's face had gone pale. His hands tightened on his bike grips, his knuckles whitening.

"Sophina," Kevin said, "whatever this is about, we don't have time!"

"Then make time," Sophina growled. "You need to hear this." She grabbed Finley's handlebars and hauled Finley and his bike to the side of the road. "Should I tell them, Finley, or would *you* like to do the honors?"

Finley's lips trembled, but no words came out. A bead of sweat rolled down the side of his face.

What was going on?

Sophina whipped her head around, looking at the rest of us, but she didn't let go of Finley's handlebars. "GEEKs, allow me to introduce you to the Fair Valley Tattler."

Thursday, April 14, 11:45 p.m.

Observations & COGITATIONS

(Possible Spies & Haters of Elmwood & the GEEKs)

— <u>The Tattler</u>: Spotted at ground-breaking ceremony at Bamboozleland . . . outside Elmwood Middle School . . . at Grove Park Challenge kickoff . . . at the dock . . . at the inn . . . outside Grove Park Middle School basketball game . . . and by Bamboozleland train tunnel; takes photos and posts them in FVT blog

  ↪ HOW DOES HE ALWAYS FIND US SO QUICKLY?

  ↪ WHERE WAS HE ON THURSDAY?

  ↪ WHY, WHY, <u>WHY</u> DOES HE HATE US SO MUCH?!?!?

— <u>Lambert J. Schoozer</u>: Wants to expand Bamboozleland; businessman interested in profits; no personal history in Elmwood

  ↪ WOULD HE SABOTAGE HIS OWN CHALLENGE TO HAVE AN EXCUSE TO GET OUT OF THE BAMBOOZLELAND DEAL?

— ~~Jerry Smokes: Threatened us with a frozen fish and chased us away from his boat the first time we saw him; lifetime resident of Grove Park~~

➥ NO WAY. JERRY ENDED UP <u>HELPING</u> US.

— <u>Eggy</u>: Injured ankle at basketball game because of us

➥ EGGY HAS MOTIVE FOR DISLIKING GEEKS, BUT WE DIDN'T INJURE HIS ANKLE UNTIL AFTER THE TATTLER STARTED "REPORTING" ON US

➥ WHO'S ACTUALLY HIDING BENEATH THAT EAGLE OUTFIT???

35

The Fair Valley Tattler. Sophina's words knocked the air from my lungs like a punch to the stomach. For a moment, the only sound was the White Bend River rushing beneath the bridge. I thought of the journal entry I'd written the night before. I'd listed plenty of people who might have reasons to dislike the GEEKs, but . . .

"Picking stupid clothes for us was one thing." Elena plucked at one sequined sleeve. "But now you've hopped the train to fantasyland."

"It's not a fantasy," Sophina spit. "I'm *right.*"

"But we already know who the Tattler is," Edgar protested. "We've seen him!"

"He's followed us everywhere," I added. "I just want to know *why* he's been after us."

"*Pff*. Wilton Snivley?" Sophina swatted away our arguments like they were nothing more than buzzing houseflies. "He's just a freelance paparazzo."

"But how do you—"

"I followed Wilton yesterday and used his own tricks against him. I snagged video of him firing off roman candles at the Grove Park High football field after the boys' basketball team won some tournament and everyone was celebrating. A quick bit of research showed that Grove Park town ordinance twelve-dash-zero-three includes roman candles on the list of prohibited fireworks. Breaking the ordinance carries a two-hundred-dollar fine." Sophina's eyes sparkled like they were fireworks too. "I confronted Wilton and told him he'd better stop following you GEEKs and tell me everything I wanted to know. Otherwise the police would be getting evidence related to illegal fireworks, and *he*'d probably be getting a two-hundred-dollar ticket."

I climbed off my bike and parked it on its kickstand along the edge of the road. "You're not making sense, Sophina. Even if this Wilton Snivley character is a freelance paparazzo, that doesn't mean he isn't the Tattler. You just have to look at the facts." I cut my eyes toward Finley, who had stayed silent through all this. Why wasn't he defending himself? Why wasn't he telling Sophina how off base she was?

"You want facts, Gina? No problem." Sophina let go

of Finley's handlebars with one hand so she could tally them on her fingers. "Fact one—Wilton had a deal with a blogger. Fact two—Wilton didn't know who the blogger was. They just exchanged information using an anonymous email address. Fact three—the blogger tipped Wilton off about where the GEEKs would be, and in return, Wilton let the blogger use some of his photos."

"That doesn't make Fin the Tattler," Elena said. "Now we have to go."

Sophina reached out with her free hand and grabbed Elena's handlebars too. "Not yet. Not with Finley along." She glared at Finley, who sat slumped on his bike, staring at the ground. "After talking with Wilton, I reread the FVT blog posts and realized the Tattler mentioned a source who confirmed breaking and entering at Van Houten Toys. I went to the one person who would definitely know about that—security guard Cy Porter. And guess what? Cy had only talked to one person recently whom he didn't know. A boy about our age who chatted with him and shared a box of Mrs. Dupree's maple leaf cookies. A boy who had—in Cy's exact words—'the finest head of wavy black hair that ever made a bald man jealous!'"

Every single one of us turned and stared at Finley Brown. His wavy black hair hung below the edges of his bike helmet, the wave in the front still swooping across his forehead.

Elena threw up her hands. "This is ridiculous. Finley's the only one who's been covering us fairly. Right, Fin?"

Finley hesitated. Then he whispered two words that somehow seemed as loud as fireworks: "I'm sorry."

Wait. What?

"Finley?" His name escaped my lips like the croak of a frog. I recalled how he'd ducked into the shade when we'd run into Cy at the entrance to Bamboozleland. Had he been hiding?

Finley picked at the rubber grips on his handlebars, his eyes focused down the steep, muddy bank toward the river. "Back in September, after my big exposé of the cafeteria fraud, I thought I'd be getting the New England Youth Journalist of the Year award. Then you came along with all your articles about your treasure hunt and the Van Houten fortune, and suddenly . . ." Finley's voice trailed off. He swiped under his nose with the back of his hand.

My head felt ready to explode. I'd thought Finley *liked* me! But this whole time, he'd been upset that I'd beat him? "So, what then?" I said, my voice rising. "You went out and spread lies about us because you were jealous of some award?"

Finley flinched at my words. For the first time since Sophina's arrival, he met my gaze. "No. I . . ." Finley scrubbed at his eyes with the heels of his hands. "I didn't know I was writing lies. Someone I trusted came to me with a tip that your discovery of the Van Houten fortune was all a big, elaborate hoax. I thought I had the biggest scoop of my life. And"–his head drooped again–"I was all too willing to trust them."

"*Who?*" I demanded, my voice tight. "Who was your source?"

"Lily Grove," Kevin and Edgar said at the same time.

Elena, Sophina, and I all gasped.

Finley gave a slow, wordless nod.

"That's why we didn't come to the library this morning," Kevin said. "Edgar got suspicious last night, so we did a little research. It turns out Lily is a distant cousin of Maxine Van Houten's husband, Harold."

I glanced over at the bundle in my bike basket, which held the clock that had become a part of George and Louis's feud.

"It seemed strange that Lily never mentioned her family connection to Maxine," Edgar said. "Especially after all the other stuff."

"*What* other stuff?" Elena asked, reading my mind.

"On the boat last night, Lily acted like she didn't know about Elijah Sánchez being from Elmwood, but that didn't make any sense. She made the treasure hunt specifically because she knows every little tidbit about Grove Park's history. Plus, to be honest"–Edgar grimaced–"Lily's a pretty lousy actor. She stood way too rigidly, and she drummed her fingers like she was nervous. I could tell she was lying."

I thought back to the boat ride the night before, when Edgar had looked lost in thought. Now I knew what he'd been thinking about–Lily's suspicious behavior.

Kevin took off his mirrored sunglasses and waved them around as he went into lecture mode, explaining even *more* facts he and Edgar had put together and that I'd somehow missed.

FACT #1: Lily Grove bought maple leaf cookies from Mrs. Dupree.

FACT #2: Jerry Smokes had a box of maple leaf cookies on his houseboat. But . . .

FACT #3: Jerry said he didn't even like maple leaf cookies that much.

"So it was a simple deduction," Edgar said. "Lily bought the cookies and gave them to Jerry Smokes when she told him not to help us. She knew exactly what lead we would follow, and that we would end up on that houseboat. She was trying to slow us down."

Finley stayed silent, his hands clamped to his handlebars.

Finley's hands. I was reminded of the muck I'd noticed on his hands after he'd gotten sick following our ride on Jerry's houseboat. At the time, I'd figured he'd gotten something on his hands while kneeling on the pier, throwing up into the river. *Only now* . . . I glared at Finley. "You weren't really sick at the lighthouse, were you? You faked it, then sabotaged Oakley's motorboat."

Finley blinked. Nodded. "Lily got the idea from Elena's YouTube channel. She gave me—"

"*Tums.*" I practically spit the word. I thought about when Finley had stuck his hands into the pockets of his windbreaker as we'd sat on the couch in Oakley's cottage. The rattling sound. "She gave you a bottle of Tums."

Finley's shoulders slumped. "Lily told me to kill the boat battery. That way, by the time she came to get us off the island, it would be too late to get the clue from inside the church. But Pastor Bailey stayed late, and you got the next clue after all. So then Lily booked the nine o'clock tour at Grove Manor, trying to slow you down even more."

The nine o'clock tour. I suddenly remembered what Annabelle had said as we'd rushed from the museum: *But you paid for the full ninety-minute immersive experience.* That had been Lily too.

Finley rubbed at his throat. "It was all for show. She made up this whole challenge for you, but she really doesn't want you to win."

Sophina shook Finley's handlebars. "It sounds like *you* don't want them to win!"

"I didn't know at first. I swear." Finley held up both his hands. "I thought Lily was telling the truth, that you guys had lied and cheated. She even gave me evidence—the picture of Gina wearing that golden necklace in fourth grade."

"A blurry picture of plastic costume jewelry!" Elena growled.

"I realize that now," Finley said. "But I didn't know it *then*. That's why I let Lily talk me into starting the FVT blog. And then people liked the blog and posted comments and shared it and talked about it around town. More people read FVT than anything else I'd ever written, which made me feel important. Plus, Lily said I was doing the right thing. So." Finley swallowed. "So I kept up with it."

"But what about the facts?" I said, each word fluttering down like a dead leaf in fall.

"I guess . . ." Finley kicked at a piece of gravel, sending it skittering off the road. "It was easy for me to believe you were a bad person, Gina, because if you'd lied about the Van Houten fortune, then I didn't have to feel guilty about being mad that you'd won the youth journalist award. It meant you'd made up your story, but I hadn't made up my article about the school

285

exposé! I thought if I uncovered your dishonesty, you might lose your spot as the winner and I'd get it instead. But I chose to believe the story that I *wanted* to believe. I see that now."

I walked over to Elena's bike and picked up Sauce, blinking away tears. Sauce licked at my face and whined, seeming to understand my distress. I'd trusted Finley. *Liked* Finley. *And all this time?*

Finley's eyes were locked on mine now, begging, pleading. "You've got to understand, Gina, I didn't know you yet. But the more I watched you–*all* of you–I realized how great you are. How smart and nice and the real deal, not fakes or frauds or any of that." Finley blinked back tears of his own. "When Lily told me to kill Oakley's battery, I knew it was wrong, and by then I'd stopped texting updates to Wilton, so he couldn't follow us anymore. But with the battery . . . Lily . . . I just caved."

I thought of when Finley had come into Oakley's cottage, pale and sweaty and sick. I'd thought it was from the boat ride. Now I knew differently–he'd felt sick about what he'd done to sabotage us.

Finley forced himself to look each of us in the eye. "I'm sorry."

Sauce seemed to be the only one ready to offer forgiveness. He wriggled from my grasp and jumped to the ground, then waddled over to lick Finley's pant leg.

I grabbed his leash and pulled him back to my side,

too shocked to know what to say anymore. Elena didn't have that problem. She rolled forward on her bike and bumped her tire against Finley's. "You'd better make like evaporating water molecules and disappear, Tattle Boy. Right now."

"Elena, I—"

"Right. Now." Elena rolled back a few feet to clear a path for Finley to escape. "Before I do something we'll *both* regret."

Finley hung his head and pedaled away. He crawled slowly over the bridge we'd all been ready to blast across only a few minutes earlier. Back when we'd thought Finley was our friend.

"I'll follow him," Sophina offered, retrieving her bike from the middle of the road. "I'll make sure he doesn't do any more damage."

"Thanks, Sophina," Kevin said.

"No problem." Sophina gave Kevin a nod and a half smile. "It's the sort of thing one sixth-grade co-president should do for another. And, Elena." Sophina studied Elena's makeshift cape and grimaced. "We *will* discuss your style choices." Then Sophina took off toward Grove Park, trailing behind Finley Brown—the Tattler.

Kevin turned to the rest of us and held up his phone. His entire body sagged. "That delay doomed us. There're only forty minutes left, and everyone's already at Bamboozleland."

"I could call my mom to drive us," Edgar said. "But it'll take her ten minutes to get here."

"We need a miracle," Elena said, pulling the fedora down over his eyes.

Honnnnk! A rusty pickup truck coming from Grove Park laid on its horn and veered to our side of the road.

I yanked the leash backward to pull Sauce out of the truck's path and accidentally bumped into my bike. The bike began to topple. My eyes snapped to the bike's basket—to the bundled antique clock.

"*Nooo!*" I lunged for my bike's handlebars.

So did Edgar and Kevin.

We were all too slow.

My bike clattered onto its side. The bundled clock rolled from the basket. I watched in horror as the priceless Grove family heirloom started sliding . . . tumbling . . . down, down, down the steep, muddy bank, heading straight toward the rain-swollen White Bend River.

36

I didn't want to watch, but I couldn't look away. The loose end of the scarf flapped from the bundle like the tail of a kite. Edgar's leather jacket might have been padding the priceless clock enough to protect it from serious damage, but once it hit the river, none of that would matter.

The bundle slid past a tree. Bumped over a rock. Continued toward the water. Closer, closer, closer.

Twenty feet. Ten feet. Five feet.

And then it happened.

The flapping, shimmering end of the scarf snagged on some brambles growing along the river's edge. The scarf stretched. Pulled tight. Held.

One foot away from a plunge into the river, the bundle and its historic cargo was yanked to a stop.

I had to climb down and get it before it broke loose and disappeared forever!

"Hey, GEEKs!" Elena stood by the rusty pickup, waving me and Kevin and Edgar over. "It's Cy! He was heading to Bamboozleland for the ceremony, but he said he can give us a ride to Cloud Tapper Hill instead. Edgar asked for a miracle, and we got it! But we've gotta roll. *Now*."

It was just like Cy to pull over and offer us a ride. For a security guard, he sure was thoughtful . . . and trusting. It was no wonder Finley had been able to trick him into talking about us breaking into Van Houten Toys. Cy didn't have a suspicious bone in his body, and I knew he wouldn't have done anything to hurt us on purpose. But right now, that wasn't what mattered.

I glanced down the slope to the bundled-up clock. Then back to Cy's pickup. The clock was pretty far down the slope, and it would take time to get down there, safely retrieve it, and figure out a path back.

But if Cy was willing to drive us right now, we might still have a chance to make it to Wizard Rock and retrieve the Bolt in time.

Still, I couldn't bring myself to move. If we left and came back, would the clock still be here? The bundle was holding on by a thread, literally! If we left now, the clock would end up in the river. And that would mean losing a piece of history that meant a lot to *both* our towns.

I took a deep breath and slowly let it out. "I can't go."

Elena smacked her forehead. "We can't let Lily win!"

"But we can't leave the clock. It's a piece of history." I pointed down the slope. "It belongs to Grove Park. At least if we save it, we'll salvage *something* from this treasure hunt. It doesn't matter what Lily did. The people of Grove Park deserve to have this piece of their town's history returned."

"But I've made some rough calculations," Kevin said, tapping on his phone. "Assuming that Cy averages thirty-five miles per hour, and we're able to climb Cloud Tapper Hill at a rate of–"

"The math doesn't matter, Kevin," I said with a sigh. "This whole mess started because people didn't believe in who we are. I'm not about to prove them right by letting a priceless Grove family heirloom be lost forever."

"Maybe we should vote on it," Edgar suggested.

"No." I shook my head. "I couldn't live with myself if I left. You guys go on without me, and I'll meet you at the ceremony."

"You're sure, Gee?" Elena asked.

"I'm sure. You guys go! Take Sauce with you."

I handed Elena his leash, then turned and began to slowly inch my way down the slope.

The climb would have been easier with help, but I knew the others needed to finish what we'd started.

The previous night's rain had made everything muddy and slick, but small saplings and bushes provided some hand- and footholds. I gripped a thin branch of a bush and used it like a rope. I lowered myself slowly, slowly, until I ran out of branch.

I was looking down, trying to find a rock or tree root where I could put my foot, when the branch snapped.

"Ah!" My feet shot out from under me. My butt smacked into the mud, and I began to roll. I was going to fall, right into the frigid river.

Then something locked around my wrist.

"We've got you, Gina."

I spit out a mouthful of New Hampshire mud and looked up.

Kevin lay in the wet grass at the top of the slope, his hands fastened around my wrist like a vise. His extended arms mushed against the sides of his face, twisting his sunglasses. Elena and Edgar held his ankles. Not to be left out, Sauce had his slobbery jaws clamped on to the cuff of Edgar's khakis, his butt in the air, tail wagging.

I locked my hands around Kevin's wrists too, my fingers slick with mud. "I thought you left," I gasped.

"If I learned anything from our last treasure hunt,"

Kevin said, "it's that GEEKs stay together. No matter what."

"Everybody, hold tight and pull!" Edgar said.

Edgar and Elena (with some questionable but enthusiastic help from Sauce) dragged Kevin backward, towing me along for the ride. I slid through the mud and wet grass until they got me safely back to the top.

Cy stood over us, his eyes wide. "You kids all right? I was fishing in the back of my truck for some rope, but you all beat me to the punch!"

"We're fine," Elena replied.

"And . . . never mind about the ride," Kevin added. I could tell by the way he gritted his teeth that it pained him to say it.

"Ya sure?" Cy asked, bending down to pet Sauce.

"*Are* you sure?" I asked, disbelieving. "What about being class president? The petition for your resignation?"

Kevin sighed. "Real leaders lead by example," he said. "And saving that clock is the right thing to do."

"Yeah," Edgar said, and turned to Cy. "Thanks, though. Guess we'll see you at Bamboozleland."

"All righty then," Cy said. "If you're sure there's nothin' I can do for ya."

"Actually," I said, "wait a second. Can I ask *one* favor that would make things a lot simpler for us?"

A minute later, Cy was back in his truck, raising his hand in farewell as he drove off. Sauce sat on Cy's lap, head out the window, howling happily as his ears lifted in the wind.

Once Cy and Sauce were safely on their way to Bamboozleland, I turned to my friends. "You guys, seriously, you could have still gone after the Bolt."

Elena shrugged. "Kevin's right. GEEKs gotta stay together, no matter what. Plus, even if you got down there"–she flapped her hand toward the muddy slope–"how would you get back up without help? And *double*-plus, I'd let Sophina pick my clothes for a year before I'd let you have all the fun without me. Especially when there's mud and danger involved."

Edgar picked up his fedora, which had fallen off his head and gotten stepped on at some point during the rescue. He held the crumpled hat over his heart. "And I think fondly of my beloved heifer and ask myself: *What would Ollie do?* She knows the herd sticks together!"

I smiled at my three best friends. "In that case, how about we go and save an irreplaceable antique clock before it plummets into the White Bend River?"

It turned out Elena was right: the task would have been impossible without all of us working as a team. Elena clipped our bike helmets together, looped them around a sapling at the top of the slope, and attached them to Edgar's belt, turning him into our anchor. Next came Kevin, holding on to Edgar, then Kevin's blue silk shirt, then Elena's cape, then Elena. And finally—connected to Elena by a twenty-foot-long, doubled-over strip of heavy-duty duct tape—was me.

(When I asked Elena why she'd had a roll of duct tape stuffed into the pocket of her sequined shirt, she pointed at the duct-taped *S* on her cape, rolled her eyes, and said, "Duh, Gee. Ninja scientists have gotta be prepared.")

With a lot of slow, slippery shuffles, I managed to descend the slope, glad I was spared from worrying about the stringy-haired reporter since Finley—the *real* Tattler—had stopped letting the guy know where to find us. I detached the jacket-scarf bundle from the brambles (thank goodness for wild raspberries!), and my friends helped haul me back up. At the top, I collapsed onto the wet grass, breathing hard, cradling the bundled clock. Then slowly, carefully, I started untying the sleeves of the jacket.

"Is it damaged?" Edgar asked, unbuckling himself from his helmet-belt anchor.

"Give me a second." I peeled away the mud-covered leather jacket, unwound the scarf, and pulled out the Grove family clock.

Edgar and Kevin huddled around as Elena took the clock from my hands and turned it this way and that so we could all examine it for damage. By some miracle, the glass of the clock face hadn't cracked or broken, and the carving of the elm tree and eagle on top seemed undamaged.

It was when Elena gently turned the clock over to inspect the bottom that Kevin frowned. "What's that?"

I squinted. Carved on the underside of the clock was an inscription:

LOUIS, LOOK INSIDE.
LOVE, GEORGE

"Wait, that's a message from George to Louis. So Louis *didn't* steal it?" I asked.

Edgar threw his hands into the air. "It was a gift!"

"That doesn't make sense," I said. "If George *gave* it to Louis, why did everyone think Louis stole it?"

Kevin pointed at the inscription. "We need to figure out what it means by *look inside.*" Then he held up his phone. "And we'd better be fast. There's only twenty minutes left until noon."

"Remember what the guide said during our tour of Grove Manor?" Edgar said. "George and Louis liked to give each other puzzles. This clock must be a puzzle!"

"But how do we get inside it?" Elena asked. She ran her fingers around the edges, searching for some way to open it, but other than a brass key sticking from the back of the clock to wind it, there was nothing to be found. Elena gave a few quick turns of the key, which made a ratcheting sound. The clock began to tick softly.

"It still works!" I said, relieved.

"Yeah, but it's also still closed," Elena said, continuing her examination of the antique. She shut her eyes, mumbling to herself. "Now if I were the engineer of a secret compartment in a totally ancient clock . . ." The rest of us barely breathed as Elena rested her forehead on the clock as if she could absorb its secrets directly into her super science brain. Her eyes popped open. "Got it!"

Elena once again reached for the brass key on the back of the clock. However, this time, instead of twisting it, she pressed it with her thumb.

Click.

The entire back of the wooden casing sprang open on a hidden hinge. In a shallow compartment beside the gears and inner workings, the back of the clock held one final surprise.

My fingers trembled as I reached in and pulled out a leather tube.

We could hear Lily Grove's words booming through the sound system of the Bamboozleland amphitheater before we could even see the stage. "Good people of Grove Park and Elmwood," she was saying, "it is with a heavy heart that I complete the countdown to the noon deadline for the Grove Park Challenge. Unfortunately, I have no choice. Our young treasure hunters now only have five . . . four . . . three . . . two—"

"*Wait!*" Elena, Edgar, Kevin, and I screamed from the top of the amphitheater. We hopped from our bikes right as a giant digital clock on the amphitheater stage flashed 0:00:00. The others charged down the amphitheater steps. I trailed a little behind, not wanting to risk tripping and tumbling on the crumbling cement stairs. I cradled the Grove family clock in my arms, re-wrapped in the scarf and leather jacket.

Lily's mouth dropped open. She staggered back from the podium in the center of the stage. Although she only whispered to herself, the microphone picked up her single word and carried it into the crowd: *"No."*

Lambert J. Schoozer, who stood beside Lily, reached out a hand to steady her before stepping forward to take her place at the podium. "My goodness, folks, it looks like we may be receiving a Grove Park Challenge surprise!"

As the other GEEKs bounded onto the stage, there was a mix of cheers, boos, and gasps from the crowd. It was probably a good thing I couldn't see Sophina's face in that moment, because if appearances mattered as much as she thought they did, we were in trouble.

Elena's usually perfectly braided hair had sprung free and was shooting out in wild tangles. Mud-soaked fuzzy bits of shawl drooped from her neck like a giant caterpillar that had been caught in a storm. The once-sparkling sleeves of her sequined shirt were dulled by mud.

Kevin and Edgar looked no better. Kevin's mirrored sunglasses sat crooked and bent on the end of his nose, and his blue silk shirt had a large tear in the left armpit where it had snagged on a briar while we'd rescued the clock. Edgar's fedora was cockeyed and crumpled, and he no longer wore his leather jacket. Both of the boys were muddied from head to toe.

I choose not to detail or discuss my own appearance.

As I joined the other GEEKs onstage, I tried to absorb everything around us. A royal-blue banner had been strung above the stage, and its gold lettering reflected in the noonday sun. GROVE PARK CHALLENGE: BOLT OR BUST! Just like on the day of the aborted ground-breaking ceremony, the amphitheater was packed. Annalise Richardson and the TV crew from Channel 6 News were back. I also spotted Wilton Snivley–the would-be paparazzo–and hoped he wouldn't be a problem.

Mr. Schoozer smiled as if he thought his too-white teeth might shine so brightly that they would blast the mud straight from our clothes. He gestured toward the bundle in my arms and leaned toward the microphone attached to the podium. "It appears you have something to show us. Has your treasure hunting led you to the Bolt?"

Someone started a chant that was picked up by the rest of the crowd: "Bolt! Bolt! Bolt! Bolt!"

Kevin stepped forward, raising his arms to silence the crowd.

The chanting faded.

"Thank you, everyone, for coming this afternoon." Kevin nodded toward the audience and then toward

Mr. Schoozer. "I am happy to report that we figured out each clue in the Grove Park Challenge."

Cheers. Applause. A shout of "Show us the Bolt!"

Kevin raised his arms again and waited until quiet returned. "Unfortunately," he continued, "we ran out of time to retrieve the Bolt at Wizard Rock—where the last clue led."

"We knew you were fakes!" someone called.

"That's what you get for being cheaters!"

It didn't feel great.

However, even though angry voices filled the air, I spotted friendly faces in the crowd—my mom, blinking back tears . . . Cy, holding Sauce, who was fast asleep in his arms . . . Elena's abuela, staring down some red-faced guy who'd been booing. I even saw Jerry Smokes, who gave me a thumbs-up when he caught my eye.

Mr. Schoozer tried unsuccessfully to quiet the crowd, and no amount of arm waving from Kevin or fedora flapping from Edgar had any effect either.

I just stood there, still cradling the bundled-up clock. Would we be forced to leave without having a chance to explain what we *had* accomplished, what we *had* found?

Then Finley Brown appeared onstage. He stepped to the microphone and quieted the entire amphitheater by shouting a single declaration: "STOP!"

The noise began to die away.

"If you won't listen to them, then listen to me . . . the Fair Valley Tattler!"

The sudden silence reminded me of the time when the *Tribune*'s press had broken down in the middle of our Friday print run. The stillness was immediate and complete.

Elena glared at Finley.

"I am the Fair Valley Tattler," Finley repeated, more quietly than before, commanding the audience's attention with his words, not his volume. His statement sent a fresh stab of pain through my heart. "I'm the one who wrote the FVT blog. I'm the one who accused the GEEKs of fraud." He took a deep breath and gazed out at the sea of faces. "I'm the one who was spreading lies."

The crowd gasped. My heart lurched. Finley was confessing?

Finley's knuckles whitened as he gripped the sides of the podium, but he kept his head high, his eyes on the crowd. "I wrote the FVT blog, but the things in it weren't true. Or, at the very least, they lacked context."

Murmurs rose but no shouts. Brows wrinkled in confusion and doubt.

"Did the GEEKs go on someone's houseboat uninvited?" Finley asked. "Yes, but only because they misunderstood one of their clues. Did they cause an injury to Eggy the mascot? Yes, but only by accidentally bumping into a rack of basketballs. A misunderstanding is not criminal trespassing. An accident is not an assault. You see how easily the truth can be twisted to fit the story you want to tell? Or hear?"

More murmuring. A few heads beginning to bob in agreement.

"But they faked the first treasure hunt!" a voice shouted from the crowd. Within seconds, other voices were chiming in to agree.

Finley shook his head. "*Did* they, though? Are you sure? Just because there's a picture of Gina wearing a necklace that looked *sort* of like a necklace they found? And because I pointed out that some important Elmwood citizens were close to the kids who found the treasure? That doesn't mean it was faked, but it was enough to make you believe it was."

Finley glanced at me, but I looked away. I wanted to forgive him, but it was still hard to believe that our new friend Finley had been the cause of all our troubles over the last few weeks. It would take time to get over that.

"What about that fellow being an actor?" a voice called out. "You know. James Hatcher. There are photos of him conspiring with some of the kids' family members."

"I have no reason to believe he's an actor," Finley admitted. "He was in Elmwood for some time, so of course he interacted with a bunch of the townspeople, including Edgar's mom. He's being held in jail until his trial, where he'll likely be found guilty and sent *back* to jail. Would an actor hired to do a job go along with that?"

Grumbles went through the crowd, then murmurs of discussion.

"The thing is," Finley said, his voice rising, gaining strength, "I've been with the GEEKs every day as they chased down clues and raced to complete the Grove Park Challenge. What I witnessed wasn't a group of fakes or frauds. What I witnessed were four friends who overcame every challenge, solved every clue, and cared about our towns and each other in a way that should make us *all* proud."

"Hear! Hear!" Jerry Smokes cried from the crowd. "These four are welcome on my houseboat anytime! They got my computer online so I can finish my degree. Without them, I'd be a college dropout!"

A titter of laughter rippled through the crowd. A few more heads began to bob.

Then Oakley Seasons stood up in the front row. As he prepared to speak, I realized he was holding the hand of Elizabeth Baldoni, who rose to stand beside him. *No way!* I nudged my friends, who nodded and grinned. Even from several yards away, I could see the green turtle pendant on Elizabeth's necklace sparkling in the sunlight.

"These fine young people gave us the courage to re-kindle our love after more than fifty years," Elizabeth said. "Thanks to them, we have a second chance at happiness."

"And I've finally reached Asteroid Harvester status on Space Farm Defenders!" Oakley added, winking at Edgar.

More laughter from the crowd. Some clapping. An "Amen!" that sounded a lot like Pastor Bailey from Grove Park United Methodist.

At the top of the amphitheater, a tall boy I didn't recognize stood on crutches, his right foot encased in a cast. He brushed his floppy brown bangs from his eyes. "I'm Eggy, and I hate polyester!" He raised his right leg, waggled his casted foot around, and smiled. "It may have been an accident, but the GEEKs finally gave me an excuse to escape my itchy Eggy outfit!"

Yet more applause from the audience. A shout of "We still love you, Eggy!"

"See?" Finley said, stepping back to the microphone. "The GEEKs are not what many of you have been led to believe. They're not what *I* led you to believe. I smeared them on my blog. I hurt their reputations while trying to help my own. And through it all, I had one person pushing me to turn the GEEKs into fakes and frauds. I had"–Finley turned from the podium and stabbed a finger toward Lily, who had eased her way toward the back curtain and was one step from ducking out of sight–"Grove Park mayor Lily Grove!"

A collective gasp went through the crowd. Lily's face drained of whatever color had been left. She grabbed the curtain to steady herself, then started to slip behind it.

"Ms. Grove!" Lambert J. Schoozer boomed. "This accusation warrants a reply!"

Lily halted. She forced herself to stand tall, tugging at the lapels of her blood-red pantsuit. Her jaw tightened. "Fine!" she snapped, half stalking, half stumbling back to the podium. "I admit it! I wanted the GEEKs to fail!"

Shouts exploded around the amphitheater like fireworks on the Fourth of July, drowning out my own shouted question: "But *why*?"

"You people think that what's good for Elmwood

is good for Grove Park, but that's the thing–nothing that's good for Elmwood has *ever* been good for Grove Park!" The ghostly paleness that had taken over Lily's face a minute earlier was now colored by bright red splotches. "Don't you understand? Can't you see? I had to create this treasure hunt. Not so these children could prove how good and smart they are, but so you could see how Elmwood and its citizens have always–*always!*–been destined and determined to try to destroy Grove Park!"

I exchanged glances with the other GEEKs, sure that my eyes were just as wide as all of theirs.

Mr. Schoozer tugged at the collar of his shirt. A bead of sweat rolled down the side of his face. "Ms. Grove . . ." He rested a hand on Lily's shoulder, but she shook him off.

"In the beginning, Grove Park had all it ever needed," Lily said. "Then Louis Grove, the younger son of our great town's founder, split the town in two, taking all the best timbering land with it. Grove Park struggled to recover, and eventually we did. We found a new way to flourish. We built the premier riverboat in the northeast. What did Elmwood do? They destroyed it! Next, Grove Park bought land across the river to construct a pleasure park and convinced the New Northern Rail Company to build a train to connect it. Once again, the town prospered. But then Elmwood's greedy logging destroyed our train, just as they'd destroyed our riverboat!"

"The riverboat crashed because of steam fog!" Elena shouted, but she couldn't be heard over the sound of Lily's amplified rant.

"Was Elmwood ever punished for any of this?" Lily cried. "No! They walked away with a highway connection. Elmwood flourished, while Grove Park suffered." Lily leaned forward, her mouth nearly swallowing the microphone. "And it didn't stop there. When Maxine Van Houten took over as CEO of Van Houten Toys, did she pour resources into Grove Park, the town of her birth? No, of course not. She did everything for Elmwood!"

I thought of the letter tucked away in my journal, written by Maxine's mother but never postmarked, never mailed. If only Lily knew the full story.

"Of course, after Maxine's children ran her company into the ground, Grove Park finally seemed to catch a break. Janson Harland, an executive at Van Houten Toys, left the company and started Fair Valley Technology Solutions in Grove Park. At last, things were good for our town again! We were able to build a new library, new schools. More people moved to town. Then, suddenly, the closure of Fair Valley Technology Solutions was announced. And why did this happen?" A bitter smile twisted Lily's lips. "Because the Elmwood GEEKs went and discovered a fortune."

"But, Ms. Grove," Kevin said, "you can't blame us for Fair Valley Tech leaving!"

"Oh, but you're so *inspiring*!" Lily threw out air quotes with her fingers. "With all the press coverage about your discovery of Maxine's treasure, Janson got inspired to spend his golden years as a treasure hunter himself. He sold Fair Valley Tech to some competitor in California that plans to shift all the operations out there. Goodbye, Janson Harland. Goodbye, jobs in Grove Park. Our town was originally Maxine's home, yet it's Elmwood that has all of her fortune, and because of that fortune, Grove Park is once again left with nothing!"

There was bitterness in Lily's words, but more than that, there was hopelessness. As messed up as she'd been to sabotage us and our treasure hunt, I realized it was because she truly and deeply cared about Grove Park. Still, the facts she thought she knew weren't the full story; there was more that needed to be told.

I took a step toward her, the muddy jacket-scarf bundle clutched to my chest.

"With Fair Valley Tech leaving," Lily continued, "I knew I needed to do what the Grove family has done for over two hundred and fifty years—fight for my town. If only I could show the world Grove Park's history, they would fall in love with our town the same way they'd fallen in love with Elmwood."

I took another step toward Lily. The bundled clock was growing heavier in my arms.

Lily turned toward me and the other GEEKs. "If you

couldn't find the Bolt in time, plans for Bamboozleland would fade away. I could convince Mr. Schoozer to develop a newer, bigger, better theme park in Grove Park instead." The bitterness seemed to have faded from Lily's voice, with only the hopelessness remaining. "Grove Park and Elmwood have been oil and water ever since the Grove brothers split up. Our towns will never be united, just like the Grove brothers never were."

As Lily's last words settled over the crowd, I took the final step to join her at the podium. She flinched but didn't step away.

In that moment, I knew we couldn't have looked more different as we stood side by side—her, tall and professional with highlights streaking her glossy brown hair; me, short and mud-splattered, my messy bun of blond hair a tangled mass. Yet I also knew we were more alike than Lily or anyone else in the amphitheater probably realized. Because we both loved our towns more than we could ever express.

I gently placed my muddy bundle on top of the podium, then stood on my tiptoes, craning my neck toward the microphone. "But the Grove brothers *were* united," I said. "And my friends and I would like to show you how we know. . . ." As I unwrapped the Grove family clock, the other GEEKs joined me at the podium.

Kevin stepped up to the microphone and quickly

explained the clock's history and the inscription we'd found on its bottom.

Then Elena said, "And we discovered a totally rocking secret compartment in the back of the clock, so prepare to be amazed by what we found inside!"

Edgar took his cue. With the dramatic flair of a medieval knight drawing his sword, he reached into the pocket of his khakis and withdrew the leather tube that had been hidden in the back of the clock. He carefully slid out the two brittle sheets of parchment rolled inside. In a clear, strong voice that was surely destined for Broadway—or at least to play the lead in our local production of *Oliver!*—Edgar read aloud a letter from George Grove to Louis Grove, written in 1779, the year following their father's death. Then he read the last will and testament of Thomas Grove, which had been signed in 1776, right after Thomas Grove had joined the Continental Army.

The letter and the will shone a new light on long-hidden facts:

FACT #1: In the will, Thomas Grove stated that he wanted his sons to split the land between themselves, using the White Bend River as the dividing line . . . just like Louis Grove had claimed.

FACT #2: In the letter, George Grove explained that he had truly thought their father had wanted them to keep the land together . . . until George had received the items their father had had in his possession when he'd died at Valley Forge, which included the will.

FACT #3: George apologized to Louis and asked for his forgiveness.

FACT #4: The hiding of the letter and will inside the clock had been meant as a final puzzle from one brother to the other, just as they'd done for each other "as young lads."

When Edgar's dramatic readings were finished, the silence hung over the amphitheater for only a moment before it was shattered by Wilton Snivley: "I bet it's another fake! If that will and letter are real, why didn't the brothers ever make a public reconciliation?"

I didn't like Wilton's approach to journalism, but I couldn't deny he'd actually asked a good question. I just wished I had an answer. "I . . . um . . ." There had to be some key fact we still didn't know. A logical explanation. But we'd discovered the will and letter only minutes before arriving at the ceremony. We hadn't had time to figure everything out.

Lily Grove stepped forward, a grim look on her face. Was she going to blast apart everything we'd uncovered? Was she going to twist our discovery in some way to prove her claims that it was always and forever going to be Grove Park versus Elmwood?

"I think *I* should answer that question," Lily said, her voice shaky and weak. She steadied herself on the podium. "My ancestor George Grove died in a skirmish against the British in Morrisania, New York, on August 5, 1779, which was only a month after Elmwood split from Grove Park. He left behind a wife and a young son of his own. It seems he gave the clock to Louis and then died in battle without telling the world what he'd found out about his father's will–only his letter and the will could do that. And they were hidden in a clock that no one else in his family even knew George had given away."

"Then why didn't Louis Grove set the record straight!" Wilton Snivley shouted.

Lily stood a little straighter, seeming to find strength as the truth of the letter and the will settled in. "Louis died from consumption in 1782, and he had been ill for quite some time before his death, which is why he hadn't joined the Continental Army himself. It seems likely that even though Louis received the clock from his brother, he never noticed the inscription on the bottom. He never knew his brother had uncovered their father's will and sought reconciliation. He never knew there was one final puzzle, one final . . . truth." Lily hung her head, deflating again. "And I–I didn't know either."

The crowd sat, stunned. Even Wilton Snivley kept his mouth shut.

Elena, Edgar, Kevin, and I all glanced at each other. By the looks in my friends' eyes, I knew they were thinking the same thing as me. Without any need for discussion, we gathered around Lily Grove and rested our hands on her shoulders. Elmwood and Grove Park . . . united. And then we—the Elmwood GEEKs—began to talk.

We shared what we'd learned about the mudslide, about the riverboat and the steam fog, about the missing postmarks on the letters to Maxine Van Houten. With two towns listening, a TV crew filming, and a rich CEO standing only a newspaper toss away, we shared the stories our two towns needed to hear.

"So you see," I said as we finished, "maybe it's felt like Elmwood and Grove Park have often struggled *against* each other. But almost two hundred and fifty years ago, George Grove realized what our towns could be. What they *should* be." My eyes fell on the Grove family clock, the elm tree rising from its top, the eagle perched high in its branches, and for the first time it dawned on me how the carving represented the symbols of our two towns—the elm tree and the eagle. I held the clock high for everyone to see, knowing what our final message had to be. "George Grove gave this clock to his brother because he realized our towns are stronger–are *better*–when we stick together."

There was no cheering, no applause. Thoughtful silence hung in the air of the amphitheater like an eagle gliding on a spring breeze.

Lily sniffled. "I'd only seen my side of the story, the side that fit my view. I'm sorry."

Mr. Schoozer coughed behind us and cleared his throat. "Well, *er*, this afternoon has certainly taken an unexpected turn, and I . . . um . . . have a lot to think about before I"–he tugged at the collar of his shirt–"before I talk to the Deepsight board."

My friends and I nodded. There was nothing left to be said.

We didn't know what would become of Bamboozleland or Elmwood or Grove Park, and somewhere out there on Cloud Tapper Hill was a Bolt still waiting to be found. But even though we'd failed in our treasure hunt, we'd accomplished something much more important.

We'd shown everyone that it wasn't Elmwood versus Grove Park. We'd pushed for teamwork between the towns, not tug-of-war. And, sure, some of what we'd said had been only our own opinions. But you know what? Even newspapers have opinion sections. And a well-presented opinion is always supported by the facts.

The Fair Valley Tattler

THE TRUTH ABOUT TRUTH

FINLEY BROWN • Friday, April 15 • 10:49 p.m.

I used to end all my posts with a tagline: *"The Fair Valley Tattler—Finding. Verifying. Truth."* I failed to live up to that claim.

In recent weeks, I wrote this blog and gained readers. I built a platform and found people willing to follow what I had to say. Unfortunately, I used that for my own advantage and interests. I became more concerned with *claiming* I was finding and verifying truth than I was with actually doing so. This was wrong. It was unfair to my readers. It was unfair to the Elmwood GEEKs at whom so much of my writing was targeted. Now all I can say is this: *I'm sorry.*

My writing did not reflect what journalism is all about. It did not reflect who I thought I was and still hope to one day become. My writing cost me my integrity and—even worse—my friends. All I'm left with is the lessons I've learned.

I learned that total lies make the truth hard to find, but it can be trickier than that. Sometimes the truth just gets buried under half-truths. Other times, it gets

316

twisted by misleading facts. Yet the main thing I've learned is that truth is always worth searching for.

The truth can hold us together, and I—for one— am done with tearing us apart.

The Fair Valley Tattler

39

After school on Monday, Lambert J. Schoozer invited all the GEEKs to the Maple Leaf but didn't tell us why. He waited until Mrs. Dupree set Maple Bacon Barbecue Burgers, fries, and Cokes in front of us before he got down to business.

"As you might imagine," Mr. Schoozer said, "the outcome and revelations at Friday's ceremony were"—he pursed his lips and drummed his fingers on the table, searching for the right word—"*interesting.*"

"We tried our best with the challenge, sir!" Kevin blurted. "But the delays . . . the sabotage. Everything was rigged against us!"

"Never mind all that." Mr. Schoozer waved away Kevin's concerns. "I realize there were extenuating circumstances. Although you didn't finish the treasure hunt, the revelations from the closing ceremony made it quite clear why that was the case. By the time I met with the Deepsight board the following day, every board member had already seen news coverage of the event. You all left quite an impression."

I thought of our muddied and torn clothing as we'd stood on the amphitheater stage. What kind of impression had we left?

"The board held a lengthy discussion, and . . ." Mr. Schoozer raised his glass of Coke. Then he flashed his super-CEO smile. "I propose a toast in celebration of the board's unanimous approval of the Bamboozleland Improvement and Expansion Project!"

The rest of us raised our glasses too, but Mr. Schoozer must have noticed the glances we all exchanged with each other.

"Is something wrong?" he asked.

"Well . . . ," Edgar said.

"The Death Drop ride we've heard rumors about totally sounds better than a chocolate-dipped jalapeño," Elena said. "And it would be applesauce awesome for Elmwood. But . . ." She snatched up a French fry and took a bite. "We've been chatting and have an idea that would totally rock even more."

Mr. Schoozer arched a skeptical eyebrow. "More than a bigger, better, expanded Bamboozleland?"

"The thing is," Kevin said, "as a long-time student-council representative and current sixth-grade co-president, I understand the sort of political and personal pressure Lily Grove must have felt to help her town. Sure, what she did was terrible. But she's apologized, and we forgive her. We don't want Grove Park to suffer just because of what she did."

"Plus," Edgar said, "in a way, Lily was right—with Fair Valley Tech getting sold and moved, Grove Park needs a new theme park more than Elmwood does."

"Besides," I said, "if you expanded Bamboozleland, you'd have to cut down more of the woods. That's land we'd hoped could become part of the nature preserve."

"I'm sorry, kids." Mr. Schoozer rubbed his nose. "I appreciate the way you want to help both towns as much as possible, but we already own the Bamboozleland property, and the appeal of the project has always been its connection to the original theme park."

"Exactly," I said. "The *original* Bamboozleland. It's a reminder of the history of this area, and it only needs to be restored—not expanded—in order to fit perfectly back into Elmwood and to preserve its history."

Mr. Schoozer shook his head. "In today's competitive theme-park market—"

"You have to stand out," Elena said. "You have to be different. We totally get that."

"What we think you should do is use the Fair Valley Tech land to give Grove Park the big, shiny, new theme park," I said, "while also restoring Bamboozleland to its original glory. Then you can connect the two parks with a classic train ride, just like Grove Park connected to the original theme park all those years ago."

"So you'll have the classic Bamboozleland *and* the bigger park with the Death Drop and all that," Kevin said.

"The old and the new connected," Edgar said. "It'll be the *Hamilton* of theme parks!"

"See?" Barbecue sauce dripped down Elena's hand as she pointed her Maple Bacon Barbecue Burger at Mr. Schoozer, using it to punctuate each of her next points. "Better for Elmwood. Better for Grove Park. Better for Deepsight Development." She plucked a strip of bacon from the middle of her burger and chomped it in half. *"Bam."* Elena let go of her hamburger, which plopped back onto her plate. "Mic drop."

I rested my forehead in my hands. Heaven help us—and the rest of the world—if Elena ever decides to become a businesswoman instead of a scientist.

For a moment, I thought Mr. Schoozer was about to laugh. Either at Elena or at our idea. Or at both. Then he rubbed his chin and stared for a long moment at the Maple Leaf's ceiling, thinking. "You know what?" His eyes came back and met each of ours. "You kids may actually have a pretty good plan. . . ."

40

"One . . . two . . . three . . . *now*," Kevin said.

All five of our golden-handled shovels bit into the ground as cameras clicked and the crowd cheered. Elena, Edgar, Kevin, Sophina, and I all grinned as we posed alongside Mr. Schoozer with our shovelfuls of Bamboozleland dirt. The park filled with music from the Elmwood and Grove Park High School bands, which had combined together for the ceremony. Then we dumped the dirt back to the ground and smiled our way through more photos and official handshakes as I tried to take it all in.

Citizens from Elmwood mixed and mingled with townspeople from Grove Park, chatting and laughing and celebrating the official kickoff of renovations at Bamboozleland and the soon-to-be-under-construction

Fair Valley Adventure Zone in Grove Park. It was just the sort of event I'd have loved to cover for the *Elmwood Tribune* . . . *if* the other GEEKs and I hadn't been so busy being the guests of honor.

It seemed like everyone we knew was there, and one by one they wandered our way to say hello and offer congratulations. People like Mrs. Dupree, Cy Porter (who apologized at least a dozen times for unwittingly helping the Tattler during the Grove Park Challenge), Mrs. Sánchez, Jerry Smokes, and Oakley Seasons and Elizabeth Baldoni (who were now engaged and held hands the entire time). But no matter who came up to greet us, my gaze kept wandering over the crowd, looking for the Tattler despite everything he had done.

No, I had no interest in the greasy-haired Wilton Snivley, and I wasn't worried about him and his clicking camera anymore either. I was scanning the crowd for the *real* Tattler—Finley Brown.

"I know who you're looking for, Gee," Elena said.

"Huh?" I widened my eyes, wishing I was as good an actor as Edgar. "I—who . . . ?"

"Finley, of course. Though, you know you're too good for him, right?"

My face warmed. "How did you know I liked him?"

"I may wear glasses, but I'm not totally blind, Gee. Plus"—Elena smiled and nudged me with an elbow—"you and I *are* best friends, you know."

Before I could figure out how to respond, someone wedged in between me and Elena, smelling like a mixture of flowery perfume and breath mints.

"This is Annalise Richardson, Channel 6 News, and I'm live on location at Bamboozleland amusement park in Elmwood, New Hampshire!" A Channel 6 cameraman appeared in front of us, camera rolling, and Ms. Richardson gave both of us a dazzling smile. "With me are Gina Sparks and Elena Hernández, two of the fine young fortune hunters who have led the revitalization of the Fair Valley communities of Elmwood and Grove Park."

I shifted from foot to foot, trying not to think about the fact that we were suddenly on live TV.

"Gina, Elena," Ms. Richardson said, "I can't help but be impressed by your puzzle-solving talents. And for any of our viewers who don't recognize you, I must point out that you look quite different than you did during your *last* public appearance here at Bamboozleland." Ms. Richardson laughed lightly at her own joke.

Elena tugged shut the front of her Sophina-selected leopard-print sweater, though I imagined the TV camera had already caught Albert Einstein's face on her T-shirt underneath.

I cringed at the memory of our mud-splattered outfits on the final day of the Grove Park Challenge, but then looked down and admired my latest, surprisingly comfortable outfit–cropped jeans, a creamy blouse, and a camel-brown cardigan. When I caught Sophina watching the interview from right behind the cameraman, I winked at her, then smiled at Ms. Richardson. "I'd like to mention that we have a talented local stylist–Sophina Burkhart–who helped outfit us for today's event."

Sophina looked ready to pass out from joy, though I'm pretty sure I heard Elena mumble, "Why do you have to encourage her?"

"Now, in your efforts to save Bamboozleland, I know there was some conflict with the Grove Park mayor, Lily Grove," Ms. Richardson said, turning more serious. "With the growing connection between your two communities, how have you handled that relationship? What are your thoughts on her offer to resign?"

Ms. Richardson was good at her job. She'd used her compliment about our puzzle-solving and talk about our clothes to put us at ease before asking the tougher question about Lily, who had tried to resign the day after the Grove Park Challenge ended. I'd seen my mom use the same interview technique when working on articles for the *Tribune.* But the thing was, even though Ms. Richardson had asked a tough question, the answer was still pretty simple.

"We forgive her," I said. "She was desperate to save Grove Park, just like we were desperate to save Elmwood when we went hunting for the Van Houten fortune last year. We're glad the citizens of Grove Park refused to accept her resignation. She's the right person to lead her town into the future."

Ms. Richardson continued to ask us questions for a few more minutes, but even while getting interviewed on live TV, I found myself scanning the crowd, thinking of Finley. He wanted to be a TV news reporter himself someday, and I couldn't help but picture him in the role of Annalise Richardson, his wavy swoop of dark hair brushing his forehead, his smile lighting up the camera.

And then the interview was over. Annalise Richardson and her Channel 6 cameraman walked off toward Mr. Schoozer. Elena got into an argument with Kevin about the metric system versus inches, ounces, and pounds. Edgar started singing "Be Back Soon" from *Oliver!*

And I felt a tap on my shoulder.

"Gina?"

The voice. The last time I'd heard it was on the final day of the Grove Park Challenge. I had heard it over and over in my dreams. *I am the Fair Valley Tattler.*

I turned.

There stood Finley Brown, his dark eyes lowered, that wavy swoop of hair TV-ready.

"I just wanted to say I'm sorry, Gina." Finley scuffed the ground with his sneaker. "You have every right to hate me now, and I'll understand if you do. But I . . . I like you. And I respect you and your journalism. I just wanted you to know that. And if you can ever forgive me, can we at least be friends?"

He likes me.

I shoved my hands into my cardigan, my fingers curling around my brand-new phone. My mind flashed back to when my old phone had shattered after Finley and I had dived from the Old-Time Express. So many things had been broken during our hunt. My phone. The model W-48. My trust in Finley. But perhaps that last one could be fixed?

"I understand, Finley. Journalism is tough business, especially when people only want to read what they want to hear. So . . ." I released my phone, pulled my hand from my pocket, and rested it on Finley's arm. "We can still be friends."

For the first time since he'd appeared, Finley's eyes rose to meet mine. "Friends."

"Yes," I said, "friends. Though, nothing more than that. At least not right now." The beating of my heart was somewhere between heartache and hope. "There's a lot of trust to earn back."

Finley smiled and stuffed his hands into the pouch of his hoodie. "I'll take whatever I can get, since it's more than I deserve. See you at the wedding?"

He meant, I knew, the wedding between Oakley

Seasons and Elizabeth Baldoni, which would take place in two weeks on the Elmgrove Bridge. Burkhart Bakery was making the cake, in the shape of a turtle. Lion's Pizza was catering the reception. My fellow GEEKs and I were going to be bridesmaids and groomsmen. And my mom was covering it for her newly reinstated column in the *Boston Globe*.

"Yeah . . . see you there," I said.

He pulled something from his pocket, pressed it into my hand, and curled my fingers around it. "And that trust thing? Maybe this can be a down payment."

Then—with one final smile—Finley Brown melted back into the crowd, leaving me with something cool and jagged pressed into my palm.

I looked down and slowly opened my hand. The golden Bolt—dug from somewhere up by Wizard Rock—sparkled in the Fair Valley sunlight.

I smiled. And this time, the beat of my heart was pure hope.

ACKNOWLEDGMENTS

It's hard to believe that I'm already here again, at the end of another book, preparing to hand out another batch of THANK-YOUs that is bound to accidentally overlook some of the countless folks who helped make this book and series possible. Yet so many people deserve thanks and recognition that I'll forge ahead anyway and hope for the best. Now, without further ado . . .

My first and biggest thanks must always and forever go to my wife, Amy, who lets me be a writer instead of telling me to go get a real job. Of course, her willingness to let me write and work from home may just be so I get stuck doing all the laundry. She's tricky that way. But still . . . THANKS, AMY!

Additional thanks go to my children, Ramona and Lincoln, and to my almost-kind-of-child, Caroline Lenore Malloy Diaper Wipe Scooby Snack Sciba. You've all three grown up. But only kind of. And your ever-present goofiness continues to inspire.

Thanks, Dad, for once again counting syllables and checking rhythm and rhyme. As with the GEEKs' first foray into treasure hunting, the poetic clues in this book are much better because you helped shape them.

As always, I owe a never-ending stream of thanks to my fellow authors and critique partners Jan Gangsei, Amie Borst, and Pete Barnes. Your boundless support and feedback continue to shape my writing and my life.

Not to be overlooked is the entire team at Working Partners: a bonus supersized "THANK YOU!" to Ali Standish, who continues to put up with my many questions, requests, and random ideas. Thanks also to the sensitivity readers—yep, that includes you, Moukies!—who provided valuable insights and feedback that strengthened my GEEK-y cast of characters. And, of course, plenty of gratitude must be reserved for the team at Penguin Random House, and especially for Diane Landolf, who spotted the GEEKs' potential early on and has now skillfully guided their development through two treasure-hunting adventures.

Finally, I want to thank all the students, teachers, librarians, bookstore folks, and other readers who have embraced this series. I hope the GEEKs' second puzzle-filled escapade didn't disappoint!